The Gallery

The Gallery
Fredrica Alleyn

BL

This book is a work of fiction.
In real life, make sure you practise safe, sane and
consensual sex.

First Published by Black Lace 1997

2 4 6 8 10 9 7 5 3 1

Copyright © Fredrica Alleyn 1997

Fredrica Alleyn has asserted her right under the Copyright, Designs
and Patents Act 1988 to be identified as the author of this work

This edition first published in Great Britain in 2009 by
Black Lace
Virgin Books
Random House, 20 Vauxhall Bridge Road,
London SW1V 2SA

www.blacklace.co.uk
www.virginbooks.com
www.rbooks.co.uk

Addresses for companies within The Random House Group Limited can be found at:
www.randomhouse.co.uk/offices.htm

The Random House Group Limited Reg. No. 954009

A CIP catalogue record for this book
is available from the British Library

ISBN 9780352345332

The Random House Group Limited supports The Forest Stewardship Council [FSC], the
leading international forest certification organisation. All our titles that are printed on
Greenpeace-approved FSC-certified paper carry the FSC logo.
Our paper procurement policy can be found at www.rbooks.co.uk/environment

Mixed Sources
Product group from well-managed
forests and other controlled sources
www.fsc.org Cert no. TT-COC-2139
© 1996 Forest Stewardship Council

Printed in the UK by CPI Bookmarque, Croydon CR0 4TD

Chapter One

Cressida Farleigh lay with her head against her lover's chest and tried to glance at the bedside clock without him noticing. It wasn't that she hadn't enjoyed herself – she had. As usual the sex had been highly satisfying, but she had to be up early the next morning for a special meeting and wanted to get back to her own home for a proper night's sleep.

Tom clearly sensed that she was restless and tightened his right arm across her back. 'What's the matter?'

Cressida sighed. 'I'm sorry, Tom, but I've got to get home.'

'Why? Honestly, Cressida, I don't understand you. We both live alone, we're single and answerable to no one but ourselves, so why is it that you're always dashing off after we've made love?'

'It's the job,' retorted Cressida, slipping free and swinging her feet to the floor. 'We both keep such ghastly hours that we need our sleep, and we never sleep when we're together!'

'I don't think the job's got anything to do with it,' he muttered, watching her put on her policewoman's uniform and feeling himself stir again at the sight of her long

1

legs in the black stockings. 'I think you're afraid of emotional commitment.'

Cressida smiled at him. 'So you're becoming a psychiatrist now, are you? I think I prefer you as a detective sergeant – far less intrusive.' Bending down she kissed him on the corner of his mouth. 'I had a lovely time. Think of me tomorrow morning.'

Tom nodded. 'Of course I will. Hang on, let me put on a robe and I'll show you out.'

'There's no need. After two and a half years I think I know the way!' laughed Cressida. At the bedroom door she hesitated. 'You really don't know what this meeting is about, do you, Tom? As it's CID I thought you might have some idea.'

Propped up on one elbow, Tom tried to keep his face expressionless as he shook his head. 'No, honestly, I haven't a clue, but I'm sure it's nothing to worry about. If you were in trouble someone would definitely have told me!'

'I'll let you know what it was about as soon as I leave,' Cressida promised him. 'You're off tomorrow, aren't you?'

'Yes,' said Tom, feeling incredibly guilty because he wouldn't be off at all. He would be at the meeting, a meeting that his department had been planning for the past week, only he was sworn to secrecy and it was more than his job was worth to tell Cressida anything about it before she was interviewed by the top brass.

'Sleep well,' murmured Cressida, then she was gone and he heard the front door close quietly behind her. Turning on his side, he stared at the brown and cream striped curtains that covered his bedroom windows. He'd known Cressida for three years and been going out with her for over two, but she still maintained an emotional distance that drove him to distraction. She said that she loved him, and he knew that she was totally faithful, but at the back of his mind there was always the fear that what she felt wasn't really love at all and one day she might realise this.

If he was totally honest with himself, it wasn't an all-consuming passion either, he thought, as he drifted off to sleep. She was responsive and he seemed to satisfy her, but he'd never yet seen her totally lose control of herself in the throes of sexual excitement. Considering what lay ahead of her after tomorrow's meeting, he found this more than a little worrying. His only consolation was the possibility that Cressida wasn't capable of anything more than she gave him, in which case he had nothing to fear.

Totally unaware that Tom was in any way concerned about her or their relationship, Cressida arrived at her tiny terraced house in west London, gave her long-haired grey cat Muffin some food and then went straight up to bed where she fell asleep immediately. Unlike her lover, she never spent much time analysing herself or their relationship. As far as she was concerned they suited each other, and being in the same line of work they both understood the stresses and strains the days could bring.

If anyone had asked Cressida that night if she was happy she would have said yes, completely happy. And this was the reason she'd been chosen for the meeting the following day. It was simply unfortunate that everyone, including Cressida, was wrong.

At 10.30 the next morning, Cressida – wearing a straight, dark blue skirt that ended on the knee and a cream long-sleeved tunic top because she'd been ordered to appear out of uniform – was ushered into the chief superintendent's office.

She was surprised at the number of people sitting round the oval-shaped table. Most of them were unfamiliar to her, but when she saw Tom sitting there her eyes widened in astonishment and he looked away, clearly embarrassed at having lied to her the night before.

3

'Sit down, WPC Farleigh,' said a tall, bald-headed man who Cressida assumed must be in charge of the meeting. 'I'm sorry we've had to keep you totally in the dark about all this, but we're engaged in an extremely tricky under-cover operation and we need your help.'

'By "we" do you mean CID?' asked Cressida as she sat down.

'Yes. Detective Sergeant Penfold here knows all about it, but even he wasn't allowed to breathe a word to you until we'd had our say.'

'I see,' said Cressida, glancing at the hapless Tom. 'Well, he certainly obeyed orders.'

A man sitting to the right of the bald-headed man leant forward slightly. 'How much do you know about art, WPC Farleigh?'

Cressida blinked in surprise. 'Art? Not a lot. I know a Picasso from a Monet, but that's about all. It isn't a particular interest of mine.'

'Pity,' murmured the man, sitting back in his chair again.

'Nonsense,' said the bald man firmly. 'WPC Farleigh's an intelligent young woman. She can learn all she needs to know in ten days or so I'm sure. I think,' he added as he saw the bemused look on Cressida's face, 'that we'd better start at the beginning.

'First of all, I'm Detective Chief Inspector Williams and I'm from the fraud squad. We're very interested in an art gallery that opened about ten months ago in Elgin Crescent in west London. It's called Room With a View. Do you know it?'

Cressida shook her head, totally bewildered by the entire conversation.

'No, well, you wouldn't have any reason to, but the fact of the matter is it's vital that we get someone inside the gallery who can report back to us. We've made a start – WPC Hinds here has been working there as a junior assistant-cum-receptionist for the past three months – but it hasn't worked out the way we hoped so we're pulling her out and you've been chosen to take her place.'

Cressida looked across at WPC Hinds. She was young and small, with curly blonde hair, and she had a cheeky smile that she flashed at Cressida. She and Cressida could not have been more dissimilar, which made the choice totally bizarre.

'I don't know anything about being a receptionist,' she pointed out. 'Neither do I look at all like WPC Hinds.'

'Exactly,' said Detective Chief Inspector Williams with obvious satisfaction. 'That's why we've chosen you. Susan here was chosen because we thought she looked right for what we wanted her to do, but now it seems that we were wrong. This time we're going for someone who's the opposite of Susan, and the general feeling in the station was that you and Susan have nothing at all in common!'

Cressida, who was now more confused than when the conversation began, felt that this was probably not a compliment. Susan Hinds was clearly very attractive, sexy and lively, which Cressida felt reflected badly on her own rating on the scale of sexuality and feminine charm.

'What was it that you wanted WPC Hinds to do?' she asked quietly.

One or two of the high-ranking officers sitting round the table averted their eyes and Tom turned a delicate shade of pink. Detective Chief Inspector Williams, however, had no qualms about telling her.

'We wanted her to get very close to the owner of the gallery. His name's Guy Cronje and women seem to fall for him if he so much as glances in their direction. Naturally we don't really want you to fall for him, but we want him to believe that you have.'

'How do I achieve that?' queried Cressida, looking over at Tom, who still refused to meet her eyes.

Detective Chief Inspector Williams cleared his throat.

'Well, I'm sure I don't have to spell it out to you. You're a woman of the world, a good policewoman and in a steady relationship with Detective Sergeant Penfold here. You know how many beans make five!' There was some nervous laughter round the table.

'The thing is, Cressida,' said her usual boss, Inspector Cross, 'those of us who know you well appreciate that you're not the kind of girl to do anything silly. One of the reasons you're so good at your job is that you don't get involved emotionally. People trust you, and they sense that you care when they're in trouble, but you always keep this barrier around you and that's what counted most strongly in your favour. Let's face it, Tom here wouldn't be pleased if you got carried away by Guy Cronje's charms and really fell for him, would he?'

'I imagine not,' said Cressida dryly, thinking that Tom was going to have a lot of explaining to do when they were next together. She also thought that her chief's summary of her made her sound rather aloof, which wasn't very pleasant. However, she knew that she had to sit there and listen to whatever they had to say and then go out and do the job because if she turned it down it would always go against her, and Cressida was ambitious.

'Well?' asked Detective Chief Inspector Williams. 'What do you say?'

'I still don't understand what it is that I'm expected to do, apart from pretend to fall for the owner of this gallery. What's he done wrong?'

'Inspector Cross will fill you in on all that later. What I need to know is, are you willing to take on the job? WPC Hinds here will help you in a crash course on art, and she'll recommend you as her replacement when the interviewing starts. You'll have to do your bit, but they've no reason to suspect Sue's motives. She never blew her cover or anything of that nature – it simply didn't work out.

You'd have to dress better than you have today, of course, but again WPC Hinds can give you some tips.'

'How kind,' muttered Cressida through gritted teeth.

'Inspector Cross agrees that you're perfect for the job, so do we have your agreement?' persisted the detective chief inspector.

'Yes, I suppose so,' said Cressida. 'It's just that I don't understand what I'm going to be doing at the gallery, apart from pretending to be an artistic receptionist.'

'No, well, once you've signed the secrecy agreement you'll get full details,' said Williams, rising to his feet. 'I'll leave all that to your chief and WPC Hinds here. The fraud squad's a busy place, I'm afraid, and I've spent long enough here already. Good luck, WPC Farleigh. Having seen you I'm sure you'll handle the detective side of it very well. I just hope that Guy Cronje – ' He pulled himself up abruptly. 'Sorry, I was thinking aloud there. Once you're safely ensconced in the gallery you'll report directly to me on a number you'll be given by Inspector Cross. Good luck. I hope to hear you've been taken on very soon.'

Cressida stood up as he left the room and watched as most of the other people who'd been sitting round the table left with him. When the door finally closed only Inspector Cross, Tom and WPC Susan Hinds remained in the room with her.

'Confused?' asked Inspector Cross with his familiar smile.

'Very,' said Cressida, who was also feeling rather annoyed.

'I'm not surprised, but when God visits you have to let him take charge! Now sign the secrecy agreement and then Susan here is going to take you off for the rest of the day and fill you in on the details. No doubt you'll spend the entire evening discussing it all with Tom, and tomorrow morning you can come and see me with any questions that are still unanswered. But once you've got the job at the gallery you'll be on your own. Poor Tom will have to take a back seat for a time, but he knows this, isn't that right, Tom?'

'Yes, sir,' replied Tom in a muted voice.

Susan Hinds touched Cressida on the arm. 'Come on, let's get out of here. We'll lunch at the Italian place round the corner and I'll explain everything. Don't worry, it'll be fun. I wish I'd done better, but you can't make a man like short bubbly blondes if his taste runs more to tall enigmatic brunettes, can you?'

As Cressida got to the door, Tom moved to her side. 'I'll call round tonight, at eight,' he said urgently. 'I'm really sorry I couldn't tell you about any of this but I'd have lost my job.'

'I understand that,' said Cressida calmly, and logically she did, but somewhere deep inside her she couldn't help feeling that he'd let her down.

As both Cressida and Sue were officially off duty, they were able to drink plenty of the rough red Italian house wine with their pasta, so by the time they were halfway through their meal Cressida was feeling very relaxed about the whole operation.

'Let me make sure I've got this right,' she said, dipping her spoon into a delicious strawberry ice cream. 'When Lord Michael Summers died in a car crash recently, the people who came in to check the value of his estate discovered that two of the paintings from his collection, a Rembrandt and a Monet, were forgeries, yes?'

'The real point is,' said Sue, 'that when Lord Summers inherited the title on the death of *his* father, those paintings were the real thing. At some stage during his time as a peer of the realm they were replaced by copies.'

Cressida nodded. 'And his widow, Lady Alice, is saying that her husband used to visit the gallery this Guy Cronje owns and buy works done by new artists?'

Susan nodded. 'That's what she says, and there are

records at the gallery of purchases by the late lamented Lord Summers.'

'But the fraud squad think that Guy Cronje and his partner . . . what's her name?'

'Marcia Neville.'

'I must remember that. OK, so they think Guy and Marcia somehow managed to swap two incredibly valuable paintings from the estate's collection for two copies. I can't imagine how it would be done, though, can you?'

Sue shrugged. 'Well, there are ways. For one thing, Guy and Marcia were socially friendly with Lord and Lady Summers and used to go to their house. It's possible that Lady Alice, who's only thirty and had a husband of sixty-nine, might have taken a shine to Guy and helped him, in return for favours – and a share of the money, no doubt.'

'It's all rather nebulous, isn't it?' queried Cressida. 'I mean, why this urgent need for us to get someone inside the gallery? Two paintings missing from one estate is hardly earth shattering. Bad for the Summers family if the news gets out, but not large-scale crime.'

Sue grinned. 'You didn't listen to me properly – it must be this potent cheap plonk! This kind of thing has been happening all over Europe in recent years, and every time Guy Cronje was an associate of the deceased owner. Interpol have had their eye on him for over three years. Naturally now it's happened here we'd like to be the ones to catch him.'

'You said you were pulled out because Guy didn't fancy you,' said Cressida slowly. 'I take it he's meant to fancy me?'

Sue nodded. 'He certainly is! I had to give the top brass an Identikit picture of his kind of woman, and they came up with you! To be honest, I don't think it's going to work this way because he and Marcia are very close and by all accounts he can have any other woman he wants too.

9

Why should he start a fling with a lowly assistant at his own gallery?'

'I don't know,' agreed Cressida. 'Well, I don't mind. In fact, the sooner I'm pulled out the happier I'll be.'

'I enjoyed myself there!' laughed Sue. 'I didn't manage to get close to Guy, but there were other compensations, I can tell you. Some of the artists are fantastic lovers.'

Cressida stared at her. 'You mean you actually slept with them?'

'No, but we had fantastic sex! Come on, Cressida, what do you think men and women do when they fancy each other? Hold hands in the back row of the cinema? If Guy does get interested in you, I don't think you're expected to act like a timorous virgin – that's not his scene at all.'

'But I'm sleeping with Tom Penfold,' said Cressida.

Sue's eyebrows rose. 'I suppose someone has to! Seriously, Cressida, these men knock spots off Tom and the beauty of it is, you're only obeying orders!'

'No one told me I was expected to sleep with Guy Cronje, or any other man come to that,' protested Cressida. 'I couldn't. It takes me ages to get to know a man well enough to do that.'

Sue frowned. 'No one told you because they couldn't possibly order a woman to sleep with a suspect. Suppose it came out in court? They'd be done for enticement. I've no doubt Detective Chief Inspector Williams assumed you'd understood the sub-text. Your Tom will have done, which probably explains his long face at the meeting.'

'Well, I'll find out what I can, but there's no way I'm getting sexually involved with anyone,' said Cressida firmly. 'If I string this Guy along, assuming he even looks twice at me, that should be enough.'

Sue looked at Cressida carefully. She was tall, about 5 8", and her dark brown hair was cut in a very attractive gamine bob, but she seemed totally unaware of how attractive she could make herself with more effort. Also, in Sue's opinion, her clothes were a disaster. She wondered, with some amusement, how long Cressida's resolve would hold out once she became part of life at the gallery.

'You'll have to play it by ear,' she said casually, aware that to press her replacement would be a mistake. 'The only thing is, once I've given you your crash course in art and got you a phoney degree in fine art, you'll have to do something about the clothes you wear. They like their staff to look glamorous but sophisticated at the gallery, and full make-up is expected at all times.'

'I can't afford glamorous, sophisticated clothes,' retorted Cressida.

'That's one of the perks of the job; the force gives you a *very* generous allowance and I'll come round the shops and help you choose some outfits. It's vital that you get it right for the interview. Marcia's capable of rejecting you on sartorial grounds alone if you wear the wrong tights or shoes! I'm going to recommend you and say you and I have been friends for years, ever since we met while taking a year out before university, but while that will help it will be up to you to clinch the position.'

Cressida was beginning to hope she failed the interview – it was all starting to sound very complicated and not at all her kind of thing. 'What's Guy Cronje actually like?' she asked tentatively.

'I didn't ever get to know him that well,' admitted Sue. 'He's certainly got something, but it isn't conventional charm. He's quite tall, very slim, dark haired and pale, but he gives off this air of repressed danger. He's like a simmering volcano that you feel might erupt at any moment. I think it's that dangerous quality that draws all the women.'

'I don't like strong emotions,' admitted Cressida, ordering an espresso coffee. 'That's why Tom suits me; he's wonderfully lacking in danger. I like to know where I am with people.'

'I think this job will do you good,' commented Sue.

11

'You sound as though you need a fresh perspective on life, particularly in the sexual area.'

'I'm quite happy as I am, thank you!' laughed Cressida. 'After all, this is a job, not a life-long commitment. Do *you* think there's anything criminal going on at the gallery?' she added.

'I think there's something going on, but I'm not sure what,' said Sue slowly. 'Sometimes there was a very strange atmosphere, but I never made out if the undercurrents were due to law breaking or sexual tension.'

'You make it sound as though it should be vice, not fraud, handling this job,' commented Cressida.

'What's wrong with a bit of vice?' asked Sue with a grin. 'At least when I'm old and grey I'll have some good memories to look back on, and quite a few of them will have come from my time at the gallery. Unfortunately, not with Guy Cronje though. He always seemed to think of me as a total airhead, and I didn't dare enlighten him in case he went into my background too carefully. That's one thing to remember, Cressida. Be on your guard. He's very sharp, and if you make a mistake then he'll spot it.'

They paid the bill and left the restaurant together after arranging to meet up the following day for Cressida's crash course in art to begin. What with the wine and her head buzzing after all she'd learnt, Cressida headed for home and slept for the rest of the afternoon, only just waking in time to get herself bathed and changed before Tom arrived.

It was clear from the moment he walked in the door that he was in a bad mood. Normally nothing troubled Tom, and Cressida felt irritated that her new job was already causing trouble in her tranquil private life.

'Do you want to go out for a meal?' asked Tom, sinking down on to the sofa as he spoke.

'No thanks; I had lunch with Sue Hinds at that Italian place round the corner from the station, so I'm not hungry,' she assured him.

'I suppose I ought to say sorry about this morning,' he said at last. 'I knew what was coming days ago, but it was highly confidential. You're not annoyed, are you?'

'I was, but I'm not now,' Cressida replied, realising to her surprise that this was true. 'I don't suppose you're any happier about it all than I am.'

'No, I'm not!' said Tom vehemently. 'I've read all about Guy Cronje and he's the last man on earth I'd choose for you to work for.'

'I don't think I'll be in any physical danger,' said Cressida. 'He hasn't got a record for violence, has he?'

'No, nothing like that, but he seems to be a danger to women.'

'Only silly women, and I'm not a silly woman,' said Cressida sharply.

'No, but you *are* a woman all the same, and sex is a funny thing,' muttered Tom. 'Who'd have thought he wouldn't fancy Susan Hinds. Every man at the station fancies her.'

'Is that a fact?' asked Cressida, her temper rising.

Tom quickly tried to retract his statement. 'I don't!' he exclaimed. 'You know me, Cress, I'm a one-woman man – but she is sexy.'

'You mean I'm not?' asked Cressida quietly.

Tom frowned. 'I think you're sexy, but it isn't in an obvious way. You know that, Cressida. You're just not a siren, and you wouldn't want to be, would you?'

'I might not mind,' she retorted. 'In fact, I'm beginning to think this job might be fun. After all, I'll have my mind improved with all this artistic education, and my dress sense improved with a shopping expedition in the company of the sexiest WPC in west London. What more could a girl ask for?'

Tom looked baffled. 'What are you angry about? I always thought you were comfortable with yourself, that's one of your attractions. I hate women who spend all their time fussing about clothes and make-up. You look nice, and you're always neat and tidy; you don't need anything else. It's you as a person I like. Isn't that what women want these days?'

'It would be better,' said Cressida slowly, 'if you thought I was a desirable person in every respect, not just "from within" as it were. I had no idea Sue was so popular.'

'Look, if this is going to cause trouble between us, why don't you tell Williams you can't go through with it?' suggested Tom. 'I mean, you could say that art just isn't your thing, which it isn't to my way of thinking. There are plenty of get-outs that won't go against you. Let's face it, Detective Chief Inspector Williams can't afford another failure.'

'I won't be a failure,' said Cressida, suddenly absolutely determined to make a success of the assignment. 'I shall turn myself into a highly desirable and sexual woman, gain Guy Cronje's confidence, discover exactly what's going on at the gallery and then when I've broken up the entire dastardly operation I shall be given an award by the queen for bravery in the face of blatant sexism!'

Tom put his head in his hands. 'I knew this was a mistake,' he complained. 'Why they picked you I'll never know.'

Resisting the urge to pick up a vase and break it over his head, Cressida sat down next to him. 'I won't take that as a personal insult,' she said softly, 'but don't push your luck, Tom. There are limits even to my self-control.'

He turned and put his arms round her. 'You know how much you mean to me, Cress. I'm crazy about you, but I don't want people changing you. I like you as you are – the last thing I want is a pale replica of someone like Susan Hinds.'

'I won't be a pale replica of Sue, I'll be a super-charged version of myself,' Cressida promised him.

'You won't fall for this man, will you?' persisted Tom.

'I couldn't bear it if I had to stand by and hear how well you were doing at your job if I thought it meant you and he were . . . well, you know what I mean.'

Cressida did know, and she felt a frisson of excitement run through her. Of course, she knew that nothing would happen at the gallery. Even if she got the job, the chances of Guy Cronje fancying her and her reciprocating the feeling were negligible, but just the same a whole new world was opening up to her and she realised that she was beginning to feel a sense of excited anticipation.

'Let's go up to bed,' said Tom suddenly, pulling her to her feet.

Cressida was about to make her way upstairs, but then, already acting quite out of character, she had an overwhelming desire for them to make love in her front room. She stood by the post at the bottom of the banister rail and began to unbutton her long crinkle-cotton dress. 'Let's stay here,' she said softly.

Tom stared at her. 'The sofa isn't big enough,' he protested.

'Then we'll use something else. 'I know, my swivel chair, the one in front of my computer, that'll do. Luckily it hasn't got casters or life might be difficult!'

Watched by a startled Tom, Cressida moved over to the chair and then sat back in it, her head hanging slightly to the side and her hands gripping the arms of the chair as she swivelled her lower body towards where Tom was standing.

'People can see in!' he protested.

'They can't!' said Cressida, wishing that he'd just follow her mood and start making love to her quickly. 'I haven't cleaned the windows for so long I can't even see out!'

Now she was moving against the seat of the chair, her hips wriggling provocatively, and finally Tom too was overwhelmed by desire. Quickly he unfastened his trousers and let them fall round his ankles as he knelt between her legs. Cressida wrapped her calves around his lower back and he pushed urgently at her bra, until his fingers could caress her already hard nipples.

Cressida began to ache low in her belly and what she wanted most was for him to lower his head and let his tongue wander up and down the exquisitely sensitive moist channel below her clitoris, but this was something Tom rarely chose to do and tonight was no exception. Instead he pulled his erection free of his boxer shorts and she felt the swollen tip brushing against her pubic hair for a moment, until her growing excitement caused her sex lips to swell and part so that his glans was now against the flesh of her vulva. She rotated her hips urgently as she tried to get some kind of clitoral stimulation. Her breathing was rapid and noisy in the slowly darkening room, and Tom's breathing was harsh as his hands continued to fondle her breasts while his mouth nuzzled against her neck.

She could feel her breasts swelling, and the tension in her pelvis increased so that she thrust upward against his penis, frantic now for some direct contact against her clitoris. Tom's hips were thrusting backward and forward as he slid up and down the length of her outer channel, and when at last her swollen bud was touched by the underside of the ridge of flesh beneath his glans she gasped with pleasure and felt her belly begin to tighten.

'Do that again, Tom,' she whispered, but Tom either didn't hear or didn't understand because almost immediately she felt him slide inside her and begin thrusting in earnest, lost in his own journey to satisfaction.

Luckily, because she was able to angle her body as she wished, Cressida managed to maintain some indirect stimulation of her clitoris, but despite this and the first thrilling moments when her entire body tightened in anticipation of sexual release, Tom still came before she did and she heard him gasp and then cry out with delight as his orgasm rushed through him.

'I'm sorry,' he muttered as he collapsed against her. 'I got over-excited. Don't worry, I'll make sure you're all right too.'

'Go down on me,' begged Cressida. 'Please. I want to feel your tongue on me, then I'll explode, I know I will.'

'Leave it to me,' murmured Tom, and as he kissed the base of her throat and rubbed the palm of one hand across the surface of her nipples, his other hand went between her thighs and she felt him slide two fingers slowly up and down the side of her clitoris.

Now her body tightened again and Cressida was almost crying with need as he circled around the hard mass of frantic nerve endings, until suddenly there was an explosion of white light behind her closed eyelids and then her whole body convulsed in a climax.

At last Cressida was able to relax and her whole body felt limp and strangely weightless. Tom stood up and began to straighten his clothing. 'That was great!' he enthused. 'You didn't mind coming last, did you?'

'Of course not,' said Cressida with a smile, and it was true. She didn't mind and she'd had a very satisfying orgasm, but she couldn't help wondering why Tom hadn't done any of the things she'd wanted, and for the first time since she'd been sleeping with him she started to wonder what it might be like with a different man – a man who was more adventurous.

'We make a good pair,' Tom said, with what Cressida thought was a rather smug smile as they sat drinking coffee a little later. 'I'm sorry I was in a bad mood when I got here. It was stupid of me. I should have known you're not the kind of girl to have her head turned by a man like Guy Cronje, even if he does fancy you.'

'Yes, you should,' murmured Cressida, resting her head against his shoulder. Luckily Tom couldn't read her mind, because she resolved there and then that she'd make this Guy Cronje fancy her if it was the last thing she did, just to shock everyone who knew her and seemed to think the chances of that happening were virtually nil.

Tom stayed over that night, and the next morning they made love again, but in their usual, more conventional, fashion. When he left her house he looked and felt extremely pleased with himself, not realising that Cressida was now very anxious that she got the job as receptionist at Guy Cronje's gallery, Room With a View.

'Today's the big day then, Cressida,' said Inspector Cross, smiling across his desk at her. 'How do you feel?'

'Nervous,' she admitted. 'I think I'm all right on the actual art side, I've been studying art books day and night and gone round more galleries than I knew existed! I'm more worried about the rest of the interview. Suppose Marcia Neville doesn't like me?'

'It's your job to make her like you,' pointed out her superior. 'It shouldn't be a problem; you certainly look the part!'

For the first time that Cressida could remember, Inspector Cross was looking at her as an attractive woman rather than one of his WPCs, and she realised what a difference her new style of dressing had made. Cross had often seen her in casual clothes, but he'd never looked at her in that way before.

'Susan chose this outfit,' she admitted, glancing down at her V-necked collarless black jacket with large gold buttons that ended just below her hips. With it she was wearing a short, straight black skirt and a cream satin blouse with a draped neckline that made it look as though she was wearing a scarf rather than a blouse. 'I wouldn't have chosen any of it, but now I've got it I can see that Susan was right.'

'She certainly was,' he said appreciatively. 'From the look of your expenses sheet you've bought a few more outfits like it too.'

'Susan said it was essential,' said Cressida. 'If you think we overspent then – '

'Good heavens, no!' he exclaimed quickly. 'Chief Inspector Williams would never forgive me if I spoilt his operation by penny pinching. Susan was quite right. Appearances count for a lot in this kind of job. You're the face of the gallery, just as here you're the face of the police force.'

'I think I'm going to miss the excitement of the work here,' admitted Cressida. 'I doubt if there'll be many robberies, domestic assaults or drunks in the gallery.'

'If the fraud squad are right, the crimes going on at that gallery are far more serious,' Inspector Cross reminded her. 'Don't forget that either, will you? People who commit dangerous large-scale frauds are usually totally ruthless, however charming they may appear on the surface.'

'I won't forget,' she assured him.

Inspector Cross nodded with satisfaction. 'I know you won't. Luckily you're not the type of girl to get carried away by the thrill of an illicit dalliance. I told Detective Chief Inspector Williams that you've got a mind that's more like a man's. He was very relieved to hear it, I can tell you.'

Cressida was slightly less than thrilled, and as she made her way out of the station and hailed a taxi to take her to Elgin Crescent, she thought that it would serve them all right if she totally lost her head over this Guy Cronje and ended up having a mad, passionate affair with him. Although she prided herself on her common sense and emotional reserve, she didn't enjoy hearing other people talk about her in the way they had over the past week. They'd succeeded in making her sound passionless, which she knew she wasn't.

Her annoyance at Inspector Cross's remarks helped to drive some of her nerves away, and when she climbed out of the cab and walked through the heavy swing doors

19

into the shining white brightness of the gallery she was feeling relaxed, confident and positive.

'Can I help you?' asked a pencil-thin, raven-haired girl at the desk by the door.

'My name's Cressida Farleigh. I've come about the position of receptionist,' she explained.

The girl raised her eyebrows. 'Really? I thought the job was taken. Just a moment, I'll speak to Miss Neville.'

Cressida's confidence drained away immediately. If the job had gone she was in serious trouble, but Sue hadn't mentioned the possibility and she couldn't imagine how it could have happened, unless they'd taken on a personal friend.

As she stood by the side of the desk an immaculately groomed blonde woman in her early thirties walked down the long main area of the gallery towards them. Her caramel-coloured dress fitted her like a glove and she was fastening a matching jacket with cream-coloured spots as she moved. Cressida noted the small gold earrings, the tiny gold chain round the base of the woman's throat, and also her rings, three on each hand. It was all expensive but plain jewellery, while her blonde hair was drawn back off her face with just a few strands falling over the right side of her forehead.

She wasn't as tall as Cressida but she was equally slim, except for her breasts, and they seemed strangely at odds with the rest of her. Cressida wondered if they'd had some assistance from a plastic surgeon.

'Hello, I'm Marcia Neville,' she said in a low voice. 'I do hope Saskia here hasn't been telling you the position's filled?'

Cressida glanced at the dark-haired girl. 'Well . . .'

'Too silly! We've been holding it for you, because you know Susan Hinds and she's spoken so highly of you. Never mind, that's the problem with temps – they get everything wrong. Come through to my office – hopefully Saskia can manage to bring us some coffee. Remember, mine's decaffeinated, Saskia.'

Saskia nodded, her face blank but beautiful.

'There, now sit down where I can take a good look at you and tell me all about yourself,' Marcia said with another of her practised smiles once they were in her office.

After a moment's hesitation, Cressida launched into her well-rehearsed tale of qualifications, past experience and burning desire to work in a gallery where new artists were given a chance to launch their careers, and all the time she talked Marcia never once took her eyes off her face.

After she'd finished, Marcia proceeded to ask her a series of searching questions and as the time went on she became more and more grateful to Sue for her insistence on thorough preparation. When Marcia finally settled back in her chair in silence, Cressida felt exhausted by the strain of it all.

Marcia, however, seemed very pleased. 'Susan was right to recommend you to us,' she said with a smile. 'You look right, your experience is just about sufficient, and I think you probably know more about the Impressionists than Susan does. She's stronger on the Renaissance side, but I'm sure you know that?'

'I've always thought of the Surrealists as being Sue's speciality,' said Cressida, and Marcia nodded. Cressida gave a silent sigh of relief. That had clearly been a trap, and she'd negotiated it safely.

'Of course, Surrealists! I was getting her confused with her predecessor,' murmured Marcia. 'Now, I've checked out your references already and they're highly satisfactory. If I were to offer you the position, when could you start?'

'I'm free from next week,' said Cressida.

'Then I suggest that you start with us on Monday morning at ten,' said Marcia, holding out her hand. 'I have a feeling that you're going to fit in with us all very well, Cressida.'

'I hope so,' responded Cressida. 'This is exactly the kind of gallery I've always wanted to work in.'

'The owner of the gallery isn't in the country at the moment,' remarked Marcia, leading Cressida out into the corridor. 'I expect Susan told you about Guy, did she?'

'She mentioned him.'

'Luckily he's perfectly content to let me make decisions over staffing matters. He's more involved with the artists and the collectors, as you'd expect.'

'Of course,' murmured Cressida, anxious not to show too much interest in Guy at this stage.

'Is there anything you'd like to ask me?' queried Marcia, glancing at her watch to make it clear that if there was, Cressida had better hurry up and do so.

'No, I think you covered everything,' Cressida assured her.

'That's wonderful! It's so unsatisfactory when you've got temporary staff at the desk. First impressions are very important, and you make a very good impression indeed.'

'Thank you,' said Cressida, and with a final handshake and smile the two women parted.

As the swing doors closed behind Cressida, Marcia Neville stood by the desk and looked down at Saskia. 'I may have to watch that one,' she said quietly. 'There's more to her than meets the eye, and Guy does like a challenge, as you well know, Saskia.'

The dark-haired girl blushed scarlet. 'I'd really rather not –'

'Remember the other night? Yes, well, that's perfectly understandable, although personally I found your cries of ecstasy highly arousing, even though the setting was, shall we say, a little bizarre! Incidentally, Guy asked me to give you his best wishes and to say how much he appreciates all you've done during your brief time at the gallery!'

Saskia kept her eyes down until Marcia had walked away, and then stared around her. She'd always known it was only a temporary job, but she'd never expected to learn what she had during her stay. At the memory of what had taken place only two nights earlier between her, Guy Cronje and Marcia, she shivered with guilty pleasure.

Somehow she couldn't imagine Cressida Farleigh becoming personally involved with the mysterious and exciting owners of Room With a View – but if she did, her life would almost certainly change for ever.

Chapter Two

A s Cressida dressed for her first day at the art gallery, she realised that she was feeling decidedly nervous. It was strange, because during all her time as a police-woman, and there had been some very tense moments over the years, she'd never had the sensation of butter-flies dancing in her stomach before.

Being out of uniform was part of the problem. Once she was wearing that, Cressida ceased to exist as an individual and became part of the police force instead. There was no such disguise now, nothing for her to hide behind. She had to cope as herself, and the prospect was unsettling.

At least her clothes looked right, she thought with satisfaction. The short cropped navy-blue jacket with gold buttons sat neatly on her hips, and the matching straight skirt that rested two inches above her knees emphasised her excellent legs. She'd obeyed Sue's instructions and was wearing opaque navy hold-ups, but as an individual touch knotted a red scarf at the base of her neck. This dash of bold colour helped lift her naturally pale skin tone and she felt quite pleased with herself. After a final check in the full-length mirror she threw a light raincoat over her arm and left the house.

Luckily it was only a short drive to Elgin Crescent, but as usual the London traffic meant it took longer than she'd anticipated and by the time she'd found the parking space Marcia had told her was reserved for gallery employees, it was five minutes past ten. Not a very good start, she thought wryly.

Luckily Marcia was also late, and the gallery was still locked. Five minutes passed before the blonde woman arrived, and then she didn't bother with an apology. In fact, Marcia was surprisingly distant, and didn't even give a smile of greeting.

'Make me some coffee when you've put your coat and things away, would you, darling?' she asked Cressida, lighting a cigarette. 'You'll find all you need in the small room behind the front desk. I like mine strong and black.'

'What if anyone comes into the gallery?' asked Cressida nervously, seeing her new employer walking off to her own office. Then you'll have to deal with that first,' said Marcia sharply.

Luckily no one did come in, and Cressida was able to take Marcia her coffee quite quickly. 'I hope it's strong enough,' she said with a polite smile.

Marcia, who'd been sitting with her head in her hands, looked up and this time managed to smile back. 'I'm sure it will be perfect,' she murmured. 'I've got such a headache I can hardly bear the light of the day.'

She certainly didn't look too well. There were dark circles beneath her eyes that even her make-up couldn't conceal, and around her eyes the skin was puffy with what looked to Cressida like lack of sleep.

Leaving Marcia to recover in her own time, Cressida returned to the desk and started going through the very comprehensive list of instructions that Sue had typed out for her. After twenty minutes, when she'd read them through twice, she left her desk and walked down the L-shaped gallery to look at the pictures.

The walls on either side of the longest part of the L-shape were covered with fairly conventional paintings – landscapes, portraits and the occasional still life – but at the far end, where the room branched off into the bottom of the L-shape, there was an alcove, and once through that Cressida felt as though she'd entered another world.

Both walls were covered in stark black and white sketches of men and women, but men and women as Cressida had never seen them before. The women were nearly all in chains, either sitting provocatively in chairs, naked with their wrists and ankles chained, or else suspended from doorways or wall brackets, their forward-thrusting breasts emphasised by the constraints of their chains and the careful positioning of their bodies. Each picture also contained a man, but he was always faceless, a shadowy figure secondary to the woman despite being larger and clearly in a position of power.

She moved closer to see the name of the artist and as she did so she noticed that the expression on the faces of the women were not quite what she'd expected. There was certainly fear there, but also a strange glitter of triumph and superiority, as though they had obtained some special knowledge that nothing, not even their chains, could take away from them. She just had time to mentally file away the name of the artist, Rick Marks, when she heard the bell that went when the gallery door was opened and had to hurry out to the main desk again.

For the next hour she was quite busy. People came in and browsed, or asked to see the latest work by their favourite artist, while others ordered well-known prints, usually by Picasso or Salvador Dali. She was searching for a supplier for Dali's 'Persistence of memory' when Marcia finally emerged from her office and took over.

'Go and have a break, Cressida,' she said with a smile. 'You deserve it. I didn't mean to leave you to cope on your own for so long but a problem cropped up which I had to deal with immediately.'

Cressida retreated gratefully to the back room and made some more coffee, adding cream and sugar to her own cup. After she'd drunk it she went back to the desk and Marcia glanced up from the order book.

'We aren't usually this busy on a Monday, Cressida. I hope you didn't have too many problems?'

Cressida shook her head. 'Everything was fine.'

'Good. I've had Guy on the phone. It seems that he's promised a friend of his, Sir Peter Thornton, that his daughter can come and work at the gallery for the next few weeks while she takes time out to "find herself" – whatever that phrase means. It's a nuisance because the girl's only eighteen and isn't particularly bright, but an extra pair of hands is always useful I suppose. Her name's Leonora, and she can act as your junior. If she can "find herself" making endless cups of coffee and trying to sell some of those contemporary Parisian photographs we mistakenly decided to stock, then she's brighter than I thought.'

'Do you know her father too?' asked Cressida.

Marcia nodded. 'Guy and I dine with Sir Peter and his wife about once or twice a month and I remember that Leonora was due to finish at boarding school at the end of this term. His wife isn't Leonora's mother, of course, she's far too young. I think she's the result of his second marriage. He's had three, and it's difficult to keep track with these men!'

'Perhaps her stepmother wants her out of the way while she "finds herself",' suggested Cressida.

'I'm sure she does. Rose is only twenty-three herself, so an eighteen-year-old stepdaughter is bound to cause trouble, but then what do these men expect? Tell me, have you had a chance to look round the gallery?'

'Yes, I think I've seen everything,' said Cressida.

27

Marcia looked thoughtfully at her. 'What did you think of Rick's work?'

'The ones in the alcove?' asked Cressida. Marcia nodded. 'Well, they're certainly powerful,' conceded Cressida slowly, 'but I also found them very disturbing. I don't think I'd want one hanging on my bedroom wall.'

'The perfect place, I'd have thought!' laughed Marcia. Then she seemed to decide that wasn't the right thing to say and stopped laughing. 'It's all a question of personal taste,' she remarked briskly. 'Personally I think he's incredibly gifted and Guy's convinced he's going to be very famous indeed one day, but the dark side of his work isn't to everyone's taste.'

'I couldn't stop looking though,' admitted Cressida.

'Really?' said Marcia slowly. 'That's interesting. I'll tell him when he next rings. Like most artists, he's so insecure that any praise helps him keep faith in himself.'

It was difficult for Cressida to believe that a man who could create such powerful drawings would need anyone to boost his self-confidence, but she knew from what Sue had told her that all the artists were insecure and neurotic and clearly this Rick was no different.

The rest of the day passed quickly. In the afternoon Cressida was joined by a young woman called Polly who was responsible for making sure all the reproduction orders went through quickly and also took orders for her own framing business which she ran from her home on the opposite side of Elgin Crescent. Cressida decided that Polly might be able to give her some useful information, and just before the gallery closed for the day she managed to engage her in conversation.

'Do you know any of the artists who display here?' she asked.

Polly shook her head. 'Not on a personal level. They come in from time to time and we chat, but that's all there is to it. I'm not one of the chosen ones, if that's what you mean!'

'Chosen ones?'

'Yes, Marcia and Guy take a fancy to a gallery assistant now and again, and then they take them round some of the parties and dinners where artists and collectors meet up. From what I've heard they're very interesting evenings, but that's only gossip. As I say, I've never been invited.'

'Was the girl before me invited?' enquired Cressida.

Polly raised her eyebrows. 'She's a friend of yours, isn't she? Why not ask her?'

Cressida cursed herself for the slip. 'I know her family,' she explained quickly. 'Sue might not want to tell me everything.'

'Then far be it for me to talk out of turn. I tell you who they did take a fancy to, and that was Saskia. She was just a temporary receptionist – she only did about eight weeks part-time in all – but they took her around with them almost from the day she started here. Of course, she was very attractive, and that makes all the difference to Guy Cronje.'

'All the art I've seen here is modern. Don't they go in for anything else?' asked Cressida casually.

'Like what?'

'Well, paintings in the style of some of the Renaissance painters or – '

'There's no point,' Polly cut in. 'You can get prints of all the famous artists of that time. What this gallery does is offer an outlet for new artists, the greats of the future as it were. Most of our collectors have their family homes stuffed full of tiny Holbeins and Rembrandts anyway, and they're the genuine article. Why would they want something similar by an unknown artist?'

'I hadn't thought of it that way,' admitted Cressida, who was beginning to wonder how the gallery could possibly be involved in any kind of fraud involving old masterpieces when they were so committed to modern works.

'Your friend Sue seemed to think there must be money in reproduction work too. I mentioned it to Marcia. She said that wasn't the way that Guy wanted the gallery to go, and I can't say I blame him. He's building up quite a nice little name for himself, not just here but in France, Italy and Germany too. Why spoil a good thing?'

'Quite,' said Cressida quickly, deciding it was time she changed the subject. 'Rick Marks does some strange work. Does it sell well?'

Polly smiled to herself. 'Yes, but it's very specialised. Some people are totally obsessed with his pictures and buy almost everything they can afford. Others refuse even to view it. I can see their point too; it's pretty kinky, don't you think?'

'I don't know what I think,' admitted Cressida. 'Tomorrow I'm going to study it more closely if I get the time.'

'My partner likes his work,' said Polly as she got up to leave. 'He says that every picture expresses a different aspect of genuine sexuality, as opposed to society's glamorised view of it. I say give me the glamour any day! See you tomorrow.'

As soon as Cressida got home she punched out the number she'd been given by Inspector Cross and was immediately put through to Detective Chief Inspector Williams. She told him about her day and could tell that he was disappointed she hadn't yet come into contact with Guy Cronje himself.

'He's been abroad,' she explained. 'Marcia hasn't said when he's due back, but to be honest, so far I haven't seen anything that makes me think this gallery can possibly be a front for the kind of fraud you're interested in. It doesn't deal with that kind of clientele, and the paintings are about as far removed from Rembrandt as you can get!'

'You've only been there a day,' he reminded her sharply. 'I think you can safely leave it to us to decide whether or not we have grounds for being suspicious. I don't expect the kind of people we're talking about to wander round the shop ordering a few prints. These are important people, and they have special relationships with Cronje.'

'In that case, how am I ever going to get to meet them?' she asked in bewilderment.

'You'll have to use your initiative there,' he responded curtly.

'There was a Sir Peter Thornton mentioned,' said Cressida, and she heard Detective Chief Inspector Williams draw in his breath sharply. 'His daughter's coming to work at the gallery for a few weeks. She's just finished school, and reading between the lines I think her stepmother wants her out of the house. Does his name ring any bells?'

'It certainly does. Sir Peter is one of our wealthiest industrialists, retired now of course – he must be mid-sixties – but he's a patron of the arts and has a vast private collection of his own. You must get friendly with his daughter, WPC Farleigh, because through her you might get access to their home and find out just how well he knows Guy Cronje.'

'From what Marcia told me, he knows him pretty well,' said Cressida.

There was a long silence at the other end of the line. 'He's a good friend of mine,' said Williams at last. 'I don't want him ending up in trouble because of this conman, so keep your wits about you and watch every move that's made where he's concerned, understand?'

'Yes, sir,' said Cressida politely, but when she put the phone down she was less than pleased. She'd intended to keep her wits about her in any case – just because Sir Peter was a friend of the detective chief inspector, it didn't mean he was any more important than other people who might be being tricked by Guy Cronje and Marcia Neville.

'It's the old boys' network,' Tom told her when she rang him. 'Same school, same university, maybe even the same doddering nanny when they were tiny! You have to learn to live with it, Cress. It's what makes the world go round, I'm afraid.'

'Well, why isn't there an old girls' network?' demanded Cressida.

'I expect there will be before too long,' responded Tom. 'Take care now. I'll come round and see you tomorrow night. We can get a take-away in and talk things through.'

Cressida agreed, although she wasn't sure how long she and Tom were meant to carry on seeing each other now that she'd started her undercover work.

The following morning was bright and unusually warm for early May. Cressida looked through her new wardrobe and picked out a sunshine yellow and white striped skirt with a matching scoop-necked sleeveless top and short-sleeved collarless jacket. The colours suited her and by the time she'd applied her make-up she felt very pleased with her appearance.

It was only as she was driving to the gallery that she realised how quickly she was changing. A few weeks ago she would have crawled out of bed, pulled on her uniform, made sure she looked neat and tidy and then never considered her appearance for the rest of the day. But given a new wardrobe and a change of working environment, she was already thinking differently, even to the extent of worrying that she was wearing the wrong shade of lipstick. Although she told herself that this was because everyone had emphasised the importance of looks for the assignment, she knew that wasn't the whole truth. She was enjoying herself, and this realisation was rather disturbing.

'You're still a policewoman, Cressida,' she murmured as she turned into the parking area. 'This is a glamorous piece of undercover work, nothing more. When the party's over the gown goes back to the shop!'

This time Marcia had already opened up when Cressida arrived, and very soon after that the first of the day's customers began browsing through the gallery. Marcia had impressed upon Cressida that she must always watch the browsers carefully. 'They mustn't feel they're being watched,' she'd explained, 'but if you're not on your toes we can easily lose a small painting, or even a large one. Don't ask me how they do it, but they do.'

Luckily, watching people unobtrusively was something Cressida had had plenty of practice at doing, and she found that she could take phone calls and liaise with Marcia without missing anything that was going on in the gallery itself.

By 11.30 it was quieter, and when a tall, elderly man, smartly dressed and beautifully spoken, arrived for an appointment with Marcia, Cressida showed him into the other woman's office and then decided to have a second look at the paintings of Rick Marks.

In the centre of the back wall, lit by a spotlight, there was one that drew Cressida almost against her will. The woman was standing with her arms up level with her shoulders, her wrists cuffed, and long thin chains extended upward into the air like marionette strings. Her hands were hanging down limply from the wrists, and her upper torso was angled slightly forward although the expression on her face was still visible. In the bottom right-hand corner of the picture stood a man, his naked back displaying tension in every line of the straining muscles and the whole scene made Cressida feel very strange.

Her chest felt constricted and her breathing grew more rapid the longer she studied the picture. Moving closer she looked at the title. It was called 'The Puppet'. Cressida gazed into the woman's eyes, trying to work out what the expression in them conveyed, but she found it impossible to tell. They were dark and enigmatic and from certain angles it almost looked as though she was mocking the man in the corner, despite her chains.

Cressida tried to imagine what it would feel like to be in that position – to stand, totally naked and defenceless, in front of a man who desired you so desperately. To be restrained in chains so that no matter what you wanted, it was the man who called the tune and touched your body how and when he wanted.

Her stomach fluttered and she realised that her mouth was dry. She wanted to look away, to go back into the brightness of the gallery and look at some of the land-scape paintings designed to soothe rather than disturb, but she couldn't. Instead she stayed where she was in silent contemplation of the picture.

She studied it for so long that she became the woman. She could feel the chains around her wrists and the discomfort of the muscles in her arms as she waited for the man to make his move.

'Who's really the puppet do you think?' murmured a male voice in her ear, and with a cry of shock she spun round to see a man standing at her shoulder.

'I thought he'd spoken,' she blurted out.

'Who?' asked the man softly.

Cressida had never felt so foolish. 'The man in the picture,' she muttered.

'Ah, yes. I can understand that. She's clearly waiting for him to move or speak, but look at her eyes. She's a woman in control. He thinks she's the puppet, but she knows better. He's as much her slave as if he was wearing the chains. It's his desire that enslaves him.'

Feeling suddenly hot, Cressida turned and hurried out into the main gallery. 'I'm sorry, I didn't hear the doorbell ring. I would have come out sooner. Can I help you at all?'

The man looked thoughtfully at her. 'Not at this moment, but possibly later. I'm Guy Cronje, the owner of

Room With a View. You, I imagine, are Cressida Farleigh?'

Cressida, who was still trying to get her breathing under control, nodded. 'Yes, that's right.' She held out her hand. 'Again, I'm sorry I wasn't at the desk.'

'That's not important. I came in the back way so the bell didn't ring. You know, you're exactly as I pictured you. Marcia described you very well.'

Cressida smiled politely. Guy Cronje wasn't at all what she'd expected. He fitted Sue's general description: tall, slim and pale with dark hair cut quite short at the front and sides but brushing his collar at the back. However, nothing she'd been told had prepared her for the air of repressed tension that he exuded. His dark eyes seemed to burn right through her, they were so intense, and as he moved and talked he used his hands and arms to emphasise every point.

He was wearing a light brown suit with a white shirt and fawn tie but he continually fiddled with his jacket, and now and again he'd touch the knot of his tie in a series of nervous gestures that seemed necessary to soak up some of the energy that was consuming him. He was charismatic, intriguing and the least relaxing person she'd ever met.

'Well?' he asked with a half-smile.

Cressida frowned. 'I'm sorry?'

'You were examining me very carefully. I wondered what the verdict was.'

'I'm sorry, it's a terrible habit of mine. I like painting portraits in my spare time, and I was trying to work out how I'd paint you,' she lied, hoping he never asked to see any of her work because the only thing she could draw was breath.

'I'll sit for you some time,' he promised, and then he turned quickly on his heel and walked swiftly down the gallery and into Marcia's office.

Cressida returned to the reception desk, and had just

started thinking about 'The Puppet' again when a woman walked in with an enquiry about another of the gallery's artists, so she tried to push the unsettling image out of her mind.

About half an hour later, Guy emerged from Marcia's office, paced up and down the gallery, put two new paintings up and then walked out of the building without even glancing in Cressida's direction.

When Polly arrived after lunch, Cressida mentioned the meeting to her. 'He seems quite volatile,' she said casually. 'Not that he was in a bad mood or anything, but he's got a lot of nervous habits and does everything at twice the normal speed. I imagine he's capable of being difficult if things don't go right.'

Polly shrugged. 'I don't know him well enough to say. He and Marcia have been together some time now, I think, so she obviously doesn't find him that difficult. Or if she does she thinks he's worth it. Saskia was very smitten!'

'He's not my type,' said Cressida truthfully, ignoring the fact that despite this she couldn't get him out of her mind. 'I prefer reliable men.'

'You could probably rely on him giving you an exciting time!' laughed Polly. 'I know what you mean, though. He isn't my type, but I wouldn't mind spending a night with him, just to see what all the fuss is about.'

'Fuss?' asked Cressida.

'Yes. In the time I've been here we've had three or four slightly hysterical women on the phone demanding to know where he is and why he doesn't return their calls any longer. They're all married women, of course, which means he can discard them and there's nothing they can do about it.'

'Did you know any of them?' enquired Cressida, hoping for some names that she could pass on to Detective Chief Inspector Williams.

'No, although there was one voice I thought I recognised.'

'And Marcia doesn't mind?'

'Who knows what Marcia really thinks,' responded Polly. 'She certainly never shows that she minds, but then she never really lets on that she and Guy are an item either. Not here, at the gallery. Of course, they're often seen out together, but again they can claim that's business. It isn't, Saskia told me, but the whole affair is kept pretty secret. it makes sense. Far better for everyone if they don't mix their business life and their private life.'

'Did Saskia go out with him?' asked Cressida.

Polly gave her a strange look. 'You're just like your friend, Sue, always asking questions. Yes, I think she did but from what she said they only had a meal and a couple of drinks.'

'I'm always interested in other people's lives,' confessed Cressida. 'So is Sue. That's probably why we get on well!'

'I prefer to remain in ignorance, it's usually safer,' said Polly enigmatically, and then she went off to see about some picture framing, leaving Cressida to go over what she'd said and work out if any of it was important as far as her undercover work was concerned.

At 5.30 Marcia handed her a set of keys. 'Could you open up for me tomorrow morning, Cressida? I'm out tonight and it will be late before I get back. I used to open the gallery at midday on Wednesdays, but we're busier now and you've picked things up so quickly I feel quite happy leaving you in charge for a couple of hours.'

'Of course,' said Cressida, feeling a surge of triumph. If she was alone in the gallery from ten until noon then she could search Marcia's office and go through all the filing cabinets, which was something Sue had never done.

'I'm very pleased with how you're doing,' Marcia continued. 'Guy told me you're interested in Rick's work. He's due in tomorrow afternoon, so you'll have a chance to meet him. Maybe he'll ask you to pose for him!' She laughed.

Cressida shook her head. 'I'm definitely not nude model material, I'm afraid.'

Marcia raised her eyebrows. 'What nonsense. You've got a lovely figure, and wonderful legs. Guy noticed them at once.'

'How flattering,' said Cressida, embarrassed but at the same time relieved because at least it meant that she might manage to get closer to him than Sue had done.

'Yes, well, Guy does notice most attractive women,' responded Marcia, her smile slipping briefly. 'The only problem is, once he's completed the chase he loses interest, which leads to a lot of broken hearts.' Cressida didn't reply, and after a moment's hesitation, Marcia walked back into her office.

Ten minutes later, Cressida left the gallery, and as she got into her car she noticed a black XJS parked next to her. Guy Cronje was sitting at the wheel but he had his head bent over a book and didn't seem to see her. However, as she reversed out he watched her go in his driving mirror, and didn't return to his book until she was out of sight.

When Marcia finally joined him he glanced at her in a slightly questioning way, as though he'd never seen her before, and she felt a flicker of unease. Guy didn't realise it, but whenever he looked at her like that it meant that he'd been thinking about someone else and that Marcia's appearance had given him a surprise. She was used to it now, and could often head off the threat before too much damage was done, but sometimes she failed and then she suffered torments of jealousy until her lover's insatiable desire for trying fresh conquests was temporarily slaked and he turned all his attention back to her.

'What did you think of Cressida?' she asked lightly, certain that it was their new assistant who'd caught his attention.

Guy looked puzzled. 'Cressida?'

'Cressida Farleigh, the new girl at the gallery,' explained Marcia, wondering who on earth it could be if it wasn't Cressida.

'She seems very suitable and she's a great improvement on the last one. As I remarked, she got good legs, and if you're happy with her work then let's keep our fingers crossed that she stays.'

'Are we going out tonight?' asked Marcia. 'I gave the gallery keys to Cressida because I thought I might need a lie in in the morning. Monday was bad enough, but I had to get there on time then as it was her first day.'

Guy manoeuvred the car out into the fast-moving traffic. 'Is that wise? How do you know she's trustworthy?'

'There's no money on the premises! Besides, she was probably a Girl Guide or something, she's so clearly a thoroughly decent girl.'

'As long as she doesn't go poking about in our private papers,' muttered Guy, swearing as a taxi cut him up.

'Why on earth should she?'

'Why indeed? I have a suspicious nature, that's my problem. Now, about tonight. I thought that since she sent her solicitor to see you this afternoon, we should perhaps pay a call on Lady Alice Summers. She's expecting me, but I'm sure that seeing both of us will only double her pleasure.'

Marcia settled back in the passenger seat and smiled to herself. 'I'm sure it will,' she said softly. She then closed her eyes and began to picture the possible delights of the forthcoming evening.

Chapter Three

*I*t was a little after eight when Tom arrived at Cressida's
house that evening. She'd already telephoned Detective Chief Inspector Williams and, as she'd expected,
he'd been delighted that Guy Cronje had spoken to her
and made admiring comments to his partner. He'd also
been pleased to learn that in the morning she would have
a chance to search the whole gallery, but he reminded her
to take care to replace things where she found them.
Remembering Guy's edgy nervousness, Cressida
thought this was probably very good advice.

'Good day?' asked Tom, throwing his scruffy zip jacket
over the back of a chair.

Cressida picked it up and hung it on a hook in the
lobby. 'Yes, it went well. I met the boss and I've been
given the keys so that I can open up the gallery
tomorrow. Not bad after two days, is it?'

'They can't have anything there that matters,' said Tom
dismissively. 'No intelligent criminal would let a
stranger loose in the place if there was anything there to
hide.'

'Perhaps he isn't a criminal,' said Cressida, intensely
irritated by this put-down. 'Maybe he's what he seems –

a successful promoter in the world of art – and your lot in CID are all totally wrong about him. Have you thought of that?'

'Hey, what's wrong? Have I said something I shouldn't?' asked Tom, clearly startled by her response.

'I was feeling quite pleased with myself until you spoilt it,' said Cressida shortly. 'Even the great Detective Chief Inspector Williams said I'd done well, but apparently Detective Sergeant Tom Penfold knows better.'

'I hope you do find something,' he assured her. 'It's just hard to believe he'd make it that easy for you.'

'Let's forget work, shall we?' suggested Cressida. 'Do you still want to order a takeaway?'

Tom smiled. 'Later, perhaps. I thought we might find something else to occupy us for a while.'

Cressida, who was still aroused by the memory of looking at 'The Puppet', felt a rush of excitement. 'That sounds a good idea,' she agreed. 'Come on, let's go upstairs.'

Once they were in the bedroom Tom started to take his clothes off in his usual methodical way, but this time Cressida wanted to inject some of the urgency that she'd sensed in Guy Cronje into her sex life, and she quickly took off her own clothes and then began to undo the buttons on Tom's shirt.

'You're in a rush!' he exclaimed, taking a step back.

'Let me undress you,' suggested Cressida, but Tom still helped and when he was finally naked he stood in the middle of the bedroom floor, apparently uncertain how to proceed.

'What's the matter?' asked Cressida.

'I'm not sure what you want. You seem in a funny mood.'

'I want you, Tom,' she whispered, and then she began to push him towards the bed until he was lying on his back, his head supported by three pillows.

Cressida was feeling more excited than she had for a

long time, and images of the woman in chains and the watching man's taut muscles kept flashing through her brain as she joined Tom on the bed. Slowly she knelt over his body, facing his feet so that she could press her breasts and belly against his stomach and chest as she lowered herself on to him, and then she gently lifted his slowly stirring penis into her mouth.

With her legs spread wide across his chest, Cressida knew that she was totally exposed to Tom's view, and her entire vulva felt as though it was already swollen with desire. She wriggled her hips slightly to encourage Tom to touch her there, but he didn't respond so instead she concentrated on him.

She held the base of his penis in her left hand and then licked up each of the sides of the shaft in turn, running the blade of her tongue up from base to tip in firm leisurely strokes that soon had his penis fully erect while the glans darkened in colour.

Now she began to flick her tongue softly across the ridge on the underside of his erection, and when he finally uttered a tiny moan of pleasure she moved the tip of her tongue and ran it round the ridge instead until he groaned once more. She kept repeating this pattern, alternately crossing and circling the incredibly sensitive ridge, and at the same time she tightened her grip on the base of his penis and moved her hand rapidly up and down until the moment she felt his hips lift and his belly harden beneath her breasts. Then she stopped and lifted her head.

'Don't stop!' gasped Tom. 'I was just about to come.'

Cressida turned her head and looked at him over her shoulder. 'What about me?' she asked softly.

'I'll see to you later,' he promised. 'Just do what you were doing before.'

'I want you to make me come first,' said Cressida, and Tom's eyes widened in shock. 'Touch my bottom,' she urged him. 'Use your imagination for once! I want us to come at the same time.'

Tom didn't reply, and Cressida pressed her breasts down more firmly against his lower stomach, rubbing the hard peaks of her tiny nipples to and fro against his flesh, which at least stimulated her breasts for her, but she still refused to move her mouth back to where Tom wanted it and finally she felt his hands cupping the cheeks of her bottom.

He stroked her tentatively at first, but then his fingers wandered beneath her and she pushed her bottom higher so that he could easily massage the whole of her vulva. The moment she felt his fingers caressing her there she began to writhe desperately against him as the simmering excitement that had started back at the gallery began to build towards an orgasm.

When she felt his fingers part her outer sex lips and slide along the damp inner channel until he reached her swollen clitoris, she finally took his penis back into her mouth and this time she not only licked the ridge beneath the glans but also sucked on the glans itself.

Tom's hips lifted off the bed as he felt his heart rate increasing, and the sexual tension at the base of his penis increased to the point where he always lost control. He'd never known Cressida behave like this before, but at this moment he didn't want to think about that – he simply wanted to come and he knew that in order for that to happen she had to come too. Swiftly his fingers located the small hard bud of pleasure and he ran them along each side of the mass of nerve endings before gently brushing the side of the stem itself.

Cressida's breathing was shallow and every muscle tight as he at last touched her where she most wanted to be touched. Now the almost unbearable tension made her hips jerk instinctively and for a moment Tom lost contact with her clitoris and the build-up towards her release faltered. Luckily he quickly pulled her back down to him and then he was softly massaging all around the clitoris once more and she felt a sharp flash of pleasure, so intense it was almost pain, dart through her lower belly.

This always happened just before she came, and knowing that her own release was near Cressida moved her hand up and down the full length of Tom's shaft while her tongue whirled around the glans, dipping into the slit on the top so that she tasted the tangy salt of the clear fluid that had gathered there earlier. When the tiny point of her tongue dipped into the slit and her mouth continued to suck on him, Tom lost all control and with a shout he thrust up off the bed, his chest rubbing hard against Cressida's softly rounded belly.

This added pleasure on Cressida's already engorged pelvic area, and meant that her climax rushed through her with unexpected speed. She heard herself cry out only seconds after Tom and then the wonderful hot pleasure spread through her body until at last she slumped, limp and sated, on top of him.

For several minutes they lay together in silence, and Cressida was just about to say how wonderful it had been when Tom rolled out from under her. 'What on earth got into you tonight?' he asked, sounding less than pleased.

Cressida reversed herself until she was lying with her head next to Tom's. 'I felt like doing something different. Didn't you enjoy it?'

'I wasn't given much choice,' he muttered.

Cressida couldn't have been more shocked if he'd slapped her. 'What are you saying? That you didn't like it? You seemed keen enough; I had to remind you that I needed attention too, you were so lost in the pleasure of it all.'

'I'm not saying I didn't have a great orgasm, I did. It just wasn't ... Well, it isn't the way you usually behave and it made me feel strange.'

Cressida remembered Guy's words about the woman in the picture. 'You mean, you don't like women being in control, is that it?' she demanded.

Tom sighed. 'Let's not argue. It made a nice change, but I always like making love to you and you aren't naturally an aggressive sort of person so I think that in future I'd rather we stuck to the kind of thing we normally do.'

'Perhaps I should just lie back and think of England,' snapped Cressida. 'God, Tom, you can be incredibly boring sometimes.'

'If you ask me, it isn't doing you any good mixing with this arty set,' muttered Tom. 'The sooner your under-cover job's over the better as far as I'm concerned. 'You've already changed. Heaven knows what you'll be like in a few weeks' time.'

'I'm sorry you don't like it, but since you disapprove you'll probably be relieved to hear that Detective Chief Inspector Williams says we have to stop seeing each other for a while,' said Cressida. 'I wasn't going to take any notice, but after this I think he's definitely right.'

'Why?' demanded Tom.

'He wants me to seem unattached, and if we were seen out anywhere together that would show I wasn't. We can't afford the risk.'

'But we could still meet like this,' Tom pointed out.

'I think that's a very bad idea,' said Cressida, climbing off the bed and pulling on her robe. 'You make it very clear that you don't like what I'm doing, but I'm under orders and I've got no choice. I don't want to be pulled in two directions at once and it will make things easier for me as well if we stop seeing each other until this job's over.'

Tom held out a hand to her. 'I didn't mean to spoil it tonight, Cress. I admit I'm not happy about what you're having to do and that makes me feel threatened. When you took over in bed as well it was the last straw, but I did enjoy what we did and – '

'I'll order the takeaway,' said Cressida, walking out of the bedroom.

At the same time as Cressida was picking up the phone, Guy and Marcia were drawing up outside the late Lord Summers' house on the outskirts of London. Guy spoke his name into the security phone at the gates, and as they swung open he eased the car between the tall brick pillars.

The house, set in half an acre of land, was magnificent. It was split level, and the mixture of light and dark bricks together with imitation wooden beams on the top third of the outer front wall made a very striking impression.

'Rather large for our Alice to live in on her own, isn't it?' asked Marcia.

'I doubt if she'll stay here,' responded Guy. 'No doubt she'll sell everything she's allowed to sell and buy herself a nice place in sunny Spain where she can meet another wealthy older man. Once the problems over the estate have been sorted out, of course!' He smiled to himself.

'Here she comes,' murmured Marcia as the slim figure of Lady Alice appeared at the top of the steps. 'Not a twin-set and pearls day it seems!'

Guy surveyed Alice with interest. She had a capacity to surprise him that he found highly stimulating, and although he was annoyed with her over the visit from her solicitor, he was still fascinated by her sexuality, a sexuality that was totally at odds with her appearance.

Alice was 30, but didn't look a day over 22. Her naturally blonde hair was enhanced with ash-blonde streaks. She had recently grown out the layers from her urchin cut in an effort to cultivate a more sophisticated look, and while it was at the difficult in-between stage she'd taken to gelling it back off her fine-boned face, which if anything made her appear even younger. Only the heavy lidded dark grey eyes hinted at her real nature.

Marcia was right; it wasn't a twin-set and pearls day. Alice was wearing a deep red ankle-length silk wrap skirt, split to mid-thigh, and a startling red silk bustier that clung tightly just above her breasts and was heavily embroidered in gold and silver. On her feet were high-heeled silver sandals with slim ankle straps.

'I didn't expect to see Marcia,' remarked Alice as Guy kissed her on the cheek.

'I didn't expect to see your solicitor earlier,' responded Guy. 'However, I didn't let it spoil my day, and I'm sure Marcia won't spoil tonight for us. After all, we've spent many an enjoyable evening together in the past, haven't we!' He laughed, but Alice looked doubtful.

'That was when Michael was alive. I'm not sure it will be the same with three of us rather than four.'

'We'll just have to find out then, won't we?' said Guy briskly, putting a hand between Alice's shoulder blades and propelling her back up the steps and into the house.

Behind him, Marcia smiled to herself. She could imagine how Alice must be feeling. She'd anticipated a night with Guy, visualised Guy pleasuring her to the point of ecstasy for hour upon intimate hour. Now it was spoilt. There would be pleasure – exquisite pleasure – but of a different kind. It was a clever move by Guy, and one that should ensure they didn't have any more visits from Lady Alice's solicitor.

The room into which Alice led them was one that always made Marcia shudder. She understood the powerful impact clear lines and austere furnishings could make, but this looked like something out of a science fiction movie. It had been dreamt up by a very new and popular designer, and although the late Lord Summers had voiced his displeasure, Alice had told him it was perfect and he was behaving like an old fogey. That had been enough to silence him, at least in public.

The floors were bare pine, light coloured and so polished that you could see your reflection in them. Large glass tables of varying heights were dotted around the vast room, and ergonomically correct chairs in varying shades of greens and pinks were placed around them. Large green palms and what Guy always described as jungle vegetation stood in pots round the walls, and the large windows were protected by continental-style blinds.

'I've often wondered if Mark thought your late husband was a dentist,' commented Guy, sitting down in one of the few comfortable chairs at the far end of the oblong room.

'His name's Marco, and I'm surprised you don't like the design more,' retorted Alice. 'You're meant to have an eye for new talent.'

'If he came to me with a painting like this I'd suggest he tried another job,' said Guy shortly. 'Come along, Alice, you're neglecting us. How about some champagne?'

'I'll ask Mrs Rogers to fetch some,' said Alice quickly. 'Then shall I tell her she won't be needed any more tonight?' She looked hesitantly at Guy, clearly uncertain as to how the evening was going to proceed now that Marcia was here.

'I shan't be needing her!' laughed Guy. 'How about you, Marcia?'

Marcia, who was examining an abstract painting hanging behind some of the potted vegetation, shook her head. 'She's not my type either!'

As Alice left to organise the drinks, Guy glanced around him thoughtfully. 'I think that table by the wall might be useful,' he murmured. 'Let's move it nearer this chair, and pull the other comfortable chair over here. Alice will be spending quite a lot of time on the table top, and I want us to be able to see her, and her us.'

A few minutes later Mrs Rogers brought in the champagne, together with an ice bucket and three glasses. 'It's nice to see you again, Mr Cronje,' she said with a smile. 'I know how much poor Lord Summers valued your company, and Lady Alice is rather lonely now he's no longer with us. It's very kind of you to take the time to call. So many friends seem to disappear once a husband dies, isn't that right, Lady Alice?'

A frown creased Alice's normally smooth brow. 'I hardly think Guy's interested in my social life, Mrs Rogers. That will be all for tonight, thank you.'

'How to keep the servants happy!' remarked Guy sarcastically. 'Really, Alice, you still haven't grasped the way to deal with the domestic help, have you? I'm afraid your background shows when you're rude to Mrs Rogers.'

'I've no idea what you mean,' said Alice, looking annoyed.

'I was remembering your mother and what a sociable young lady she's reputed to have been. Still, no doubt that's all long forgotten. Or is it? Why does Mrs Rogers think you're being neglected by your friends?'

'Because she isn't blind,' snapped Alice, losing her composure. 'No one calls any more, not since they heard whispers about problems with the estate. I can't imagine why they think it's got anything to do with me. I don't know the first thing about art.'

'Or interior designers,' murmured Marcia to herself.

'I suppose that's why you asked your solicitor to call on me,' said Guy slowly. 'Knowing that I'm something of an expert in that field you presumably thought I might be able to help him track down the missing paintings, is that right?'

Alice chewed on her bottom lip. 'In a way,' she muttered.

Guy smiled. 'I thought I must be right. After what we've been to each other I didn't imagine you'd suggest I was in any way involved in the disappearance of these paintings. It's just unfortunate that your solicitor had got hold of the wrong end of the stick. Well, since that's sorted out, let's start the champagne, shall we?'

Looking immensely relieved, Alice handed him the bottle. 'Would you open it, Guy?'

'Of course. While I'm doing that, perhaps you'd be kind enough to lie face down on that glass-topped table there, the one I had Marcia move while you were out of the room.'

Alice stared at him. 'Do what?'

'Lie face down on the table,' he repeated softly. 'Come along, Alice. I thought you wanted some fun in your life again. It's a little late in our relationship to start going coy, don't you think?'

Slowly Alice obeyed him, sliding herself across the width of the table so that her upper torso was hanging over one side and her legs dangled down the other.

'Keep your head down,' said Guy softly. 'In a moment, Marcia and I will bring you your champagne. I know you like it well chilled.'

Marcia half-filled two glasses and strolled to where the prone girl was lying across the table top. Guy crouched down and slowly peeled back the top of the elaborate basque until both of Lady Alice's firm white breasts were totally exposed. Then he took one of the glasses from Marcia and they each took hold of one of the dangling breasts and dipped them into the chilled champagne.

Alice drew in her breath sharply as the cold liquid touched her warm skin. Both Marcia and Guy squeezed her breasts firmly at the top and then rotated them so that her rapidly hardening nipples and the surrounding area were thoroughly immersed in the sparkling drink.

As Alice began to tremble with rising excitement, the glasses were removed and Guy pressed his right hand softly against the exposed nape of her neck. 'Sit up, Alice. We'd like to taste the drink now.'

Without a word, Alice obeyed. She'd been in a state of

heightened sexual tension all day waiting for Guy's visit, and now that he was here and her arousal had begun she could feel an orgasm starting to build, even at this moment.

'It might be better if she lay back,' suggested Marcia. Guy nodded, and pressed against Alice's bare shoulders. She felt him pressing her backward and as soon as her spine was against the table the pair of them leant over her and started to lick the champagne from her dripping breasts.

Guy only licked for a few seconds and then began to suck, drawing her large brown nipple into his mouth and twirling the tip of his tongue around its peak while he kept up the powerful suction. Marcia sipped at the liquid in a far more delicate way. Her tongue swirled around the underside of Alice's left breast and then moved slowly upward until she could sweep it across the top of the nipple.

The contrast in the way they were using their mouths was incredibly arousing, and Alice heard herself moan softly with delight. Guy looked across her body and nodded at Marcia who nodded back at him. Lady Alice was relaxed, sexually aroused and anticipating her first orgasm. It was all going very well.

'Sit up now,' said Guy sharply. 'While Marcia and I have a proper drink we want you to keep us entertained. You are, after all, our hostess!'

'But . . .' Alice's voice trailed off as she realised that for the first time she didn't have her husband with her. She was totally alone with Guy and Marcia, and if she wanted sexual satisfaction, as she certainly did, then she was going to have to play the game their way. She could protest, but then they'd go. That was the last thing Alice wanted now, because her well-trained and demanding body was tingling with excitement and longed for sexual release.

She sat up, a slightly bemused look on her face, and

Guy's voice changed so that now it was kind and reassuring. 'That's better. What a very attractive skirt,' he added, as the material fell apart, exposing almost all of her legs. 'Panties? I think we can do without those, don't you, Marcia?'

'They'll certainly be in the way,' commented Marcia, reaching up beneath the red skirt. As Guy lifted Alice slightly off the table, Marcia slipped the whisp of white silk down the other woman's legs. 'There, now she's ready for us,' she said with satisfaction.

Turning away, Guy opened the briefcase that he'd brought with him. 'Good. What shall we use? I think this one. I seem to remember that it was a great favourite of yours, Alice, in days gone by.'

Alice, her grey eyes watchful, stared as he withdrew a soft, bendy latex vibrator from the case and then walked back towards her. 'Now, I'm going to let you play with this for a time. Part your legs, Alice.'

Marcia watched as the lean legs separated, exposing a glimpse of light brown pubic hair, and then Guy was covering the end of the soft flexible vibrator in jelly and easing it inside the trembling Alice. Once it was inserted he pulled her to the edge of the table, so that her legs dangled towards the floor and she was sitting impaled on the vibrator. Then he switched it on.

Lady Alice felt the first gentle tremors of the soft, pliable vibrator and the darts of pleasure travelled outward, spreading behind her clitoris and up through her lower pelvis. She shook with mounting desire and felt her nipples, still sticky from the champagne, hardening beneath the gaze of Guy and Marcia.

Marcia could imagine how Alice was feeling, and knew that before very long the other woman would need further stimulation because the vibrator alone had never been sufficient to bring her to a climax. This was something that Guy was aware of, and part of the reason why he'd chosen it.

Alice's breathing quickened and her face and neck started to flush with arousal. She gave a tiny whimper of excitement and her hands gripped the edge of the table as she attempted to angle herself slightly forward and increase the sensations behind her now tight bud of pleasure.

'Sit still, Alice,' murmured Guy laconically. Alice's eyes met his. She recognised the look of control in them, but decided to ignore it. She'd waited all day for this and didn't intend to wait a moment longer than necessary now that he was here.

Just the same, she didn't quite dare move, so instead she started to inch one of her hands closer to her leg. If she could only touch herself between her thighs – softly rotate her clitoris that was being continually stimulated by the vibrations from inside her vagina – then she knew she'd come instantly.

Guy knew that as well, and he saw what was happening. As Alice's hand started to lift from the table he jumped out of his chair and crossed the short space between them in two strides, grabbing her wrist in his hand. 'Not yet, Alice. I want to make quite sure that Marcia and I don't have any further visits from your solicitor, or have to listen to any more veiled threats about police involvement. Do I have your word on that?'

'Yes!' shouted Alice, trying to pull her hand away from him as the whole of her lower body started to feel tight and swollen due to the relentless squirming and throbbing of the vibrator deep within her.

'After all,' continued Guy, stroking one of her breasts softly with his free hand as she continued to shudder and whimper with sexual need, 'you too have things to hide. Things that your late husband's trustees might not approve of, isn't that true?'

Alice was beginning to pant aloud as her breath quickened. Guy's fingers were so soft against her breasts that now wonderful sensations were travelling down

53

from her nipple to join those in her lower belly. 'Yes, yes, I know,' she gabbled. 'I'm sorry, Guy. I didn't mean to cause trouble. I just wanted to get him out of here. He was driving me mad with his stupid questions about Michael and the people he mixed with. I thought you could handle him better than I could.'

'How thoughtful,' said Guy, and suddenly he began to squeeze her nipple between two fingers, very softly at first but with increasing pressure until she wasn't quite sure that it was pleasure she was feeling any more. Even if it wasn't, her body was responding in a way it had never responded before, and she heard herself sobbing for him to let her come as the tension continued to mount remorselessly.

With one final squeeze of the rapidly darkening nipple, Guy released her breasts and his hand travelled down through the valley between them and then across her stomach so that every muscle within her seemed to leap with excited anticipation.

'Then you'll keep him away from us from now on?' asked Guy softly.

'Yes!' shouted Alice. 'How many times do I have to tell you? I promise I won't let him bother you again. Now, let me come.'

'Marcia, over here,' commanded Guy. He felt Alice stiffen but ignored her resistance. He wanted Marcia to be the one to allow the desperate young woman her release, because he knew that he and Marcia would be visiting Lady Alice again and they needed to keep her in their power. She must accept them both as a source of pleasure, not just him, although he would also visit on his own because he enjoyed taking her in the privacy of her bedroom, away from any other eyes.

Marcia knelt down on the floor and spread Alice's quivering legs apart. Then, with incredible delicacy, she separated the outer sex lips. Slowly she allowed her tongue to slide up one side of the damp channel, moving the vibrator slightly to one side as Guy eased Alice's body back a little to make it easier for her, until it reached the tight mass of nerve endings that would provide the trigger for final release.

Alice felt the soft pressure moving ever upward and began to shout in a frenzy of need until finally Marcia's tongue encircled the clitoris itself, stimulating all the sides of the tiny shaft.

Guy put his hands on Alice's shoulders and as her body was wracked with a shattering orgasm and she instinctively rose up off the table, he pressed her firmly down so that even as the muscles spasmed with pleasure and her nerve endings exploded with the force of the climax she was made to endure the continued stimulation of the vibrator. As a result, her orgasm seemed to go on and on for an eternity. Both Guy and Marcia watched with interest as the slight figure screamed, twisted and shuddered in a franzy of sexual ecstasy.

Finally, when her body could take no more and her head started to fall forward, Guy signalled for Marcia to turn off the vibrator and the room fell silent.

For a few minutes Guy stroked the nape of Alice's neck until her breathing was back to normal and she lifted her head, her eyes shining and her whole body glowing with the satisfaction of her climax.

However, anxious as Guy had been to satisfy her, he was equally anxious to leave her wanting more. She had to need him, because only then could he be sure of maintaining control over her for as long as necessary.

'Sit in the lotus position on the table and watch us now,' he said quietly. 'I remember how much you and Michael liked to watch Marcia with me.'

'But that was different,' protested Alice. 'Then it turned us both on and later he and I would – '

'I do know what effect it had on you!' laughed Guy. 'Just the same, it's what I want, and when I get what I want I can be a most attentive lover, as you already know.'

Convinced by this that he would satisfy her again after making love to Marcia, Alice complied, sitting in the lotus position with her back straight and her legs crossed flat on the table top. Guy studied her for a moment and then decided to remove the basque, unzipping it at the back and peeling it off her body. Then he arranged her skirt so that her vulva was fully exposed before at last he was satisfied.

He moved across the room to where Marcia had already taken off her cerise silk dress and was standing in cream coloured hold-ups and high-heeled shoes. The only other thing she'd left on was her white satin bra, which she knew Guy loved to remove himself.

He put a hand at the back of her head and kissed her hard, his tongue invading her mouth while his free hand roamed over the tight cheeks of her bottom, stroking and kneading in a familiar rhythm that soon had Marcia thrusting her hips towards him. The watching Alice felt desire begin to stir in her again.

Then Guy released Marcia and swiftly took off his own clothes before pushing her backward. As Marcia rested her head against the stark white wall, Guy reached behind her and unclasped her bra. He then bent his head and began to lick at the tops of her breasts, pushing the cups of the bra gradually lower until at last the garment fell away and her large breasts, with their dark red nipples, were free to brush against his chest.

Marcia was desperate for him now. She'd watched Lady Alice's orgasm with great excitement and the knowledge that the other woman was watching them now, longing to have Guy penetrate her in the way he was about to penetrate Marcia, added to her desire. She wrapped her left leg round Guy's upper right thigh as he pushed his right leg forward. At the same time he wrapped his right arm round her waist and leant against the wall with his left hand to give them both support. Marcia's arms were round his neck and once more they began to kiss. This time Guy kissed around the outline of Marcia's lips and nibbled at the corners of her mouth until she heard herself whimpering, just as Alice had earlier. Guy's thigh lifted a little and Marcia ground her lower body fiercely against him so that her clitoris was stimulated and a wonderful hot tightness began to fill the whole pubic area.

Alice sat perfectly still, watching the pair of them kissing and caressing each other, and she felt herself growing very damp between her thighs. The vibrator had been switched off, but it was still inside her and she wished that the full feeling came from Guy's long, thick penis rather than the piece of latex. She also wished that the vibrator could be switched on again, but if she did it herself the other two would hear and she knew that would mean no satisfaction for her when they'd finished their erotic coupling.

Suddenly, just as Guy had begun to thrust steadily in and out of the gasping Marcia, he withdrew, and Alice saw the startled expression on Marcia's face with considerable satisfaction. It was reassuring to know that even with Marcia, Guy was unpredictable.

'Bend over that other table,' he said shortly.

Marcia stared at him. 'That's not what I want tonight,' she said quietly. Guy shrugged and stood waiting impassively for her to obey. Marcia's lips tightened into a thin line, but she knew that she mustn't break the spell and after a quick glance at Alice's shining eyes and flushed face realised that the erotic tension must be maintained.

Just the same, she bent face down over the table with a little trepidation. This wasn't her favourite position, although it excited Guy, and as she spread her forearms on the cool glass and rested her cheek against them, she wished he'd carried on in the first position. Her orgasm had been building nicely.

Guy knew this. He and Marcia had been lovers for so long that he knew everything there was to know about her responses, but he wanted Alice to see something more stimulating than a brief coupling standing by the wall.

Now he was free to start fondling Marcia's buttocks with one hand while the other ran up and down her spine, his fingers dancing along her vertebrae like a pianist playing on the keys of a piano.

Marcia started to shake with a mixture of arousal and fear. She loved having him stroke her back but she wasn't so sure about what he intended to do with her buttocks, and when he moved away from her for a moment she tensed, knowing that this wasn't going to be one of their ordinary evenings. Marcia liked to watch Guy being extreme with other women, but she wasn't so keen on him doing it to her, although it always resulted in some of her most intense climaxes.

It was the knowledge that other people were watching her earlier humiliation and were aware of her inability to control her response to it that shamed her. For Guy, it was Marcia's shame and the uncontrollable violent orgasm that always followed that provided the extra thrill.

Alice watched wide-eyed as Guy took a flat latex whip from his briefcase and then struck Marcia's very white buttocks sharply with it. Marcia gasped, her entire body went rigid, and a pale pink mark appeared across the middle of her bottom. Alice jumped in sympathy, but tendrils of pleasure also began to swirl through her. As the sting of the flicked whip reached its peak, Guy's fingers resumed their erotic dance along Marcia's spine so that she was unable to tell where her pleasure was coming from. All she knew was that she was rapidly climbing to the point of orgasm and that her body was becoming more and more alive to every form of stimulation.

Alice watched as Guy struck Marcia's tight buttocks again, and this time Marcia gave a moan of desire as the hot sting of forbidden pleasure made her press her breasts down against the cool glass table.

All at once Marcia was aware that Guy was spreading cold cream over the hot stripe marks that she knew the whip would have left. Then, while his free hand continued to play up and down her spine, the cream was massaged into the undersides of her buttocks before his hand eased its way between them. She tightened instinctively as he began to spread it around the entrance to her rear opening.

'Marcia loves this really,' Guy remarked, looking across at Alice. 'The trouble is, she doesn't like other people seeing how much it pleases her. I keep trying to break down this strange inhibition, but she still resists, don't you, Marcia?'

'No,' said Marcia shortly. She hated it when he talked about her as though she was some kind of shy novice.

'Then tell us how much you're enjoying this,' he whispered against her ear, and she felt his fingers probing gently against the clenched muscles of her rectum until finally one slipped inside and he was spreading some of the cream around, causing the incredibly sensitive nerve endings there to spark with delight. Guy pressed against the walls of her rectum with the tip of his finger, using the cream as a lubricant, and the hint of discomfort coupled with the sharp pleasure formed a combination that made Marcia begin to writhe helplessly.

Her upper torso could only be stimulated by her own movements but then Guy moved a hand beneath her belly, pulling her hips out in order to make penetration easier for him.

Her feet were planted firmly on the floor and she tried to flatten out her back so that Guy could achieve maximum penetration. Her stomach was hard and swollen now and when she heard Alice give a muffled moan of frustrated desire, Marcia knew that her own climax was only seconds away.

Guy thrust into her fiercely and without warning, within seconds of removing his finger from her rectum. The walls of her vagina tightened around him and she started to milk him in the way he loved. As he felt the velvet-soft muscles closing around his throbbing shaft, Guy stopped caressing Marcia's spine and instead used that hand to reach beneath her until he located her clitoris.

Marcia jerked at his touch as her throbbing body sent piercing tingles of electricity along every nerve as though someone had plugged her in at the mains. Behind her clitoris the orgasm was building to its crescendo and Guy, who could feel himself losing control of his own orgasm, suddenly stopped stroking the side of Marcia's clitoris and instead flicked against its head, triggering Marcia's moment of release.

She shouted out in triumph as the incredible mixture of sensations that Guy had engendered during their lovemaking all came together in one overwhelming wave of sexual ecstasy. As she shouted she heard Guy gasp aloud as he too found release inside the softly pulsating walls of her vagina.

As soon as he'd come, Guy withdrew and stepped away from Marcia, who was still supporting her upper body on the table top. She often wished that he'd spend longer inside her after his orgasm, but he never did. Once the sex was finished, Guy lost interest, and tonight was no exception.

He walked over to where Alice was still sitting obediently in the lotus position and stared deep into her eyes. 'How do you feel, Alice?'

'I want you inside me too,' she said huskily.

'I don't think I could manage that right now. Perhaps

60

another night?' he suggested, and was amused to see the look of stunned disbelief on her face.

'You can't leave me like this,' protested Alice, climbing down off the table and stepping up to Guy so that her breasts brushed against his lean, muscular chest. 'I'm ready for another orgasm now. When Michael was alive the four of us used to spend hours together. Why are you going so early?'

'I have to consult my solicitor,' said Guy dryly, and saw understanding dawn in Alice's eyes.

'You did this on purpose, to punish me!' she shouted. 'Well, you've made a mistake, because I can be just as unpleasant as you, Guy Cronje, and I know more than you think.'

Guy caught hold of one of her wrists. 'I don't think you can be as unpleasant as I can, Alice. If I were you, though, I wouldn't attempt to find out. As for knowing more than I think you know, I can't imagine what you're talking about. I don't want us to quarrel,' he added, suddenly softening his voice and caressing her marked wrist with his thumb. 'I want us to have more good times together, on our own.'

He bent his head and kissed her firm breasts, licking lazily around each of the nipples in turn until she started to squirm against him. 'I'll call you tomorrow,' he promised in a low voice. 'We'll arrange our next meeting then.'

'But I want another orgasm now,' persisted Alice. 'I'm right on the edge after watching you with Marcia.'

Guy smiled at her, but it wasn't a friendly smile and Alice remembered her earlier doubts about how far Guy could be trusted to behave. 'Give yourself one,' he suggested. 'Marcia and I will be happy to watch you.'

'Then can you and I get together another time?' asked Alice, despising herself even as she asked the question, but her body was clamouring for his attentions and she knew that she couldn't bear to lose contact with him.

'Of course,' he assured her, running a hand down the inside of her left arm until she thought she'd scream from the gently arousing touch that was adding to her frustration.

'Marcia!' Guy called to his mistress as she stood by the window, dressing. 'Alice is going to give herself an orgasm. I thought you might like to watch.'

Marcia did up the last buttons of her dress and turned towards the couple. She felt back in control now and her voice was cool and brisk. 'What a good idea. Where are you planning to do it, Alice? Isn't the glass table a little cold?'

'Marco obviously didn't realise what this room would be used for when he designed it!' said Guy with a smile. 'Let's put the cushions from the two easy chairs on to this pine floor. They'll make a good makeshift bed.'

Quickly he and Marcia laid out the removable backs and seats of the chairs, then Guy took hold of Alice's hand and drew her down on to them. 'Lie on your face,' he murmured. 'Put your hands underneath you and remember to keep squeezing your thighs together. It adds to the overall stimulation.'

Alice's face felt flushed and she was glad that she didn't have to see the expressions of the two spectators as she removed her skirt and then lay down on the soft cushions.

Her hand slid down through her pubic hair and her outer sex lips parted easily for her. She didn't need any additional lubrication because watching Guy and Marcia had been so arousing, and as her fingers slid around her rigid clitoris her body started to twist and writhe. A delicious hot sensation flooded through her genitals.

'Prolong it,' said Guy quietly. 'See how long you can make the pleasure last.'

Alice didn't need encouraging. It was bliss to be in charge of her own release at last after the frustration of the past twenty minutes. Her fingers roamed around the clitoris, moved lower to the entrance of her vagina and then she inserted two fingers just inside the entrance and rotated them until she found her G spot.

The moment she touched it her body drew in on itself as a deep piercing shaft of pleasure ran upward behind her pubic bone. Now she became totally lost in the sensations and Guy and Marcia watched as she moaned and thrashed on the cushions, her hand hidden beneath her. At last she was ready to move her fingers upward again – to touch the delicate area around the clitoris itself, an area that was now pulsating desperately as her orgasm approached.

Guy saw her bottom lift a fraction into the air, watched her toes go rigid and noted the way her head was moving frantically from side to side. She was perched right on the edge of release now, and when she uttered tiny whimpers of frantic excitement he quietly picked up the latex whip that he'd used on Marcia and at the precise moment that Alice finally climaxed he struck her twice across the back of her upper thighs.

The shock of the blows mixed with the searing hot pleasure that they caused meant that Alice's climax doubled in intensity, and she was startled to hear herself shouting out loud as her body contorted in its spasms of release. 'Again!' she shouted, sounding more desperate than ever before. 'Do that again, now! Now!'

But Guy didn't. He merely nodded thoughtfully to himself as he stored away the knowledge that this was possibly the key to controlling Alice. When the naked young woman was finally still, Marcia walked briskly out of the room, leaving Guy alone with Alice. He knelt down by her side and stroked her sweat-streaked hair.

'Did you enjoy that?' he asked kindly, trailing the latex whip softly across her shoulders.

'More than I've ever enjoyed anything!' gasped Alice, still shattered by what had happened.

'Then we'll see what we can do when we next meet up.

Be good though, or I might find I'm too busy to fit you in.'

Alice knew then that no matter how much the trustees pestered her, she wouldn't talk any more about her suspicions concerning Guy and the fact that he might have double-crossed her late husband. This evening had been far too pleasurable for her to give up the prospect of further delights.

She knew that her housekeeper was right; most of the friends she and Michael had shared had deserted her now. Not only because there was trouble with her stepchildren over the estate, but also because she wasn't 'one of them'. They thought Michael had married beneath him, and now he wasn't there to protect her from their disdain they were free to make it clear.

She was a very physical young woman who needed sex, and until she was able to free herself from the complex legal wranglings and make a new life elsewhere, she needed Guy to provide her with that. 'I'll be good,' she said slowly, and felt Guy's lean fingers massage her scalp.

'See you soon,' he promised, and then she heard him cross the floor and close the door behind him. A few minutes later there was the sound of his car starting up and she was alone once more. Alone, but at least for now she was sated, relaxed and much happier. She never had cared about Michael's art collection anyway.

'Well?' demanded Marcia, as they sped away from the house. 'Did it work?'

He nodded. 'I think it worked very well, both as a warning and as a promise. The stick and carrot method, as it were. It's a pity you can't lose yourself in some of our sex better when we've got an audience,' he added idly. 'You enjoy everything when we're alone together.'

Marcia, like Alice, recognised a warning when she heard one, and although she and Guy were tied together by far more than a sexual liaison, she knew that he was capable of ditching her should she cease to please him.

'The solicitor's visit unsettled me,' she snapped defensively.

'There's no need to let him rattle you,' Guy assured her. 'We're perfectly safe. In any case, this isn't a new problem. Just before he was killed Sir Michael mentioned to me that you seemed rather detached at times.'

'That's why I suit you,' said Marcia with a brittle laugh. 'No one could be more detached than you.'

'Where sex is involved I'm never detached,' responded Guy. 'All I ask is that you abandon yourself to every kind of pleasure when we're working, just as you do in our private life. I trust I make myself clear?'

'Perfectly,' responded Marcia. 'Perhaps you think you know someone who could fulfil my role better?' she added sarcastically.

'No,' said Guy, 'but I'm always looking.'

He laughed, leaving Marcia so uneasy that she hardly slept at all after she got home. She was very aware that Guy was ruthless, and although she couldn't believe he'd ever find anyone to take her place there was always the chance that somewhere out there, there could be a woman who'd fit the bill.

Guy too lay awake for quite some time, replaying the evening in his mind and mentally replacing Marcia with other women. He was surprised to discover that when he replaced her with Cressida, their new gallery assistant, the entire scenario took on a new edge of excitement for him. He decided that the next day he must take a closer look at Cressida, and then he fell asleep.

Cressida, blissfully unaware of everything, slept well after Tom had gone. Alice, alone in her huge king-size bed, slept the sleep of exhaustion.

Detective Chief Inspector Williams would have been very pleased with the way things were developing.

65

Chapter Four

The following morning Cressida arrived at the gallery at 8.30. She was determined to make the most of the time she had to herself, knowing that Detective Chief Inspector Williams was hoping she'd find some concrete evidence linking the gallery to the art forgeries.

She went into Marcia's office and opened the top right-hand drawer of the older woman's desk. She'd been afraid that it might be locked, but to her relief not only was it open, it also contained the key to the other drawers in the desk.

Swiftly she unlocked them and then began going through the files. The headings were vague: 'Promising', 'Rejections', 'Overseas Contacts' and 'Active' all nestled amidst files marked A - Z that could contain anything at all. With a sinking heart, Cressida realised that it would take her hours to go through everything. She'd have to choose some at random this time and hope for another opportunity at a later date.

'Overseas Contacts' sounded useful, given the fact that Interpol were interested in Guy Cronje's activities, but when Cressida went through it she found that it consisted entirely of a list of collectors in France, Switzerland, Holland and Germany, all on the look-out for promising new artists whose works they could buy at a relatively low price but who Guy considered a good financial investment.

Cressida was rather shocked by this calculated approach. It was no different to buying stocks and shares and where artistic talent was concerned she found that unforgiveable.

'Come on, Cressida, you've no time for moralising,' she chided herself. 'Keep looking for something useful.' File after file was taken out and then replaced without anything of interest coming to light, and she was about to move over to the filing cabinet in the corner of the room when purely by chance she saw one headed 'Renovations', filed by mistake under the letter E.

The file was thick and divided into several sections. One was marked 'Lord Summers' and Cressida went straight to those pages. Sir Michael's full name and address was listed, along with his wife's name and the names of her parents. Beneath that was a long list of paintings, most of which had been purchased from the gallery and had nothing to do with renovations, but then near the bottom of the page she found a note to the effect that a Rembrandt and a Monet had been brought in for cleaning at the end of the previous year.

Cressida's heart began to race. She frequently experienced a mixture of excitement and fear when on undercover work, and the fact that this time she was working in an upmarket art gallery rather than a downbeat nightclub didn't change the underlying frisson of fear that always came when she felt that she was on to something.

There was no record of where the pictures went to be cleaned, or when they were returned to Lord Summers, and so Cressida decided to start checking out other names in the file. As she flicked through the sections she caught sight of the name Sir Peter Thornton, and tried to think why that rang a bell. Then she remembered. It was the name of the man whose daughter, Leonora, was coming to work at the gallery, a man who was also a friend of Detective Chief Inspector Williams. At the bottom of his page she found a note that a Holbein had been brought in for 'skilled repair work' at the end of April.

Now she knew that Guy and Marcia had definitely had the opportunity to forge reproductions of the paintings missing from the Summers' estate. Furthermore, it seemed likely they were about to do the same to one of Sir Peter Thornton's paintings.

There was a photocopier in the small room behind her desk in the gallery and she was just about to take the two relevant pages out of the file and copy them when the door to the office opened and Marcia walked in.

'What on earth are you doing, Cressida?' she asked in astonishment.

Cressida knew that she mustn't blush or look guilty and her mind raced as she struggled to come up with an acceptable excuse for being caught going through Marcia's private drawers.

'A man called in just after I opened up,' she said swiftly. 'He wouldn't give his name, but he said he'd recently inherited a Matisse from his grandfather and it needed a good clean and possibly some restoration work done on it. I remembered Sue saying that the gallery did do cleaning work on valuable paintings and was trying to find out some details. He said he'd call back.'

Marcia glanced at her wristwatch. 'You must have opened up very early. It's only ten now but you say you've already had a nameless visitor with a valuable painting to be cleaned?'

Cressida straightened up and smiled at Marcia. She was grateful now for her years of police work and her training in keeping calm in difficult situations, because there was a definite look of suspicion in Marcia's eyes. 'I was early,' she admitted. 'I'd hoped for some private time to look over Rick Marks' work again. I can't get it out of my mind, it seems to haunt me. I suppose that says something about my sexuality, but I'm not sure what!' she laughed.

Marcia didn't laugh. 'What did the man with the inherited Matisse look like?' she asked abruptly.

'Tall, heavily built, about forty-five and with a shock of grey hair,' said Cressida, improvising wildly. 'Do you know him?'

'I'm hardly likely to know him if he came here to see whether or not we could help out, am I? Why didn't you get his name?'

'I tried,' Cressida assured her. 'He was very evasive about giving me any details. He wouldn't even say what the title of the painting was.'

'If he comes back, please show him through to me,' said Marcia.

'Of course. I'm sorry I opened your desk drawers, but I didn't think you'd mind since you'd left the key where anyone could find it.'

'Only someone who opened the top drawer in the first place,' said Marcia coldly. 'As I recall, Sue didn't mention anything about renovations on your job resumé did she?'

'No, but she must have mentioned it some other time,' said Cressida. 'It isn't a secret, is it? I mean, I didn't do anything wrong telling this man we could probably help?'

'Why on earth should anything about our work be a secret?' asked Marcia, walking over to Cressida and removing the file casually from her hands. 'If we offer a service we advertise it. There wouldn't be much point in doing it otherwise – that would prove financially rather unrewarding, don't you think?'

'I wondered if it was something you only did for personal friends,' said Cressida, trying to ease the tension in the room.

'We mention the service in our catalogue,' said Marcia shortly. 'Perhaps you should try reading that before you go and stare at Rick's work again. Guy told me it fascinated you,' she added, closing the desk drawers and re-locking them. 'Rick's calling in later this morning. You'll have an opportunity to tell him what a fan you are then.'

Cressida decided to try and cover her confusion over being caught snooping by using Rick's visit as an excuse. 'I don't think I really want to meet him,' she said, backing away from Marcia's desk and finally allowing the blush that had been threatening for the past few minutes to suffuse her face and neck. 'I won't know what to say.'

'Tell him you think his drawings are the most erotic you've ever seen. That should keep him happy. And next time you want to look through a file, please ask my permission first.'

'I will,' said Cressida hastily. 'Is Rick married?' she continued, certain that this would divert Marcia. She was right.

'His pictures have certainly made an impression on you!' laughed the older woman. 'As a matter of fact, no, he isn't married. At least, not to a woman. I think, like most truly creative people, he's probably married to his art. That doesn't stop him taking a very enthusiastic interest in the opposite sex though, so you might be in with a chance!'

'I wasn't thinking of anything like that,' protested Cressida, relieved to see that Marcia's face had lost its look of suspicion. 'But when you see images like the ones he creates you can't help wondering what kind of man he is.'

'Quite ordinary really,' said Marcia dismissively. 'He'll like you; he's always drawn to enigmatic women.'

'I don't think I'm enigmatic!' protested Cressida.

Marcia looked thoughtfully at her. 'I do, and so does Guy.'

Cressida didn't know whether to be pleased that Guy and Marcia had discussed her or not. On a professional level it was certainly what her superiors would want, but on a personal level it made her uncomfortable.

'Don't worry,' said Marcia, seeing the look of discomfort on her assistant's face. 'Guy didn't tell me that, but I always know when he's interested in a woman. Not that his interest usually leads to anything – only the occasional brief fling but never any true commitment.'

It was a warning, and Cressida knew it, but she pretended that she didn't know what Marcia was driving at. 'He doesn't look the marrying kind to me,' she admitted lightly. 'Not that I've seen much of him, but I imagine it would be hard for anyone to hold his interest for long.'

Marcia nodded. 'He and I have known each other six years now, and that's probably a record for Guy even as far as friendships go. He's rather a loner.'

'But a good business partner,' said Cressida brightly, moving thankfully towards the door and freedom from Marcia's questions and suggestions.

'Oh yes,' agreed Marcia. 'He's certainly a good partner, in more ways than one.'

As soon as Cressida got back to her desk in the reception area she started to work out how she could contact Detective Chief Inspector Williams and get him to come up with someone who would act as her imaginary caller early that morning. She knew that Marcia was still highly suspicious about the unknown man and his inherited Matisse.

While she was working out how she could get a message to him before the end of the day, a young man walked in through the door. He was tall – well over six feet in height – and had a mass of long, wavy blond hair. Coming directly to the desk he leant against the corner and stared at Cressida. 'Who the hell are you?'

'My name's Cressida Farleigh and I'm the new assistant here,' she said politely. 'Can I help you at all?'

The blond man grinned, showing very white even teeth. 'Probably, but not where my work's concerned. I want to speak to Guy Cronje. Is he in?'

'No, but Marcia Neville is. Would you like to see her?' asked Cressida.

'Sure, Marcia will do. Tell me, Cressida, how long have you been working here?'

'Less than a week.'

'And are you enjoying it?' His light blue eyes were bright with curiosity and his good humour so obvious that she couldn't help smiling at him.

'Yes, immensely. I'm fascinated by the work that's on display here. In fact, I'm hoping to meet one of the artists today.'

'Which artist is that?'

'Rick Marks. If you want to see his work it's down the far end in the sectioned-off area. It's the kind of work that some people might find disturbing – that's why it's kept separate.'

'But it doesn't shock you?'

Cressida shook her head. 'No, although it does make me feel very strange.'

'Nice strange or nasty strange?' he asked with interest.

'I can't work it out.' said Cressida. 'At first I thought it was too male dominated to be erotic from a female point of view, but the more I look at it the more I think I got it wrong first time round. I believe the artist is really saying that women hold the balance of power in sexual relationships, while men *believe* that they do. If you've got time, go and see what you think,' she added as Marcia came out of her office.

'I don't need to,' said the young man. 'I drew them, and your second appraisal is the correct one. Love the outfit,' he added, and then with a wink at her he followed Marcia back to her room.

Through her police work Cressida had long ago learnt that it was a mistake to judge people by appearances, but just the same, reconciling the open, fresh-faced amiable bear of a young man that she'd just met with the dark broodingly erotic pictures he drew was almost impossible. If Guy Cronje had drawn them it wouldn't have surprised her in the least, but Rick Marks didn't look as though he was an artist at all.

She was surprised at how much she'd liked him, and pleased that she'd chosen her cream linen shift dress with a matching waffle-textured tunic-style jacket, covered in pink and yellow flowers. It was going to be difficult for her when she had to wear her uniform every day. The upmarket clothes required for her present job were definitely gaining in appeal, and she knew that they suited her.

She was busy for the next hour and when Rick Marks emerged again he hung around, waiting until she'd finished dealing with a prospective buyer. 'How are you fixed for lunch?' he asked casually.

Cressida would have loved to have lunch with him, and knew that her superiors would approve as well, but if she didn't make her telephone call about the customer she'd invented earlier, she had a feeling Marcia might tell Guy that she had doubts about her, which meant the call had to come first.

'Sorry, I'm spoken for,' she said with a regretful smile.

'Permanently?' asked Rick.

Cressida shook her head. 'Absolutely not! I'm rather keen on keeping my freedom for a few more years yet, but I've already made arrangements for lunch today.'

'How about dinner then? Where do you live? I could pick you up at eight and we'll go to my favourite bistro at Covent Garden. They let me eat there for nothing because I did a free mural for them before they opened.'

'I don't think you're meant to tell your dates that you're getting their food free!' laughed Cressida.

'I'm making sure you know I'm a poverty-stricken struggling artist,' said Rick with a grin.

'Not for long, according to Guy,' retorted Cressida. 'He thinks a lot of your work.'

'Yes, but that's because he thinks he can make a lot of money from it,' said Rick. 'I value your opinion more.'

'Flattery will get you everywhere!' laughed Cressida. 'All right, let's say eight tonight. Here, I'll write down my address for you.'

As she was scribbling on her pad, Marcia came up behind Rick. 'What's this then?'

'I'm taking Cressida out to dinner tonight. She seems a very discerning young woman and doesn't look as though she eats too much,' responded Rick.

Marcia nodded in approval. 'She's certainly a hard worker. She may even fire you with enthusiasm for the new series Guy wants. Incidentally, Cressida, has that man called back about the restoration of his Matisse?'

'Not yet,' said Cressida, keeping her head bent over her pad.

'Well, make sure you tell me when he does. And don't forget that Leonora Thornton starts with us this afternoon. You'll have to find something for her to do that makes her feel useful, but nothing too complicated. Her stepmother says she's got the attention span of a two-year-old.'

'I hope that doesn't mean you've got to cut your lunch date short,' said Rick sympathetically as he left.

'You're a busy girl,' said Marcia. 'A lunch date and a dinner date on the same day. I always did say still waters ran deep.'

'My lunch date isn't very exciting,' Cressida said quickly. 'He's more of a friend than a lover now. You know how it is.'

'Not really,' said Marcia. 'When I stop being a man's lover then I lose interest in him as a friend. Let's be honest, most of the men we fancy aren't chosen because of their "friendly" qualities! Personally I like men who are dangerous as lovers. Men like that aren't usually interested in being "friends" once an affair's over either. Maybe you prefer a different type of man though?'

'I probably do,' said Cressida, wishing they could get off the subject of her non-existent lunch date. 'I go for men who make me feel safe and cherished.'

'You're much too young for that,' exclaimed Marcia in mock horror. 'Mind you, if that's what turns you on, make sure the man in question is both elderly and rich. That way you can have your fun later on. Rich women of a certain age never have any problem in finding a gorgeous young man.'

'I wouldn't pay for sex!' said Cressida, genuinely shocked by the prospect.

'Why not? Plenty of men do, often when they marry their third or fourth young wife as they go into their sixties! I expect they pretend it's love, but deep down they must know the truth. We see a lot of that with the people we deal with. Men who can afford expensive art collections are usually well past their prime, but never without a lithe beauty on their arm, I can assure you. Remember now, let me know when the Matisse owner calls, and enjoy your lunch. Leonora won't be here until two.'

'Fine, I'll make sure I'm back by then,' Cressida promised her.

The rest of the morning passed quietly and she found that she was thinking about Rick Marks a great deal of the time.

As soon as it was time for her lunch break, she collected her handbag and then hurried out to her car. Deciding it wasn't safe to make the call anywhere near the gallery, she used a public phone box a couple of miles away, and then had to wait while they paged Detective Chief Inspector Williams. It seemed to take an age for him to get to a phone and all the time the minutes of her lunch break were ticking away.

'What's the matter?' he demanded. 'You're not in any trouble, are you?'

'No, nothing like that,' Cressida assured him, and then she explained what had happened.

'Let me make sure I've got this right,' he murmured after listening to her story. 'The man has to be tall and well built, in his mid-forties and have a shock of grey hair, yes?'

'Yes!' said Cressida impatiently.

The chief inspector ignored her efforts to hurry him. 'And he's inherited a Monet from his grandfather, is that it?'

'No, a Matisse which needs cleaning and possibly some restoration work. He shouldn't know too much about art. I made him out to be a novice in the field to make it easier for you.'

'How kind! And where do we pick up a cheap Matisse within the next hour or two?'

'I'm sorry, sir, but I've really no idea,' said Cressida. 'I'm doing my very best this end, and I really think I'm making some progress. I can't afford to start arousing suspicion now particularly since one of the artists has asked me out to dinner tonight, and he knows both Guy and Marcia very well.'

'In that case I'll hand this over to someone with specialised knowledge immediately,' promised her boss. 'Keep up the good work, Cressida. I've got a feeling we're going to crack this one with your help. One thing, now that you're well and truly in at the gallery make sure Tom stays away from you. Right, off you go and leave everything to me. Your tall grey-haired stranger will call in during the afternoon.'

After her call, Cressida just had time to buy herself a roll and eat it in the car before driving back to the gallery. Polly looked up as she entered and tilted her head to the right. Glancing in that direction, Cressida saw a young girl standing by the wall, biting on the skin at the side of her thumb. She had shoulder-length light brown hair, hazel eyes and a pale face that wasn't helped by her navy outfit of oversize T-shirt and ankle-length baggy skirt. It drained any slight vestige of colour that she might have possessed.

'You must be Leonora,' said Cressida brightly, privately wondering what on earth Marcia would say about the girl's clothes. 'I'm Cressida, and you'll be helping me while you're here. Sorry I was out when you arrived.'

'It doesn't matter,' said the girl flatly. 'I was early. Daddy dropped me off. He probably thought I wouldn't come if he didn't.'

'If you're interested in art you'll like it here,' Cressida assured her. 'Everyone's very friendly and helpful, and the customers are generally a nice lot.'

'I'm not interested in art,' said Leonora. 'I'm only here so that Daddy's free to screw my stepmother during the day. I get in the way and stop her making a noise.' Polly snorted with laughter and quickly went into the back room.

Cressida couldn't think of anything to say in reply, so got out a catalogue and handed it to the disinterested girl. 'Have a look through this,' she said firmly. 'It tells you all about the artists whose work we display here, and the other services we offer. For example, we sell prints and can get them framed, we also clean old paintings and – '

'Is there a coffee machine?' asked Leonora, interrupting Cressida in mid-flow.

'No, we have to make our own but you have to fit your refreshment round the work, not the other way about.'

'You sound more like a teacher than an art graduate,' remarked Leonora. Cressida was grateful the wretched girl hadn't said a policewoman.

As she and Leonora Thornton stood staring at each

other, Marcia and Guy came in through the door. Guy was wearing a blue and grey checked jacket over a pale blue shirt, open at the neck, and navy trousers. His dark hair was tidier than the first time Cressida had seen him, but he looked pale and tense and there was no hint of a smile on his face as he greeted her.

Marcia, who had been smiling as she entered the reception area, stopped the moment she set eyes on Leonora. 'Where in heaven's name did you get those ghastly clothes?' she demanded in an icy voice.

Leonora's cheeks showed a hint of colour at the criticism. 'They're my favourite,' she muttered.

Guy glanced briefly at her, raised his eyebrows at Cressida and went into the office, leaving Marcia to deal with the girl. As Marcia started to tell Leonora the standard of dress she expected from her in future, the phone buzzed and Cressida was summoned into the office to see Guy.

He was sitting behind the desk that she'd searched early that morning and his face was tight with tension although he did attempt a smile, but it failed to reach his eyes. 'Marcia tells me you had a customer in this morning who was interested in our cleaning service,' he said abruptly.

Cressida looked straight into his eyes and smiled. 'Yes, that's right. He said he'd call back later today. Is it a profitable sideline?'

Guy frowned. 'Sideline?'

'I didn't think it was the main function of the gallery,' explained Cressida.

'It's one of our most important functions,' said Guy. 'It's a very specialised art, and we're lucky to have contacts in the profession who can do an excellent job. As for it being lucrative, as a matter of fact, it is. It also works on commission, so *if* this stranger does return and leave us his precious inheritance you'll find a little bonus in your pay package.'

Cressida felt very guilty but gave a polite smile. 'That would be nice,' she acknowledged.

Guy looked searchingly at her. '*That would be nice!*' he mimicked. 'I didn't realise you were fortunate enough not to have to think about money, Cressida.'

'I'm not! It matters to me the same as to everyone, but it isn't everything. I'd rather be in a job I liked and earn sufficient than thoroughly miserable but earning a fortune.'

Guy's fingers fidgeted with some paperclips on his desk and again Cressida was aware of the suppressed energy within him. 'What about sex?' he asked abruptly.

'Sex?'

'You didn't mention your love life in that interesting and worthy speech. I wondered where sex came on your list of priorities.'

'Somewhere in the middle I suppose,' she replied, wishing he wasn't looking at her so closely because all she could think about was Tom and how unco-operative he'd been when they'd last made love.

'How boring,' said Guy shortly. 'Let's hope Rick can change your mind for you. If you're to be the inspiration for his eagerly awaited next picture then he'd better. "Somewhere in the middle" doesn't conjure up a very erotic image.'

'Who told you I was going out with Rick?' asked Cressida in surprise.

'Marcia of course. She and I don't have any secrets from each other. At least, Marcia doesn't have any from me,' he added with a half-smile.

'Is there anything else?' asked Cressida, realising that she was taking far too much interest in his face; the sharp jawline and the deep brown eyes; the mobile mouth that hinted at passions she'd never even experienced.

'No, nothing else. Off you go, and try and get that dreadful girl out there into some sort of presentable state by tomorrow please.'

'I didn't choose her,' said Cressida, irritated by the assumption that she should be responsible for Leonora. 'She's the daughter of your friend, not mine.'

Guy glanced up at her in surprise. 'My word, it bites! You're quite right, she isn't your responsibility, but I thought you might do a make-over job on her more tactfully than Marcia. She goes straight for the jugular. You don't have that killer instinct; at least, I don't think you do,' he added softly.

'I feel sorry for her,' muttered Cressida.

'Why's that?'

'Because she doesn't want to be here any more than we want to have her. She's being pushed around so that her father and stepmother can have their fun and games without fear of interruption.'

'That's life,' laughed Guy. 'Her time will come. Although I can't imagine when, the way she looks at the moment. It's almost enough to make me consider taking her in hand myself, but I don't think I could cope with the teenage sulks.'

'She might think you're a bit old for her,' Cressida pointed out.

Guy's eyes widened in surprise and then he grinned. 'I'm sure you're right. What a dreadful thought, that I might go out of my way to show her the wonders of life only to be turned down because I'm past it! Back to work, Cressida. And remember, let us know the moment your Matisse man arrives.'

As Cressida shut the door behind her, she knew that despite the banter and apparent amiability Guy was suspicious of her. He didn't believe in her customer, and the fact that he and Marcia kept mentioning the man seemed to be proof that they had something to hide. Clearly Cressida should not have seen the contents of their files, and they were waiting to see if she was a spy. Unfortunately for them innocent people weren't worried about spies, but criminals were. They were starting to show Cressida that Interpol were right; the gallery had things it needed to hide.

The next two hours dragged by. Leonora had to be told everything at least three times and even then did her jobs with a very bad grace. Customers were few, which meant that there was little to distract Cressida, and every time the door did open she looked up, hoping desperately that it would be the man with grey hair.

At 4.15, when Cressida's heart was beginning to beat faster than normal with stress, the bell over the door went and a tall man in his mid-forties with a mass of thick grey hair walked into the gallery. He glanced at Polly, who took half a step towards him, and then as Cressida made a slight movement with her right hand he turned and smiled at her.

'I said I'd come back. I hope this is a better time?' he said quietly, picking up her hint.

Cressida felt a surge of relief and smiled back. 'It certainly is. If you don't mind waiting I'll go and tell the owners of the gallery that you're here. Did you bring the painting with you?'

He held a brown paper package tied loosely with string. 'Yes, it's here.'

'Wonderful! Just a moment.' Once outside the closed office door, Cressida composed herself carefully before knocking. It was vital that she didn't seem relieved that the man was here. This was meant to be run-of-the-mill work for her and she knew that both Guy and Marcia would be studying her carefully when she announced the visitor.

After a light tap on the door she went in and Marcia, who was standing very close to Guy in the far corner of the room, took a step back from him. 'Yes?' she asked irritably.

'I thought you'd like to know that the man with the Matisse is here,' said Cressida quietly. 'Shall I show him through?'

A frown creased Marcia's forehead but Guy smiled at Cressida and nodded. 'Please do. And well done,' he added. 'You're proving a great asset to the gallery.'

'We haven't seen the so-called Matisse yet,' Marcia pointed out.

'No, but I think Cressida has done her part.'

As the man sent by Detective Chief Inspector Williams was ushered through to see her employers, Cressida felt like shouting aloud with triumph. Clearly Marcia had been certain the man didn't exist, and equally clearly Guy was delighted that he did, which must mean that he liked Cressida. All in all she felt that her work was going extremely well, and she had the added bonus of dinner with Rick that night to look forward to.

When Rick arrived to collect Cressida she was still dressing, having put on and then discarded numerous outfits as either too dressy or too downbeat. Throwing a towelling robe over her underwear she showed him into her front room and then dashed off again, hoping there wasn't anything around that would give away her true profession. She'd been careful to remove all photographs of herself in uniform several days earlier, in case someone from the gallery called round unexpectedly.

Finally, dressed in an ice-cream pink sleeveless mini dress with a matching double-breasted coat, she rejoined him. He was watching cricket on the television and glanced at her appreciatively.

'Nice! Those shiny tights are all the rage this summer; they're very sexy.'

'I'm glad you approve!' she laughed. 'I wasn't sure how to dress and thought this outfit could go anywhere.'

'We don't make a very good couple,' he said in amusement, and as she looked at him and took in his old petrol-blue tunic sweater worn over a faded blue T-shirt, teamed rather incongruously with a pair of navy pin-stripe trousers, she realised that he was right.

'Shall I change?' she asked anxiously.

Rick shook his head. 'You're looking far too attractive to be the one to change, and I'm too lazy. It won't matter. They're used to me looking like this. I only ever dress up for Guy's dinner parties. As for you, they'll probably wonder what you see in me!'

Climbing into Rick's battered Ford Fiesta, Cressida was quite certain they wouldn't wonder about that. Seen out of the gallery Rick was even more attractive than she'd originally thought. His fair skin was lightly tanned, which made his grey-blue eyes all the more striking, and he had a generous mouth, prominent cheekbones and a straight Roman nose. The combination made her feel quite breathless with what she supposed must be desire. If it was, she'd never truly desired Tom, she realised ruefully.

The restaurant, small and tucked away on the edges of the Covent Garden Piazza, was designed to look like a greenhouse and when they walked in the door the heat seemed to hit her in the face. She was grateful when Rick took her coat.

The proprietor came hurrying out to greet him, shaking him warmly by the hand and ushering them to a table in the corner of the room where they were relatively private. He then brought them a bottle of house wine and left them with the menu.

'Where's your mural?' asked Cressida, wishing she could use the menu as a fan.

'Behind you,' said Rick.

Cressida turned, and saw that the wall behind her was covered with drawings of young men and women. Some were kissing, others holding hands, while a few were simply standing staring at each other, but every one of the pairs gave off a feeling of incredible sexuality. It was as though they were about to remove their admittedly scanty clothing and start making love at any moment. Cressida couldn't work out how Rick had managed to create such a feeling when there was nothing overtly sexual about what they were doing.

'Like it?' he asked nonchalantly.

'It's very powerful,' said Cressida, aware the word was a feeble one for the way the mural made her feel but unable to think of anything else to say.

He nodded. 'That's the way I wanted it to be. It's a statement you see; a statement about the contrast between what society wants people to feel and do and what they really want themselves – from an erotic point of view, that is.'

'Well, you can certainly tell what those people really want to do,' she assured him. 'I'm just not sure how you managed to get the point over.'

'It's all in the muscles and facial expressions,' he said, his face serious and his voice full of passion. 'Tension, that's the key to eroticism. There has to be sexual tension. Chocolates, flowers and a kiss on the sofa aren't real passion. They're window dressing, that's all. My drawings show us the truth.'

At that moment the waiter returned to take their order. Cressida hadn't even looked at the menu so Rick ordered mixed grill of fish for them both. 'It's one of the best meals in London at the moment,' he promised her. Cressida didn't really care. Her stomach felt as though it had closed down for the evening, and food didn't hold any interest for her. The longer she was with Rick the more she was attracted to him, and his mural had made her feel almost as strange as his drawings in the gallery.

'Guy tells me you're doing a new picture at the moment,' she remarked when the waiter had departed.

Rick, nibbling on his bread roll, nodded. 'I'm meant to be. The truth is, I haven't started yet. I've been waiting for inspiration. Now I think I may have found it.'

'That's good,' said Cressida casually, not daring to believe she might be the trigger for one of his erotically charged drawings.

Rick grinned at her. 'I mean you,' he stated. 'The moment I set eyes on you in the gallery I began to see the shape of the thing, and tonight when you came down all dressed up in that little-girl-pink outfit, like an advert for some new drink, I knew I was right.'

'But that's not your style!' exclaimed Cressida, rather put out by his description of her clothes.

'Not the exterior that you present to the world, no, but the contrast between my image of you – the way you make me feel, the things I want to do to you – and the way you dress and talk, that's my style. You're good at disguise, Cressida, did you know that?'

Considering that she was working undercover for the fraud squad at that very moment, Cressida found the remark rather ironic. 'No, I didn't,' she muttered, relieved to see the waiter approaching with their food.

The waiter placed huge plates full of a delicious-looking assortment of fish in front of them, and then put down a bottle of pink Dom Perignon. 'For the lady in pink, with the owner's compliments!' he exclaimed.

Rick was enchanted by Cressida's embarrassment. 'It's a good job Chris de Burgh isn't here – he'd probably write a song about you!' he laughed. 'I like it when you blush, it's so old-fashioned. Most girls today don't know how to blush, and it's very sexy.'

'It isn't an art that you acquire,' retorted Cressida. 'It's something that happens, and I don't like it as much as you seem to.'

'At least it means that people know when you're being honest with them. It would be difficult to lie deliberately when you blush.'

If he only knew, thought Cressida, picking at her meal and feeling more and more guilty about her deception. It wasn't as though what Guy and Marcia were doing had anything to do with Rick, but she was using him shamelessly to try and get closer to them. Worse still, she was enjoying it.

'When we've eaten, will you come back to my place?' asked Rick. 'I don't want to show you my etchings, but I would like to show you the outline I've drafted for my new idea – the idea you've inspired.'

'I'd love to,' agreed Cressida, feeling her legs going weak at the prospect.

'How many lovers have you had?' asked Rick casually.

Cressida nearly choked on a piece of grilled tuna. 'That's my business!' she said shortly.

'I only wondered. You look as though you'd be a six or seven sort of girl. Didn't you just love that scene in *Four Weddings and a Funeral* when Andie McDowell goes through her list of lovers and the list seems to last for ever? I thought that was one of the best bits in it!'

'I liked John Hannah reading Auden's *'Funeral Blues'*, said Cressida.

Rick blinked in surprise. 'Well, it was moving but hardly the highlight of a delightful comedy of modern sexual manners!'

'It was still my favourite bit,' said Cressida stubbornly.

'Perhaps sex and death are linked in your mind,' said Rick thoughtfully. 'Do you know what the French call an orgasm? A little death, and in a way it is.'

'Do you really think like this, or is it an act?' asked Cressida, drinking some of her champagne.

'I never put on an act,' Rick retorted. 'Of course this is the way I think. That's why my pictures come out the way they do.'

'It's odd, because it isn't the way you look,' said Cressida. 'You seem to be so wholesome; the sort of guy who likes rugby and cricket and belongs to his local squash club.'

'I do like cricket.'

'Yes, but dark sex is your favourite subject, and you don't look at all dark. In fact,' she added, getting braver by the minute as the champagne began to take effect, 'you look a positively conventional sort of guy. Not that different from Tom.'

Rick's eyes narrowed. 'Who's Tom?'

Cressida hesitated, cursing the alcohol and the relaxed ambience of the evening for letting her make such a stupid mistake. 'My last lover,' she said reluctantly.

'An ex?'

'Definitely an ex.'

Rick's face was happy again. 'That's all I wanted to know. How about a crême brulée for dessert?'

After that, Cressida was more careful about what she said, and by the time they left the restaurant and got into the old Ford Fiesta again, she felt that she was almost back in total control.

Rick drove carefully to his flat in Bayswater. It was over a karate club and had a huge window in the ceiling which made it perfect for his work. There was one double bedroom off the main room, and a small kitchen and toilet, but it was clear he didn't bother to clear up very often. Cressida could hardly move for sketches, paintings, discarded articles of clothing and dirty crockery.

'Sorry about the mess,' he said casually. 'I have a tidy up once a month, and the month's nearly up!'

In the middle of the floor there was an easel with a picture on it, but it was covered by a cloth and she assumed this was the outline for his new work. On the walls of the room there were dozens of rough pencil sketches. Some of them were clearly roughs for the pictures Cressida had seen in the gallery, while others were totally new to her, but they all had the same theme of a tethered or restrained woman dominating the picture while a faceless man looked on.

'Here, this is my first new rough draft, the one I did after seeing you at the gallery this morning,' said Rick after rummaging through a heap of papers. Cressida took the white sheet of paper and stared at the drawing.

A young woman with very long legs and short dark

hair was sitting on a desk, and her left knee was drawn up close to her chest while her right leg hung over the edge. Her arms were stretched out to either side supporting her. There was a thin line around her neck, which looked as though Rick might intend it to be a rope or leash, but apart from that she was quite free. What was different about this picture was the fact that the young woman wasn't naked.

She was wearing a suit that looked as though it belonged to the days of power dressing. The jacket had padded shoulders and wide lapels, but jagged tears had been created at strategic points so that one breast stuck out boldly. Every muscle and sinew at the top of the left leg could be seen and so could the opening at the top of the thighs. Her sex organs were exaggerated, like women in Eastern works of erotica, and the contrast between the business-like expression on her face and her nylon-covered right leg compared with the bared breast and vulnerable vulva was shocking and yet compelling.

'Is that how you saw me?' asked Cressida in horror.

Rick looked closely at her. 'Not literally, no, but it triggered the idea. Why? Don't you like it?'

Cressida shook her head. 'I don't think I do,' she said quietly.

'Why not?'

'I don't understand which is meant to be the real woman. The one who's in control or the one who's blatantly sexual in a way that's meant to pander to men's fantasies.'

'Can't a woman be both?' enquired Rick, equally softly, as he took a step towards her.

Cressida began to tremble as he reached out and slowly pulled her towards him. 'I think you're both,' he muttered, and then she felt his fingers starting to tear at the buttons on her pink coat as he lowered his mouth on to hers.

Chapter Five

R ick's hunger for her was so great that Cressida could almost feel the heat coming off him, and suddenly, as his mouth ground down hard against hers, she felt just as frantic for him.

As he tore at her clothes and pulled her down to the floor, she was aware of the pictures around them, and their erotic charge increased her desire. She heard herself making tiny whimpering sounds of need as he flicked his tongue around the edge of her bra before sucking at her nipples through the delicate lace. The sensation was wonderful, and Cressida reached down his body, now only covered by a pair of boxer shorts, and cupped her hands around his buttocks so that he moved closer to her and she could feel his rigid erection pressing against her.

Sucking and licking at her skin, Rick moved his mouth down lower and then began licking the inside of her thighs before nibbling gently against the shred of silk that covered her sex lips. To Cressida's amazement, a sudden ripple ran through her as she was shaken by a tiny orgasm. Rick rolled on to his back, pulling her on top of him so that when she spread her thighs on each side of his body she could feel his straining penis through both their pairs of pants.

His desire gave her a sense of power that she'd never felt before, and she began to move on top of him, knowing as he groaned and gasped beneath her that she was bringing him perilously close to the point of no return. All at once he grabbed her and rolled over again, so that now he had Cressida pinned to the floor, and as she flung her arms out to the sides she hit the edge of the easel and the cover fell to the ground, brushing against her bare arm.

She felt his hands tugging at her panties until at last they were off, and as soon as he'd removed his own she wrapped her legs tightly round his waist as he supported himself above her on fully extended arms and let the tip of his erection brush against her pubic hair. 'Beg for it,' he muttered hoarsely. 'Tell me how much you want me.'

Cressida didn't need telling twice. 'I want you inside me, now, quickly!' she whispered, but despite her words and the dampness of her frantic secret place, that wasn't enough for Rick.

'Say it louder,' he demanded. 'Shout it. Tell everyone in the street that you want me.' He let his erection brush up and down between her widening sex lips so that for one blissful moment it touched her clitoris and her whole body tightened and jerked.

'I want you now!' she screamed, totally lost in the sensations and the urgency of the moment. At her words Rick pushed hard against her and she felt him slide inside her, and then he was thrusting rapidly in and out as her orgasm built towards its climax.

Rick seemed totally out of control. She could hear him making frantic noises as his own orgasm drew nearer, and then all at once, just as she was about to come, he changed position, lying on top of her for a moment before rolling over yet again, leaving Cressida on top.

'You move now,' he gasped. 'Make us both come together.'

Cressida didn't care if they came together or not – she was totally consumed by the need to come herself – and so she angled her body forward with her head almost touching his chest and moved her buttocks back and forth while Rick's hands pulled at her nipples, which were still partly covered by the half-lace bra.

Suddenly the red-hot heat of release burst over her like surf crashing down on the beach, and she cried out with the sheer pleasure of it. Within seconds, Rick was crying out too and she felt him heaving and shuddering beneath her as his head rolled from side to side on the floor of the attic room.

For some time they lay silently together, their damp bodies entwined, until finally Rick pushed himself up and brushed the hair off his forehead. 'Fantastic!' he exclaimed. 'I was right about you, wasn't I?'

Cressida, who could hardly believe what had happened, managed to nod and look as though this was the kind of thing she did regularly. In fact, she'd only ever slept with one man before Tom and even that had been a very restrained affair. She didn't know what was to blame; the champagne, the eroticism of Rick's drawings, or his undeniable sexual charisma. Whatever it was, she wasn't about to complain.

Propping herself on one elbow, she looked around the room, and to her astonishment saw that the picture now revealed on the easel wasn't one of Rick's drawings after all. It looked to her like a half-completed Holbein portrait. Immediately her mind changed gear and she became the undercover policewoman again.

'What's that?' she asked Rick casually.

'What?' questioned Rick, his eyes still glazed with their recent passionate encounter.

'That painting there. It's not your usual sort of thing.'

Rick stood up and re-covered it with the fallen cloth.

'It's an experiment. I want to see if I can do other things apart from the stuff I sell to Guy, but I've got a long way to go before it's ready to show anyone.'

'I thought it looked good,' said Cressida. 'Can I have a closer look?'

'No way. It's private, and I guard my work very carefully. Come on, I'd better run you home as soon as I'm dressed.'

She could tell that the atmosphere had changed. He was no longer relaxed, and his desire to get her out of his flat was plain. Seeing the expression on her face he grinned ruefully.

'Sorry, that sounded pretty abrupt after what's gone on didn't it? I'm not much good at the after-sex chat and the cuddling.'

'That's all right,' Cressida assured him, knowing full well that it was her interest in the painting that had caused his change in mood. 'I'm not into all that either. I'll get dressed and then we can go.'

The drive back to Cressida's house was rather quiet. She was lost in her own thoughts, trying to work out whether or not Rick knew that he was probably being used by Guy and Marcia, while Rick seemed to have withdrawn from her completely. It was only when he dropped her off that he reverted to the Rick she'd known earlier.

'Sorry about the end to the evening,' he said. 'I'm afraid I get these mood swings and when the black dog descends on me there's nothing I can do about it.'

'Don't worry – it comes under the heading "artistic licence",' Cressida reassured him.

'So you'll come out with me again?'

She nodded. 'I'd love to. I enjoyed everything about tonight.'

Rick gave a small sigh of relief. 'That's great to hear. I'll call in at the gallery in the next few days and arrange another date. And Cressida, thanks for being so understanding.'

He walked up to her front door with her, kissed her passionately and then left, disappearing into the shadowed street so quickly that if her whole body hadn't still felt bruised and sensitive from their lovemaking, she could almost have imagined him.

The next morning Marcia joined Cressida in the coffee room.

'How was your date?' she asked with a smile.

'We had a great time,' said Cressida.

'Did you go back to his flat?' persisted Marcia.

'As a matter of fact, yes I did.'

'You're not as stand-offish as you seem then!' exclaimed Marcia. 'Rick really struck gold.'

'I just looked at his pictures,' protested Cressida, but she made sure that she didn't sound too convincing.

'I'm all for people enjoying themselves,' said Marcia. 'In fact, I hope you can inspire him with your visits. He needs a kick start at the moment. Guy's been pushing him for weeks now about a new picture.'

'I imagine artists have to wait for inspiration to strike,' replied Cressida, adding cream to her cup of black coffee.

'Quite, and with any luck you'll prove to be that inspiration. What fun! The two of you must join Guy and me one evening – that should be interesting. On another subject, when Leonora arrives she *should* be wearing something more in keeping with the gallery's style. I had a word with her stepmother, Rose, and knowing Rose that ought to be enough. If you don't think she looks right though would you let me know? Guy said it was like having a stuffed crow on display yesterday!'

'Right,' agreed Cressida, hoping against hope that Leonora had taken her stepmother's advice because the last thing she wanted was a scene from the girl. 'How old is she?' she asked.

'Nineteen! Guy thought she was twelve, or so he claims! Nineteen's far more interesting for him of course, so we must all look to our laurels.'

Cressida laughed. 'I can't seriously imagine him being interested in Leonora, can you?'

'Yes,' said Marcia. 'She's a challenge. As I mentioned before Guy can't resist a challenge.'

'Well, from what she said yesterday she already has a boyfriend called Piers, so even if Guy was interested I don't think Leonora would return his enthusiasm.'

'She might not be given a lot of choice,' said Marcia enigmatically as she walked away.

Cressida, who had no idea what Marcia was talking about, went out to her desk and began to check the morning's post.

'One other thing,' called Marcia from her office doorway. 'If anyone calls for Guy he'll be a little late today. He's got an important early-morning meeting.'

At that precise moment, Guy's important early-morning meeting was lying across a king-size bed with her waist-length, jet black hair spread over her shoulders as her dark brown almond-shaped eyes stared up into his.

As always, Guy was enchanted by the enigma that was the new Lady Thornton. The daughter of a Philippino mother and a French father she was, in his opinion, a combination of everything that was best about both cultures. Her dusky eastern beauty was perfectly offset by her exquisite French eye for fashion, and her mother's hot blood was tempered by her father's relaxed attitude to all things sexual. In other words, she was almost the ideal woman, and Guy could well understand Sir Peter's infatuation.

'Don't stop,' she begged him, her hips lifting upward off the soft goosedown duvet. Guy, who'd been crouched on the floor between her widespread thighs while his tongue worked its usual magic on her, had no intention

94

of stopping. He eased her back on the bed a little and then knelt astride her body, slowly easing his erection inside her.

Rose pulled her knees up to her chest and sighed with delight as she felt Guy's hands sliding beneath her buttocks so that he could ease her up and down. As he moved his penis in and out of her – slowly at first but in a gradually increasing tempo – Rose, assisted by his hands, rolled her thighs up and down so that at almost every stroke he touched her G spot. Each time this happened her small white teeth would catch on her bottom lip and her feet would press hard against Guy's chest.

They knew each other so well that in no time at all the right rhythm was established, and Rose felt her whole body expanding, causing the blissful feeling of tightness that always preceded her climaxes.

'How near are you?' asked Guy softly, feeling his own orgasm drawing closer.

'Just a few more strokes,' gasped Rose, perspiration dotting her top lip.

Guy smiled down at her and stopped moving. 'Is what we discussed earlier definite then?'

Some of the tightness started to fade and Rose tried to move more frantically against him. 'Keep still or I'll withdraw,' warned Guy. 'Tell me, Rose, is it agreed?'

'Yes, I told you I'd arrange it,' she gasped.

'But you don't always keep your word, as your good husband knows to his cost. You're beautiful and sexy, Rose, but you're not trustworthy. I want you to promise that what we talked about earlier is a deal. If you break your word, you'll be very sorry.'

'What about Peter?' she cried, wriggling around despite her best efforts to restrain herself. 'He'd go mad if he knew.'

'But he won't know, will he? He and I are friends, so I won't tell him – and you certainly won't talk about it if you've got any sense.'

'I don't understand why you want her!' exclaimed the frantic Rose. 'She's nothing; just a plain, boring English girl with no dress sense and cold blue blood in her veins.'

'I like a change,' said Guy. 'You want Piers, and I want Leonora. Set up an evening for the four of us, and do it soon.'

'I can't be sure,' she protested. 'I never know what Peter's doing.'

'You always know what Peter's doing,' said Guy, moving very gently inside her so that the intense searing pleasure flooded through her pelvic area for a brief moment. 'Come on, Rose, promise me and then we can finish what we're doing.'

'I . . .' Rose stopped as she felt him remove his hands from beneath her and run them up her chest until he'd grasped her nipples between his fingers. Slowly he began to roll them around, occasionally extending and then releasing them again until the sexual pleasure spread downward towards her lower belly. 'All right,' she agreed desperately. 'I promise.'

'And you'll do it soon?' He moved his hips a little and once more her G spot felt the soft caress that she adored.

'Yes, yes!' she moaned and Guy knew from the expression on her face that she wouldn't let him down.

At once he resumed their lovemaking, picking up the same rhythm he'd used earlier, and suddenly her briefly frustrated body began to throb as the orgasm, which had been smouldering inside her during the interval, started to build towards release. At the last moment, as the sheer pleasure of it all overwhelmed her, Rose uttered one tiny cry, which was all she ever allowed herself, and then her body trembled and shook as the muscles rippled at the climactic moment. Guy felt her feet jerking against his chest and thrust more fiercely so that within seconds of Rose finishing, he too had come in a highly satisfying series of spasms.

As soon as it was over he withdrew from Rose and

walked over to fetch his clothes. She watched him from the bed, her dark eyes enigmatic and her face slightly flushed with colour. 'You really do want her, don't you?' she murmured.

'Leonora? Yes, I do.'

'Englishmen are strange,' she mused. 'Even Peter's peculiar. Sometimes I think he doesn't really like women, not in a sexual way.'

'He's mad about you,' said Guy shortly. 'His trouble is, he's too trusting.'

'How do you know? Perhaps I'm just a trophy wife.'

'Believe me, I know. It's almost enough to make me feel guilty about having sex with you,' he added, and they both laughed.

'What do you feel when he and I watch you and Marcia?' asked Rose.

'I don't think about it much. I always enjoy it but I'm usually concentrating on what we're doing rather than on you and Peter.'

'But don't you think about these times? Our times together?' she persisted.

'No,' said Guy abruptly. 'I certainly don't. Now, call me as soon as you've got a date for the dinner. And don't make me wait more than a week. I'm not a patient soul.'

The gallery was relatively quiet that morning, and as a result Cressida had quite a lot of time to think.

The previous evening she'd rung Detective Chief Inspector Williams the moment she got home, telling him about the half-finished picture in the style of Holbein that she'd seen in Rick's studio. She hadn't explained exactly how the cover had come to slip off the painting, but it was clear that he guessed.

'You're doing extremely well PC Farleigh,' he'd said with considerable satisfaction. 'Now you must try and find out from this artist chap exactly how the switch is done. He obviously likes you a lot. No doubt you can use the usual feminine wiles to gain his total trust.'

'He might not be involved in anything, at least not knowingly,' Cressida had protested beginning to feel guilty about Rick.

'If he's just a pawn that they're using he won't have anything to fear from us,' the chief inspector had responded. 'We're not after the small fish here – we want the big shark. In other words, we want Guy Cronje, and we want him badly.'

'I'm hoping that through Rick I might learn more about Guy. I should certainly meet him more often,' she'd told him. 'I'm bound to go to Rick's next exhibition and that's a big event as far as Guy and the gallery are concerned.'

'Excellent! You'd better try and find out the name of the poor devil who's about to lose his precious Holbein too. I hope it isn't Peter.'

'I'll do all I can,' Cressida had promised.

'Great, and we'll tell Tom to stay well away. I gather that he's not coping too well with the situation. He hasn't caused you any trouble, has he?'

'No!' Cressida had exclaimed, finding it difficult to imagine Tom putting her at jeopardy through jealousy. He was a professional police officer too, and would understand better than anyone how vital it was that no one grew suspicious of her at this stage.

Now, however, with time on her hands, Cressida began to wonder what Tom might do if he really was upset. It was becoming difficult for her to remember what she'd felt for Tom before she'd gone undercover, especially since last night when Rick's passionate love-making had made everything she'd ever done with Tom pale into insignificance.

'Cressida!' said Leonora in a bored voice.

Cressida looked up from the leaflet she'd been pretending to read. 'Yes?'

'I've already asked you twice. What shall I do now I've finished cleaning up the coffee room?'

Cressida sighed. Leonora, who had at least taken her stepmother's words to heart and was wearing an attractive red summer dress in a soft floating material, didn't seem in the least interested in her work and occupying her was difficult.

'Why not go through our catalogues again? It's important that you know about all our artists,' she suggested.

Leonora pulled a face. 'I've read them twice.'

'Does that mean you know every name and how many of their pictures we can supply?'

'Of course not.'

'Then go through them again,' said Cressida shortly.

Leonora flounced off and sat in the far corner of the room, reading resentfully. It was quite a relief to Cressida when the bell over the door went and a customer walked in, but that relief quickly faded when she saw that the man approaching the desk was Tom.

'Can I help you, sir?' she asked with a polite smile.

Tom bent down so that he could talk softly to her. 'Why haven't you rung me for the past few nights?' he asked.

'I can't!' hissed Cressida, and saw that Leonora was now watching her with interest.

'Why not?'

'I can give you a list of all the van Gogh prints we supply,' she said loudly. Leonora went back to her catalogue.

'Never mind van bloody Gogh!' snapped Tom, keeping his voice low. 'I want to know what's going on.'

'Ask the chief,' whispered Cressida. 'He'll explain.'

'I don't see why we can't go out for a meal!' exclaimed Tom, his voice suddenly louder.

Once more Leonora lifted her head, and Cressida felt herself going pink with annoyance. She couldn't believe that Tom would be so stupid at such a vital time in the operation.

'I just can't,' she snapped, pushing a catalogue at him as she saw Marcia approaching.

'If you don't,' muttered Tom as he turned away, 'then I'll blow your cover. You're a policewoman and my girlfriend, not a prostitute.' He slammed out of the gallery leaving Cressida facing both Marcia and Leonora.

'What was all that about?' asked Marcia.

Cressida took a deep breath. 'I'm not sure,' she said slowly. 'He's a customer who's been in once or twice and seems to have some kind of obsession with me. Now he's saying that if I don't go out for a meal with him he'll throw himself under a train!'

'My goodness, you certainly have an effect on the clientele,' remarked Marcia. 'Let's hope Rick doesn't get jealous.'

'I'm sure that Rick isn't the jealous type,' retorted Cressida. 'Anyway, I'm not going. The man's clearly unstable.'

'Obsession can be dangerous,' cautioned Marcia. 'If you have any more trouble let me know and I'll tell Guy. I'm sure he'll be able to find out where the man lives and put a stop to it. He's quite attractive though, in a conventional way, don't you think?'

'He isn't really my type,' said Cressida trying to sound bored with the subject.

'Strange; if I'd had to match people from photos I'd have put you with someone like him rather than our Rick,' said Marcia. 'It goes to show, you never can tell, can you!'

Once Marcia had returned to her office Leonora put down her catalogue and walked over to Cressida. 'Are you really going out with Rick Marks?' she asked, her light brown eyes wide with surprise.

'Yes, but it's a new relationship,' said Cressida.

'You're brave,' said the girl, showing animation for the

first time since joining the gallery staff. 'I've seen his drawings here; they're dreadful. I'd be terrified to go out with someone like that.'

'People who write thrillers don't go round murdering people,' said Cressida patiently. 'Artists who draw women in chains don't necessarily go round behaving like that in their private lives either.'

'But he must be odd,' persisted Leonora. 'No normal man would draw women like he does.'

'His work represents relationships between the sexes,' said Cressida. 'They aren't meant to be taken literally. He's interested in the true balance of power between couples as opposed to the apparent reality of the situation.'

Leonora pulled a face. 'I don't know what you mean. I think he must be weird.'

'How fortunate you're not the one going out with him then,' said Cressida.

Leonora leant against the desk. It seemed that this new information had made Cressida far more interesting in her eyes. 'Piers is pretty boring,' she confessed. 'He's the son of a friend of Daddy's. I think he knows more about cricket and rugby than he does about sex.'

'Then find yourself someone more interesting,' suggested Cressida.

'I hardly meet anyone,' complained Leonora. 'I suppose it might be better when I go to Italy for a year, but that's not until the end of September.'

'In that case you'll have to put up with being bored for a few more weeks,' replied Cressida.

Leonora stared at her. 'I wonder why so many men fancy you? You look pretty ordinary to me. I mean, my stepmother's really gorgeous. She's foreign, which helps I suppose, but every man she meets goes weak at the knees, and I can understand why although it's really irritating. But you ... well, you're just like lots of other women, aren't you?'

Cressida felt herself getting annoyed but kept her voice level. 'Why don't you get back to reading the catalogues and let me do some work, Leonora,' she suggested.

'OK, but I still think it's odd.'

Cressida knew that Leonora, bored by her work but clearly intensely interested in people's private lives, would now be watching her like a hawk, and she felt even more angry with Tom for what he'd done.

That night when she got home, she rang him and told him how difficult he could have made things for her, but he still kept insisting that there was no harm in them having a meal together.

'You're allowed boyfriends, aren't you?' he shouted.

'Yes, but I'm supposed to be potty about Rick Marks. It will look rather odd if I start going out with another man just when I've begun a relationship with him.'

'You're sleeping with him, aren't you?' asked Tom furiously.

'It's none of your business what I'm doing. I'm only answerable to the chief, as you very well know,' Cressida shouted back.

Tom changed his tone. 'Please, Cressida, I miss you so much. Let's go out next Monday to that Indian place round the corner from you. No one from the gallery will see us there.'

Cressida suddenly realised that she had no desire to see him even if there wasn't any risk. She was too caught up in her affair with Rick, and deep in her subconscious was attracted to Guy Cronje. Tom was no longer of interest, but instinct told her that in order to prevent Tom from ruining everything, she had to see him just one more time.

'All right,' she agreed. 'We'll meet there next Monday at eight, but don't try and contact me before then or it's off. And Tom?'

'Yes?'

'Hasn't Detective Chief Inspector Williams told you to stay away from me?'

'Yes,' muttered Tom, 'but he doesn't control my private life as well as my working hours.'

'You should listen to him,' said Cressida. 'If anything goes wrong because of Monday we'll probably both lose our jobs.'

'It won't,' said Tom soothingly, and Cressida thought that he was almost certainly right.

As soon as she put the phone down she forgot about him and began to think about the forthcoming weekend when Rick was taking her to meet some fellow artists.

The rest of the week passed off without incident, and although Cressida didn't manage to make any progress on the case, she wasn't worried because she felt sure that her weekend with Rick would provide some useful information. She was enjoying working at the gallery more and more, and sometimes wondered how easy it would be to adjust to being a policewoman again once the undercover job was over.

At five o'clock on the Friday night she straightened up in her chair and rubbed the back of her neck. 'That's the list of framing finished,' she said with relief to Leonora. 'I hope Polly gets over her virus soon, it's made such a lot of work.'

Leonora, who hadn't contributed anything to help out with the extra workload, nodded. 'We ought to be paid more for covering for her,' she remarked. 'After all, that side of things is her business really, isn't it?'

'Yes, but it's a service our customers want and if we start turning people away they might go elsewhere,' explained Cressida.

'Who cares?' queried Leonora. 'It's not our gallery. Daddy's away tonight,' she added in a rare moment of intimacy. 'Piers and I have got to keep Rose company at some boring dinner tonight when she's entertaining one of his friends for him. We were meant to be going to a party too.'

'I'm surprised you agreed to help out,' said Cressida, well aware of the antagonism between Leonora and her stepmother.

'Rose knows things about me that I don't want Daddy to know so sometimes I have to help her,' admitted the younger girl. 'It isn't that it will be ghastly, just boring. Daddy's friends only ever talk about money and property.'

'Let's hope Piers keeps his ears open then – he might pick up a tip or two for the future!' laughed Cressida as she picked up her things, called out to Marcia and left for home.

Piers was going to pick up some tips, but not the kind Cressida was talking about.

'Why do I have to dress up?' Leonora demanded of her stepmother when she was changing later that evening. 'Piers will only be in jeans.'

A picture of Piers, his dark curly hair flopping over his forehead as his deep blue eyes stared out through their long lashes, flashed into Rose's mind and she turned away from Leonora to hide her smile.

'Never mind what Piers wears; he isn't my stepson. I'm not having you insult a friend of your father's by wearing a baggy pair of leggings and that tatty top. It's dinner we're having, not a burger and fries.'

'You're such a snob,' retorted Leonora as she pulled off her clothes and dragged on a short lilac-coloured flared skirt and a floral print cropped top. 'If you'd been born rich you wouldn't make such a fuss about things. It gives away your lack of breeding, you know,' she added spitefully.

Rose ignored the jibe. She was looking forward to the evening too much to let Leonora spoil things at this late stage. It had been such a stroke of luck when Peter had been called away to see his old and ailing nanny that she'd scarcely been able to believe her good fortune. Then, before she'd had to invent any excuse for Leonora's benefit, Peter had told her that he still wanted her to have Guy round to dinner as planned.

'I don't want to spend the evening with him on my own,' she'd protested. 'He frightens me a bit, and if you're away I won't feel safe.'

Peter had laughed, but Rose knew that he'd been flattered. 'You sweet thing!' he'd exclaimed. 'In that case, Leonora and Piers can make up a four. It will do Leonora good.'

So there it was; the whole evening that Guy had demanded handed to Rose on a plate. Now, as she pulled the ankle-length cream satin dress with its thin shoulder straps down over her hips, she realised that she was trembling with excitement at the thought of what lay ahead.

Piers, who was about her height and worked out regularly, had attracted her from the moment she'd set eyes on him, and knowing that tonight she would actually possess him and teach him things that he'd probably never even heard of before, was so arousing she could hardly bear it.

As for the thought of watching Leonora writhing in ecstasy beneath the skilful hands of Guy, well, that was a prospect that made her want to laugh aloud. She couldn't wait to see the sulky girl helplessly enslaved by what would probably be the first truly passionate encounter of her life.

'Just do as I say and try and be pleasant,' said Rose as she heard Guy's car on the drive. 'You might find the evening turns out to be more fun than you expected.'

'It couldn't be less,' snapped Leonora, and then she opened the front door and was astonished to find Guy Cronje standing on the doorstep.

Chapter Six

'*I*'m sorry, Daddy's out,' said Leonora, hoping that Guy hadn't come round to complain about her lack of interest at the gallery. 'He won't be back until about three in the morning, and we've got an important visitor for dinner so I'm afraid I can't ask you in to see my stepmother.' She was pleased about that, because if Guy was there to complain then Rose would be more likely to believe him than her father.

Guy gave a slight smile. 'I'm the visitor,' he said softly.

Leonora swallowed hard and hoped she didn't look as foolish as she felt. Wondering why Rose hadn't told her this, she stood to one side and let Guy walk into the entrance lobby.

For the first time that she could remember she was grateful to Rose. If it hadn't been for her she wouldn't have bothered to put on her skirt for the evening, and she knew very well that Guy had a keen eye for women's clothes. He was looking devastating himself, in an Italian suit that was dark taupe in colour with a single-breasted jacket. His dark blue shirt had wide-set collar wings, and the severity of the outfit was offset by a flamboyant red and blue tie with white rectangles woven into the silk.

Leonora couldn't think of a word to say to him, and she was casting around desperately in her mind for something that would be sufficiently witty when Rose drifted down the stairs. Her simple cream dress fitted her like a second skin and Leonora saw Guy's eyes light up with appreciation, just as all men's eyes lit up whenever Rose appeared on the scene.

Luckily, before Leonora could go into a sulk, Piers arrived, and soon after that they were all in Sir Peter's study having pre-dinner drinks. To Leonora's surprise Rose took an unusual amount of interest in Piers, which meant that Guy was left to talk to Leonora.

Guy, who had been able to read every single emotion that had passed through Leonora's mind from the moment she opened the front door to him, was delighted by the way things were going. He could see the attraction that Piers held for Rose. The boy was about twenty, he thought. He was well built and confident on the surface, but once Rose got to work on him that self-confidence would soon disappear and she'd have the pleasure of taking on the role of sexual teacher just as Guy intended to do with Leonora.

He knew that the gallery didn't interest Leonora – Marcia's complaints had made that clear – so he asked her about her plans for the future, and as she chatted away about her forthcoming visit to Italy he watched her face carefully and tried to picture it when she was at the height of sexual passion.

This was an unusual evening for him. Normally he spent his time with experienced women – either Marcia or else the young wives of older men who needed to gain their satisfaction discreetly elsewhere, without jeopardising their marriages. This suited him very well, although in the past few days he'd found himself thinking quite a lot about Cressida Farleigh and what it would be like to make love to her.

Leonora was clearly so inexperienced that almost

anything he did would have very satisfying results, but he did wonder now why he'd wanted her so much. He supposed that he must be getting tired of women who knew it all, but there had to be a middle path – a young woman who knew quite a lot but was still anxious to discover more about her sexuality, Leonora was almost a blank sheet. It was impossible to imagine that she and Piers did anything more adventurous than straight sex in the back of the boy's car.

At dinner the two women sat at opposite ends of the table, and by the time they were eating dessert Guy knew from Piers's flushed cheeks that Rose was already making her intentions clear. She'd probably been touching his leg beneath the tablecloth from the moment soup was served, he thought with amusement, but he himself hadn't made any move towards Leonora, who had talked endlessly about total trivia.

They moved from the dining room to the lounge for coffee, and once there Rose's intentions became even more clear as she patted the arm of her chair in an invitation for Piers to sit next to her. Guy felt Leonora's body stiffen with shock as her young lover immediately went and sat where Rose had indicated, and then heard her quick intake of breath as she watched her stepmother's hand rest on his knee, her fingers scratching lightly through the heavy denim of his jeans.

Guy, who'd been standing behind Leonora's chair, rested his hands on her shoulders and moved them over the surprisingly cool skin, skimming the surface as softly as he could so that for a few seconds Leonora wasn't sure what he was doing. Then, when she did realise, she sat perfectly still and never even turned her head to look up at him.

Rose smiled at her stepdaughter across the room and then very deliberately began to unfasten the buttons on Piers's shirt. Her hand moved inside and she rubbed his chest. 'You work out a lot, don't you?' she asked huskily.

Piers, who could hardly speak, nodded and made a sound of assent.

'I like a well-muscled body,' continued Rose. 'I work out a little myself, mostly on my exercise bike. Not that I manage to do many miles on it, but it all helps, don't you think?'

Piers nodded. 'Yes, of course,' he muttered. 'I don't think you need to worry too much, though. You've got a lovely figure.' Rose gave him one of her most enigmatic smiles and Guy had to increase his grip on Leonora's shoulders as she started to rise up from her chair.

'Shall I show you the bike?' went on Rose, getting up from her seat and catching hold of Piers by the hand. He didn't need to be invited twice and without a glance back at Leonora he followed Rose from the room.

'Well,' said Guy softly, 'I think we'd better go and keep an eye on them, don't you?' As he spoke he walked round in front of her and caught both her wrists in one hand so that for a fleeting moment he had her imprisoned in his grip. Leonora stared at him, her cheeks pink and then she too rose and followed him out of the room.

Rose had taken Piers to the second bedroom, one of the few rooms in the house that Guy considered to be tastefully decorated, and as he and Leonora entered he paused for a moment as his eyes took in the quietly sensual appeal of the room.

Two large eighteenth-century armchairs had been covered in a pink and white check design while the walls and curtains were in a soft pink and fawn Braquenie print. The same colours were picked up in the deep pile carpet, which also featured a Braquenie design.

On the walls there were numerous pictures of French origin: cafe and restaurant scenes, and one evocative painting of a couple standing outside a restaurant, their bodies half-turned away from each other as they began to part. The look of infinite sadness on the face of the woman always had a profound effect on Guy because it made him wonder why the relationship was ending. Despite the sadness there was an eroticism about the couple that made you feel that in the time leading up to the parting they'd experienced something incredible, something that would live with them for ever. He thought Rick Marks would probably like it.

The decoration of the room held no interest for Leonora, but what was happening on the large double bed did. Her eyes were wide with astonishment as she saw that her stepmother was totally naked, lying on her side watching as Piers hastily finished removing his jeans and boxer shorts. Once he was naked he was on the bed in seconds, and with a soft laugh of excitement Rose rolled him on to his back with his head on the pillows.

A strange tightness formed in Leonora's chest, and she couldn't take her eyes off the bed as Rose positioned herself on top of Piers with her carefully shaven sex lips resting just above his mouth. As she lowered herself on to him, the fingers of her right hand fondling his testicles as her mouth closed about his already rigid penis, Guy moved Leonora into the room and closed the door softly behind them.

Piers was making strangled noises of pleasure as he sucked vigorously at Rose's vulva. She turned her head back and gave him one of her strange smiles. 'Slow down, Piers,' she murmured. 'Use your tongue more. Lick me like an ice cream cone, up and down, and then swirl the tip around my clitoris. That's what I really like.'

Guy glanced at Leonora. Her face and neck were flushed and she was trembling all over. When he reached out and began to stroke the nape of her neck she gave a soft sigh and leant backward. He knew then that it was all going to work out as he'd intended. Piers and Rose were turning her on, and in a few more minutes she'd be ready for anything he chose to do; anything that could ease the desire that was already building inside her.

For Leonora it was both shocking and arousing. She wanted to look away from what was happening on the bed, but she couldn't. She and Piers had never done anything like this. She'd suggested it once but he'd reacted as though she'd asked him to do something immoral. Clearly his inhibitions had vanished now that he was with Rose.

She was also acutely aware of Guy Cronje standing behind her and the gentle touch of his hand as he stroked her neck. She realised that this entire evening had been planned, and obviously Guy intended to make love to her just as Rose was making love to Piers. Leonora didn't know whether this knowledge was making her tremble with fear or desire. All that she knew with absolute certainty was that the scene she was witnessing was making her feel more aroused than she'd ever felt before, and when Rose gave a sudden involuntary gasp of delight as Piers's tongue touched the side of her swollen clitoris, Leonora jumped and felt her nipples harden beneath her skimpy top.

Piers had never known such incredible sensations. Not only was Rose stroking and licking his testicles as she played with him, she had also pushed a hand beneath his buttocks and eased a finger into his rectum until she was able to softly massage his prostate gland. When she first started to do this Piers felt his orgasm beginning and tingles shot up his shaft as his testicles tightened and his stomach muscles contracted sharply.

Rose had expected this and she changed the pressure so that suddenly she was pressing deeply on the gland. To Piers's surprise this stopped his orgasm seconds before the point of no return so that all he was left with was a throbbing erection and the sensation of the moment of impending release dying away. He made a sound of protest but Rose ignored him. She was nowhere near ready for their lovemaking to end and the knowledge that he was frustrated only increased her own pleasure.

'When I've finished, then you can come, Piers,' she murmured and immediately Piers redoubled his efforts to please her as his own climax ebbed further away. He slid his tongue up and down the channel between her sex lips and caressed the side of her clitoris with its tip until he felt her shudder above him and then grind her vulva down hard against his mouth.

Leonora and Guy watched Rose's first orgasm, and when she tipped back her head and closed her eyes Guy knew that he couldn't wait any longer before he started making love to Leonora. She turned to face him and he peeled her top off over her head and then took off his own clothes as she removed her skirt. When she started to remove her high-legged lace panties he stopped her, and before she realised what was happening he had picked up the discarded tank top and with one swift movement drawn her hands behind her back and used it to fasten her wrists together.

Nothing Leonora had ever experienced had led her to expect this and she gave a squeal of surprise. Guy smiled at her, licked the middle finger of his left hand and then drew it down through the centre of each of her rigid nipples in turn so that both breasts started to swell.

'It will be more fun this way,' he assured her, but Leonora wasn't sure he was right. She now had no control over what happened, and that was both frightening and darkly exciting at the same time.

Rose, who had Piers's tongue deep inside her vagina, spasmed in pleasure for the second time and swirled her tongue around the ridge beneath the head of his penis as a reward for his efforts. The problem with Piers was that whenever she did something particularly delicious he threatened to climax, and she had to keep checking him. This time, just as he felt the wonderful prickling feeling in his glans, Rose squeezed firmly with her thumb at the spot where the head of his penis joined the shaft and at the same time pressed hard on the opposite side of the penis with her forefinger. He could feel her fingers curled around his shaft as she squeezed but to his dismay the firmness of the pressure in those particular spots meant that his erection subsided slightly and all chance of him climaxing vanished. He moaned with disappointment and Rose laughed softly.

'There's a long way to go yet, Piers, but it will be worth it, I promise you. I'm going to change position now and you can enter me from behind, but slide in slowly and make sure you massage my clitoris at the same time.'

Piers wished she wouldn't be so explicit in her directions. Her words only increased his excitement and he felt like a sixteen year old rather than a twenty year old as his penis grew rock hard again. The constant arousal and then denial of gratification was becoming painful, but despite this he didn't want it all to end. As the lightly tanned, slender body moved athletically round on the bed and he slid into her from behind, he knew that he'd never have the chance of making love to such a beautiful and experienced woman again and must make the most of this moment.

Because Rose was facing the bedroom door, she was able to see what was happening to Leonora, and this gave her arousal an added edge as she watched Guy lowering her stepdaughter on to the carpet before crouching over her. Because her wrists were tied behind her, Leonora automatically arched her upper torso and this meant that her breasts were in a perfect position for Guy to suck and lick at them. He began slowly but gradually increased the pressure of his tongue until finally he nipped lightly at the soft tissue around her left nipple. Leonora hissed and tried to wriggle away from him, but she was trapped by his arms resting on either side of her, and without the use of her hands there was nothing she could do.

Guy smiled down at her. 'You liked that,' he said quietly. 'Your nipples are so tight they must be painful.

You're aroused, aren't you? You want an orgasm and you want it now. Isn't that true?'

Leonora had never been spoken to like that. She and Piers rarely talked when they were having sex and in any case she couldn't imagine him asking her such a question even if he did speak. To her surprise she found that she couldn't reply; it was impossible for her to talk in the same way as this sophisticated man, especially with her stepmother on the bed uttering tiny cries and urging Piers on to greater efforts.

'You don't have to answer,' whispered Guy. 'I know what you want, and I promise you, you won't be disappointed.'

Leonora stared at him and felt herself shaking even harder as his hands moved lightly over her burning skin. All at once Piers cried out, begging Rose to let him come, but again his request was denied and Leonora began to wonder if Guy intended to play the same kind of game with her.

Guy spread Leonora's legs apart and rubbed his thumbs along the creases of her inner thighs, occasionally allowing them to stray across the tight material of her panties. Leonora started to squirm as strange prickles and tendrils of arousal fluttered through her lower body. Her hips started to twist and turn, but Guy pushed a hand firmly against her flat stomach until she was lying against the carpet again.

'I want you to keep still,' he instructed her. 'Don't move more than you can help. I want you to savour every sensation tonight, and the more you control your movements the more intense the pleasure will grow.'

As his mouth moved between her thighs and she felt his warm breath through the material of her panties, Leonora thought she was going to come immediately. The pressure behind her clitoris had never been so great and she wondered what would happen when it was finally released.

Guy heard Rose utter a single tiny cry that meant she'd had another climax and then heard Piers pleading for his own satisfaction, but again Rose denied him it. He began to utter frantic mewing noises that served as an aphrodisiac for both Guy and Leonora, who found that the thought of Piers in a state of perpetual frustrated arousal was very erotic.

After a few more minutes Guy carefully eased down the panties that had been pressing tightly against Leonora's sex. Once they were removed he spread her legs even wider apart, covered the tip of a finger with some lubricating gel that he'd taken from Rose's dressing-table drawer, and then lightly touched the acorn-shaped protruding edge at the entrance to Leonora's urethra.

He knew that this was an exquisitely sensitive place for a woman and kept his touch as light as possible, but despite this the result on Leonora was electric. Her lower body shot up off the carpet and she began to shout out as pressure inside her pelvis and lower belly ballooned until she felt that she was going to explode.

Strange searing sensations coursed through her lower body and the intensity of feeling between her thighs was almost unbearable. She felt as though she was about to come but the orgasm proved elusive. It was there, creating this terrible hot need but every time Guy touched her the sensations simply increased without her point of release growing any nearer.

Her bladder felt full and strange, and knowing that this would be happening Guy spread some more of the gel around the soft tissue that surrounded her most sensitive spot. As soon as he began, the tissue swelled beneath his touch and Leonora thrashed around even more violently, crying out incoherently as these strange, darkly exciting feelings spread through her entire body until she felt that if she didn't come soon she'd lose consciousness.

'Bear down,' whispered Guy. 'Push down so that I can lick your clitoris, then you'll come.'

Leonora obeyed, and as she bore down she heard her stepmother give another tiny cry of satisfaction while Piers shouted out, gabbling that he couldn't wait any longer and that Rose had to let him come.

Leonora felt the same, but she didn't dare cry out because she sensed that if she did Guy would simply stop everything and leave her stranded. Instead she concentrated hard on doing what he'd said and as the tip of the retracted clitoris re-emerged Guy let his tongue caress the side of the shaft before drifting across the almost unbearably sensitive head so that finally, with a scream that could have been heard all over the house, Leonora's over-excited and stimulated body exploded into the most intense orgasm of her nineteen years.

Guy waited until she was nearly still and then slid his erection into her, making sure that he brushed against her G spot as he moved in and out in a slow rhythm. 'Tighten yourself round me,' he said suddenly. 'Quickly, I want to feel your muscles gripping me.' She was already tight, far tighter than Rose or Marcia, but Guy wanted to feel the soft velvet walls gripping him even harder. When Leonora contracted her muscles it increased her own pleasure too, so that all the hot pressure built up once more and she heard herself give a cry of protest because she wasn't sure that she could bear such intense pleasure again.

Guy didn't care. He knew that she'd climax again – it was what he'd intended – and if anything this time it would be even better than the first and leave her totally sated. His hips moved faster, and at the precise moment that he felt Leonora's body draw in on itself prior to release, he heard Piers utter a strange gutteral howl of demented relief and excitement as he was finally allowed to come.

This was the trigger for both Guy and Leonora, and as

Guy's body was shaken by his orgasm Leonora uttered another scream, a scream that was almost one of despair as the sensations pierced every centimetre of her body, shattering every over-stretched nerve until at last she slumped back onto the carpet with her eyes closed.

Guy looked down at her and then up at the bed where Rose lay with her chin propped on her hands. She smiled at him. 'That sounded exciting!'

'I think Leonora enjoyed herself,' responded Guy, realising with a tinge of regret that the excitement of the moment was already over. He'd done what he wanted to do – introduced Leonora to an entirely new kind of eroticism – and that was it. The pleasure he'd gained had been fleeting, very little more than when he made love to any other woman, and he was disappointed. For some reason he'd imagined that this would be different, that it would provide more excitement than a normal seduction, but he'd been wrong.

'Piers was brilliant,' continued Rose. 'He's fallen asleep, poor boy. Do you think he and Leonora will want to repeat the evening?'

'If they do they'll have to manage without me,' said Guy shortly.

Leonora heard his words and opened her eyes, her arms reaching up round his neck. 'That was wonderful,' she enthused. 'Please, don't say we can't do it again. I couldn't bear it if we never made love again.'

Guy lifted himself carefully off her and turned away. 'I didn't make love to you,' he said shortly. 'We had good sex; it isn't the same thing.'

Leonora's eyes clouded in bewilderment. 'But you were so clever at knowing what I wanted. You made it special for me,' she protested. 'That's what lovemaking means.'

Rose laughed. 'Not to Guy. Guy's a sexual expert; he knows how to turn a woman on but not how to love. Isn't that right, Guy?'

'Yes,' said Guy, dressing quickly and glancing across at the sleeping Piers. 'I don't suppose your boyfriend's under the same illusion,' he told Leonora, trying to soften his voice a little even though the girl was now irritating him. 'He knows it was just sex.'

'I'd like to do it again with him,' Rose said softly. 'Why can't you and Leonora join us? It doesn't have to be love, as she'll come to understand.'

'I know it doesn't have to be love with you,' retorted Leonora, propping herself up on one elbow on the carpet. 'You don't even love Daddy. You just love his money.'

'It doesn't have anything to do with love,' said Guy wearily, wishing he'd never thought of the idea in the first place and desperately anxious to be gone. 'I'd be bored next time. You were a delicious novelty, Leonora, and I hope it was as pleasurable an experience for you as it was for me but that's the end of it.'

'What if I tell Daddy?' demanded Leonora.

There was a terrible silence in the room. Rose stared at her stepdaughter in disbelief and then looked at Guy, whose face had gone very pale. He fixed his eyes on the young girl lying on the floor and then spoke very slowly, softly and deliberately. 'If you tell your father, Leonora, you and your whole family will regret it. Do I make myself clear?'

For a few seconds Leonora tried to maintain her challenge, but despite his quiet tone there was something so menacing about his words that she quickly turned her head away and shrugged.

'I was only joking,' she mumbled.

'You should be careful. That kind of sense of humour could get you into trouble,' retorted Guy. He then walked past her and out of the room without giving her a second glance.

Rose scrambled from the bed and hurried down the stairs after him. 'What's the matter with you?' she asked crossly. 'I arranged this because it was what you wanted and now you're behaving as though you've been forced to go to a party that didn't interest you.'

'I made a mistake,' said Guy.

'There's no need to take it out on Leonora. You treated her shabbily.'

Guy laughed. 'That's rich coming from you! I suppose you treat your husband well, do you?'

'My relationship with my husband is a private matter,' said Rose stiffly.

'Hardly private to me or to Marcia!'

'Guy, why can't you behave like a gentleman for once?' demanded Rose.

'Look, Rose, you married Sir Peter because he was rich, good looking for his age and adored you. He *is* a gentleman, and you wanted respectability. Well, I'm not a gentleman, and that's why you like having sex with me. Don't start expecting me to behave like Peter. We're two very different kinds of animal.'

'But you *wanted* to make love to Leonora. You couldn't wait to show her what real sex, good sex, was like,' shouted Rose. 'Why are you in such a bad mood now when you virtually blackmailed me into setting tonight up for you?'

He shrugged. 'I'm disappointed that's all. I expected it to be better than it was.'

'We all had a great time. I don't see why you're complaining.'

I'm not asking you to understand,' snapped Guy, and a muscle twitched in the corner of his right eye, a sure sign that he was in a bad mood.

'All right,' said Rose quickly. 'You'd better go then. I'm sure Leonora will be able to find someone else just as good as you. I know one or two other men who might like to give her a good time if Piers proves too dull after tonight's excitement.'

'I'm sure you do. I'll ring tomorrow when Peter's back. I need to speak to him about that Holbein we're cleaning for him. It's proving a bit more difficult than our man anticipated so it will be another couple of weeks before he gets it back.'

Rose, who wasn't in the least bit interested in her husband's collection of old paintings, looked bored. 'Does it matter?'

'It might to Peter, that's why I want to speak to him myself.'

'He'll probably want it back by the end of the month,' said Rose. 'His brother's coming to stay then and he always goes round the art collection gloating over the pictures as though they're naked women.'

'Perhaps he prefers them to naked women,' said Guy. 'Right at this moment I think I would too! Incidentally, was it really good with Piers?' he added curiously.

Rose moistened her lips with the tip of her tongue and sighed softly. 'It was incredible. I had such a feeling of power. You know what it's like with Peter; I have to be so careful not to break his concentration or he can't even get started. To have a strong young man who had difficulty in stopping was bliss. Maybe I'll keep him around for a time. He seemed very enthusiastic!'

'Be careful, Rose,' cautioned Guy. 'Just because you and I have got away with an affair it doesn't mean you can do what you like, and he'd never forgive you for taking a toy boy.'

Rose pouted. 'I don't see why not. Older men always have young girls on their arms and in their beds.'

Guy smiled thinly. 'Yes, well, it's just one of those things I'm afraid. Life isn't fair and you have to accept it. Be grateful you're Peter's toy girl!'

Before Rose could say another word Guy was out of the front door and hurrying down the steps.

As Rose watched him leave from the front door, Leonora leant against the upstairs bedroom window and saw him drive away. Her whole body was tingling from the sexual excesses he'd inflicted on her, and she was determined that one way or another she'd get him to make love to her again.

Both women would have been surprised to know that as Guy drove the car through the London streets he wasn't thinking about sex at all; he was thinking about Sir Peter Thornton's Holbein.

On the Saturday evening Cressida stood by the window of her front room waiting for Rick to arrive. She'd been out shopping that morning and bought herself a navy and ivory spot-print trouser suit with short sleeves, and a pair of bright red strappy sandals. Rick had put great emphasis on the fact that his friends were a casual crowd, and that the evening wouldn't be at all formal. Because she was anxious to get it right she'd decided to buy something new for the evening.

Her undercover wardrobe that she'd already purchased had been for rather more high-powered events, and her normal everyday clothes were too conventional for artists. She only hoped that Detective Chief Inspector Williams didn't start going through her expenses with a fine-tooth comb.

She felt quite nervous as she waited. She'd become used to the gallery and the people she met and worked with there, but Rick lived an entirely different kind of life and she was anxious to fit in. If she didn't then she'd lose her chance of getting information from him; at least, that was how she justified her anxiety to herself. In truth, quite a lot of it was because she wanted him to keep seeing her so that they could sleep together again.

He arrived nearly an hour late but didn't seem to realise, and Cressida decided not to mention it. She didn't want him to know how much this evening mattered to her. He drove them to Clapham and as they walked towards a block of flats he turned to look at her and then gripped her hand. 'Why the trouser suit? Do you want to make things difficult for me later on?' he asked with a grin. Cressida felt relief surge through her at this promise of later intimacy.

'I want to see how good you are with buttons,' she replied.

'I just pull them off! Look, this place isn't much,' he added as they climbed the stairs because the lifts were out of order. 'These mates of mine are all struggling for recognition. I'm the only one who's been lucky enough to get anywhere as yet.'

'I thought most artists had to struggle for years,' said Cressida truthfully.

'That's right, they do. It doesn't mean they've got less talent than me. In fact, I'd say two of them are better, but they haven't found the right outlet. I've tried to interest Guy, but with no success.'

'Why are you telling me this?' asked Cressida.

Rick looked slightly uncomfortable. 'I'd rather you didn't mention that you were working at Guy's gallery. Sometimes there's a bit of resentment. You can't blame them for that. If they think I've got myself a stunning new girlfriend through the gallery as well then I think they'll be pretty fed up all round.'

Cressida wondered why he kept in touch with them if they resented his success so much, but before she could ask him the door to the flat had been opened for them and they were inside, swiftly swallowed up by a milling crowd of young men and women.

Rick went off to get them a drink and Cressida felt very awkward. No one showed much interest in her, and even her new outfit was out of place. Everyone else was in jeans and casual tops, with several of the men bare chested.

A tall grey-haired man who probably wasn't much over 30 finally walked over to her. 'Hi, I'm Kevin, the famous Rick's best friend. I expect he's told you about me.'

'Well, he probably has but I get a bit confused with names,' said Cressida diplomatically.

Kevin's eyes changed and some of the warmth went out of them. 'You mean he hasn't mentioned me, right?'

'I mean, I can't remember,' said Cressida carefully.

'Do you paint?'

Cressida shook her head. 'No, I'm useless. I like writing poetry, but it isn't publishable, it's just a hobby.'

'Where did you meet Rick?' demanded Kevin as a small auburn-haired girl approached him and slipped her arm through his.

'He picked me up in a cafe at Covent Garden,' said Cressida, hoping that Kevin wouldn't ask Rick the same thing. Luckily Rick was already close behind her with their drinks and heard what she'd said.

'Wasn't I lucky?' he said with a grin, putting an arm round Cressida's waist.

'Aren't you always,' retorted Kevin. 'I want to talk to you,' he added, drawing Rick to one side.

The auburn-haired girl began to chat to Cressida about the use of oil paints and how all her creative talent vanished if she had to use any other medium. Cressida listened with half an ear, nodding and giving the occasional encouraging comment, while at the same time trying to hear what Kevin was saying to Rick. All she managed to grasp were small fragments that meant nothing on their own but were enough to arouse her curiosity.

'I told you it was difficult,' Kevin said at one point. 'You should have let me do it.'

Rick muttered something that Cressida couldn't hear and Kevin gave a harsh laugh that wasn't a laugh. 'You mean you wanted the money for yourself.'

Again Rick's voice was pitched too low for Cressida's ears but she could tell that Kevin was getting annoyed. 'Doesn't he trust anyone else?' he demanded loudly.

'What's so special about you, apart from the fact that you like painting women in chains? Anyone can copy a – '

'What do you think?' asked the auburn-haired girl.

Cressida blinked. 'Sorry?'

'Do you think I should carry on as I am, or should I give in and try my hand at watercolours?'

'Watercolours do very well at the gallery,' said Cressida without thinking.

She knew the moment the words were out that she'd made a terrible mistake. Rick spun round to look at her and Kevin's head turned sharply in her direction. 'You're not another of Guy Cronje's protégées are you?' he asked with a sneer.

'Guy who?' asked Cressida, playing for time.

'Cronje, the chap who thinks the sun shines out of Rick's backside.'

'I'm afraid I don't know anything about Guy Cronje,' said Cressida.

'But I heard you say that watercolours sell well in the gallery. I thought you were a poet.'

Cressida was sweating. The room was hot and she'd made a big mistake, especially as far as Rick was concerned. Her mind raced as she tried to think of a way out of the mess. 'I didn't say I was a professional poet,' she reminded the angry-looking Kevin. 'I work in an arts centre. We sell all kinds of things from doughcraft to watercolours, all by local artists. We even sell copies of works by members of our local writers' group, so none of it's very high powered. Why? What does it matter what I do?'

She forced herself to sound aggressive, and Kevin immediately backed down. 'Sorry, no, you're right, it doesn't. The truth is, I'm trying to make contact with Guy Cronje. I think I could help him make a lot of money and Rick knows how I feel. If he'd even got himself a girlfriend through the gallery I – '

'You'd what?' demanded Cressida. 'Ask us to leave?'

The auburn-haired girl laughed. 'You tell him! He's got a real chip on his shoulder because the one time he showed his work to Guy Cronje he was told he wasn't good enough.'

'But that was my own work,' said Kevin 'I'm good at reproductions.'

Cressida felt the hairs on the back of her neck prickle. Clearly Kevin knew a great deal about Guy Cronje and what went on at the gallery, and equally clearly he didn't know that this was something he was meant to keep secret.

'At our art centre we sell bought in reproductions of famous paintings,' she said casually. 'Does this Guy prefer to pay artists to do the same thing? I'd have thought that would be very expensive. Prints are cheap. We make a good profit on them.'

Kevin laughed. 'We aren't talking about your usual Monet landscape reproduction here! No, what Guy wants are people who can – '

'Cressida isn't interested in what Guy wants,' interrupted Rick, taking hold of Cressida's arm and starting to steer her away from Kevin. 'This is meant to be a party. I don't want to talk about work all the time.'

'You usually do,' said the auburn-haired girl. 'We have to listen to all your angst about artist's block and how you can't get a girl who's different enough to inspire your next piece of erotica. Why shouldn't Kevin have his say for once?'

'I am quite interested, Rick,' said Cressida. 'It's always good to get new ideas from people and as our centre isn't doing that well Kevin might be able to give me some hints.'

'I'm surprised Rick hasn't introduced you to his mentor,' said Kevin. 'Maybe he's afraid Guy would steal you away from him. He's not only a very sharp business-man, he's also an inveterate womaniser. Isn't that right, Rick?'

Rick was clearly angry. He put his hand on Cressida's arm and pulled her towards the door. 'I don't much like your attitude tonight, Kevin,' he said shortly, with none of his usual amiability. 'I think Cressida and I could have more fun on our own. Come on, Cressida, let's go back to my place.'

Cressida didn't like to refuse, but she wished that she'd had just a few minutes alone with Kevin so that he could finish his description of the kind of artists Guy wanted. However, she couldn't afford to antagonise Rick at this stage or she'd never get the chance to meet up with Kevin again, so she gave him and his girlfriend a rueful smile and left with Rick.

Once they were outside Rick rounded on her. 'You certainly know how to make things difficult. I told you not to mention you worked at the gallery and then you have to start talking about what you do there.'

'I'm sorry,' said Cressida, with what she hoped was the right amount of humility in her voice. 'It just came out. I'm not used to deceiving people and I didn't realise it was such a big deal.'

Rick's face softened. 'No, I'm the one who should be sorry. You're one of the most honest people I've ever met, and I shouldn't have put you in that position. I can't explain, but Guy's very protective of his business and Kevin's been really difficult, pestering him to take him on in some capacity or other.'

'He's certainly on the wrong track with reproductions,' said Cressida lightly. 'I should know. I sell enough prints. I suppose there might be a market for paintings that look like the real thing though. You know, the *nouveau riche* trying to build up an "old" family art collection that's really all fakes, that kind of thing.'

'Guy wouldn't be interested in that. He loves art. He'd see it as a form of prostitution to encourage people in a deceit of that scale,' said Rick fervently.

'I'm sure you're right,' agreed Cressida as they drove

towards Rick's house. Privately she thought Rick was turning out to be less than astute when it came to summing people up.

Much later that night, when Rick had returned her home after some more passionate lovemaking in his attic, Cressida made a phone call to Detective Chief Inspector Williams and told him all she'd learnt.

'Well, that clinches it,' said her chief with satisfaction. 'All we have to do now is catch him. Be careful, Cressida. If he ever learns there's a spy in the gallery he could turn very nasty. You'll be safer if you can get him interested in you in another way, if you take my meaning. At least until we're sure we've got him cornered.'

'I'll see what I can do,' promised Cressida.

In bed that night she remembered her superior's comment and shivered beneath the duvet. She had a feeling that if she ever did get involved with Guy Cronje in a sexual way then her life might never be the same again.

Chapter Seven

The following Monday was a strange day at the gallery. Cressida, her mind full of what Kevin had said at the party on the Saturday evening, longed for a chance to go through the files in Marcia's office again, but she couldn't think how to create an opportunity for herself.

Leonora, who turned up for work in a pair of palazzo pants and a white halterneck top which left nothing to the imagination, started the day in a good temper for once. When Guy arrived with Marcia, Leonora positively sparkled and Cressida was fascinated by the change in the girl. Guy, however, looked to be in anything but a sparkling frame of mind, and when Leonora got no response she quickly retreated into her more familiar mood of apathetic silence.

Cressida watched Guy prowling around the rooms, restlessly fingering the pictures, readjusting them, changing the arrangements and generally seething with nervous energy. He also jumped every time the phone or the bell over the door went and Cressida wondered who or what he was waiting for.

After lunch she tried to draw Leonora out because the

atmosphere was getting her down and for once there was little work to keep her occupied. 'How did your dinner party go – the one with your stepmother and the friend of your father?' she asked. 'Was it grim?'

To her surprise Leonora turned her head and glared at her. 'No, it wasn't grim. Why should you think that?'

'Well, you weren't looking forward to it much on Friday afternoon,' Cressida pointed out. 'You said that you and Piers were missing a party just to keep your stepmother sweet.'

'Did I?' Leonora appeared to have forgotten all that. 'Actually it was a great evening. One of the best I've ever had.'

Cressida laughed. 'Your father's friend must have been rather special!'

'He was,' said Leonora softly. 'He was very special indeed.' As she spoke she glanced down the gallery to where Guy was standing with a framed painting in his hand, looking as though he'd like to throw it on a bonfire.

'It wasn't Guy, was it?' asked Cressida curiously.

'Of course it wasn't!' protested Leonora furiously. 'What a stupid thing to say.'

'Sorry, but I know he's acquainted with your father and – '

'How do you know?' demanded Leonora, her cheeks pink.

'Because Marcia told me,' said Cressida calmly, acutely aware that Chief Inspector Williams had told her as well. 'That's why you're working here, isn't it?'

'Oh, well, yes I suppose it is,' agreed Leonora, but it was plain she didn't want to continue talking to Cressida any more and for the first time ever she went and picked up a catalogue and started studying it without being asked.

Cressida's intuition told her that Leonora was lying. She felt certain that Guy had been the visitor on the Friday night, but why Leonora should have denied it, or enjoyed herself so much, was a mystery. She was still thinking about this when the phone went. 'Is Guy there?' asked a well-spoken woman.

'I'm not sure,' hedged Cressida, who knew that Guy hated taking unexpected calls. 'I'll see if he's left yet. Who shall I say is calling?'

'Lady Alice Summers,' replied the woman.

Cressida realised that this must be the widow of the man whose fake pictures had sparked off the investigation and she took a few seconds to compose herself before putting the receiver down on the table and walking over to Guy.

'There's a Lady Alice Summers on the phone,' she said quietly. 'Do you want to speak to her?'

Guy's eyes flickered with amusement. 'How very tactfully you put that, Cressida! Yes, I think I do. Would you mind putting it through to the office for me, please.'

Cressida did as he asked. She desperately wanted to stay on the line and listen to the conversation, but it was too risky with Leonora sitting close by. Also, she wasn't sure whether or not a light on the consul in the office would give her away if she didn't replace her receiver. It was very frustrating to see the line engaged for the next twenty minutes but have no idea what the two were talking about, and she decided to mention a possible phone bug to her chief when she next rang him.

Soon after the call ended, Guy left the gallery. He didn't look at Leonora but gave Cressida a warm smile. 'Marcia and I are planning a little party later in the week. You and Rick must come,' he said casually.

'That would be lovely,' said Cressida. 'You ought to check with Rick though. He might want to bring someone else.'

'No he won't, because I want him to bring you,' said Guy as he walked out of the door.

Leonora watched him go and promptly burst into tears. Cressida stared at her. 'Whatever's the matter?'

'Nothing!' shouted Leonora. 'I'm going home, and if Marcia wants to know why, tell her I've got depression brought on by boredom.' Grabbing her things she marched out into the street, leaving Cressida totally alone and thoroughly confused.

Luckily Marcia didn't show herself at all until 5.30 and then she seemed to assume that Leonora had just left. 'I'm sorry Polly still isn't well,' she said to Cressida. 'Are you managing all right?'

'Yes, luckily it wasn't too busy today so I think we caught up.'

Marcia smiled. 'That's good. You know, Cressida, you're probably the best assistant we've had here. You get so much done but never seem to be in the way. In fact, I often forget you're here at all. With your knack of blending into the background you'd make a good spy!' She laughed.

'I don't think I would,' retorted Cressida. 'I'm not devious enough.'

'Doing anything interesting this evening?' enquired Marcia, watching Cressida tidy her desk ready for the next morning.

Cressida remembered that she was meeting Tom, and her stomach clenched with nerves. If they were seen it could mean the end of everything, just at a really vital point in the operation. 'No,' she said nonchalantly. 'I think I'll have an early night. I'm still tired from the party Rick and I went to on Saturday.'

'I can imagine!' said Marcia with a knowing look in her eye.

As soon as Cressida had left the gallery, Marcia picked up the telephone. She didn't know why, but she was uneasy about Cressida and the sooner Guy knew this the better. They couldn't afford to have anyone working for them they didn't trust, and it seemed to her that Cressida was simply too perfect.

Unaware of her employer's doubts, Cressida hurried home, had a quick bath and then changed into a light blue belted jersey top which she wore over clinging navy leggings. She was so used to having to look good all the time now that without thinking she re-applied her make-up carefully and then sprayed herself liberally with Esteé Lauder's Cinnibar.

She didn't realise how much difference these small changes had made until she saw Tom's face when she arrived at the Indian restaurant. He leapt to his feet with far more than his usual enthusiasm and hurried to pull out her chair for her.

'You look great!' he said admiringly.

'Thanks, but – ' She stopped. It would hardly be tactful to tell him that she hadn't made that much effort for him.

They both ordered and Tom told Cressida about his work until the food arrived. Then, once they were eating, he started pressing her for information about the gallery. 'Are you getting anywhere?' he asked.

'Yes, I think I am. I'm quite sure Williams is right. There's something going on there, some kind of fraud, but I haven't yet managed to get close enough to a picture that's being cleaned to find out what,' she said quietly.

Tom's face darkened. 'You've got close enough to that artist chap though, haven't you?'

'I'm going out with Rick Marks, yes,' replied Cressida carefully. 'It's my best chance of being accepted by Guy and Marcia, and until that happens I won't make any more progress.'

'What's he like in bed?' asked Tom sharply.

Cressida looked down at her plate. 'Tom, I really don't think we should be discussing this. We're not even meant to meet, it's thoroughly unprofessional.'

'Is it part of your profession that you sleep around with artists?' asked Tom, his voice rising.

'Keep your voice down,' muttered Cressida. 'I'm not

sleeping around with numerous artists. I'm having an affair with one.'

'And that's supposed to make me feel better?'

'You're not supposed to know,' Cressida pointed out. 'This meeting wasn't my idea, it was yours. This is work, Tom. I'm not in it for pleasure. We've been through this before.'

'So you don't get anything out of it? You never have an orgasm with him, is that right?'

Cressida wanted to get up and walk out of the restaurant. She was sure that people at the nearby tables could hear what he was saying and the entire situation was rapidly running out of control. 'If you don't stop this, Tom, I'm going,' she said quietly.

'And what about Guy Cronje?' persisted Tom. 'Are you going to sleep with him too if it means you can get to see whatever there is to see?'

Cressida glanced at him and to her horror saw two familiar faces at the back of the restaurant. Their heads were close together but there was no mistaking the fact that Guy and Marcia were sitting in the same restaurant and must have seen her and Tom.

'Shut up, Tom,' she said sharply. 'We've been seen.' Tom started to turn his head. 'Don't look round,' she snapped, 'that will only make it worse. Just call for the bill, settle up and leave. I'm going now. I'll make it look as though we've had an argument.'

'That won't be difficult,' said Tom. 'We have. I want you off this case if our relationship is going to survive.'

'At this moment,' said Cressida as she got to her feet, 'I'm not sure that I care if it doesn't. I find your behaviour outrageous and insulting.' Then, with much waving of arms and fumbling with her bag, she flounced out of the restaurant hoping that her exit had been noted by the watching pair at the back of the room.

It had. Guy glanced at Marcia and raised his eyebrows. 'Well?'

'Well what?'

'Well, why are we here? Cressida's entitled to have more than one boyfriend at a time, isn't she? You've done it often enough.'

'But don't you recognise the man?' asked Marcia.

Guy studied Tom as he paid the bill. Tom's face was white and his expression shocked. 'No, I can't say as I do, but she's clearly given him a bad time! Who is he?'

'I don't know his name but he's a police officer. I remember him coming in to the gallery when we'd just bought it. He wanted to tell me all about security systems – rather amusing in the circumstances!'

'A policeman? That, I admit, is slightly more intriguing, but I suppose that policemen do have girlfriends.'

'I don't trust Cressida Farleigh,' said Marcia. 'She's too good to be true.'

'Too attractive for your liking is nearer the mark,' said Guy casually.

'I caught her going through the files, remember?' Marcia pointed out.

'Yes, but she had a genuine reason. She'd had a customer call with a painting that needed cleaning; he did come back, and we've done the job.'

Marcia exhaled a long, slow breath. 'I'm sure there's something wrong, Guy. Jealousy doesn't explain the feeling I've got about her.'

'We'll talk to her about this after the party,' said Guy. 'She didn't see us, did she? If she's honest about the man she was with then that's an end to it.'

The following morning Cressida went to work at the gallery feeling very tense. She wondered how long it would be before either Marcia or Guy summoned her to the office and asked her about her dinner date, but as time went by and nothing happened she started to think that perhaps she and Tom had got away with it after all.

Common sense told her that neither of her employers

would know Tom was a policeman, and they probably weren't the least bit interested if she was two-timing Rick. There was also the faint hope that Marcia would remember having seen Tom in the gallery and Cressida's description of him as an obsessed customer.

Marcia was very agreeable all morning, so much so that Cressida wondered if it was a trap, but deciding this was total paranoia she attempted to relax and by the afternoon was feeling far more comfortable again.

At two o'clock Rick called in, and she was very relieved to see the familiar smile on his face as he approached her. 'I'd like to make love to you right here, on the desk,' he whispered, bending his head close to hers.

Cressida grinned. 'Why don't you then?' she suggested.

'I wouldn't want to shock Leonora. Sir Peter would never forgive me.'

Cressida felt the familiar buzz of anticipation when undercover work took an unexpected upturn. 'I didn't know you knew Sir Peter,' she said casually.

Rick hesitated. 'Well, I don't know him in the same way as Guy knows him; I mean, I'm not a personal friend, but I've met him at showings and the occasional dinner party.'

'Does he collect your work?' asked Cressida.

Rick laughed. 'No, I'm not at all his style; he's far more conventional, except when it comes to choosing wives. Have you met the third Lady Thornton? She's a knockout.'

'I haven't,' admitted Cressida. 'All I know about her is that Leonora doesn't like her.'

'No women like her!' laughed Rick. 'She's competition with a capital C. Now, before I go and speak to Guy, are you free tomorrow night? Guy and Marcia are holding a party at Marcia's place in Chelsea and we're invited.'

'What kind of a party?' asked Cressida.

Rick sighed. 'You always have to dress well for Marcia's parties so casual gear's out, but it won't be a big affair. Usually there are about a dozen guests. We have a meal and then mingle and chat.'

'Are the guests mostly artists?'

Rick shook his head. 'No, usually they're collectors. I'm about the only artist that Guy mixes with socially; I'm his token bohemian!'

'Sounds nice,' agreed Cressida.

'Good, I'll pick you up just before eight tomorrow evening.

You won't recognise me – I'll be in a dinner jacket.'

'In that case I certainly won't!' laughed Cressida.

All the time Rick was in with Guy, Cressida was nervous in case he was being told about her outing the previous evening, but when Rick finally left he gave her a quick wink and she knew that she was safe. Later Polly came in for a couple of hours and Cressida was so pleased to see her back and have someone to talk to again that the rest of the afternoon flew by.

On the Wednesday Guy wasn't in the gallery and Marcia kept popping in and out, which meant that Cressida and Leonora were kept busy. She took another telephone call from Lady Alice Summers, who sounded very upset that Guy was out and asked for the number of his mobile phone. Cressida didn't have it, and was startled at the language that was unleashed by the widow when she realised she wouldn't be able to contact him.

Cressida assumed that problems about the fake paintings were increasing and she began to wonder if it was true that Lady Alice herself was involved. With any luck, she thought to herself, she might see the widow at the party that evening.

She dressed carefully for the occasion, settling on a fitted jacket made of cream lace on a coffee background worn over a long coffee-coloured georgette skirt with a fluted hemline. The jacket had short sleeves, a cutaway neckline and fastened with large pearl buttons. Worn with beige and cream strappy sandals, a faux seed pearl bracelet and large pearl earrings, it was very flattering and Cressida felt confident that she would be as well dressed as any woman there. Sue had picked the outfit and as Cressida stood waiting for Rick she knew that once again she had made a good choice.

Rick had been right. It was quite a shock to see him in evening dress and when they kissed Cressida straightened his bow tie. 'Didn't you look in the mirror before you left?' she asked teasingly.

'It took me so long to tie the thing I didn't dare put it straight in case it fell apart on me,' confessed Rick. He looked at Cressida and sighed. 'You're far too ravishing to take out. Let's go upstairs instead.'

Cressida picked up her bag and shook her head. Although her treacherous body wouldn't have minded, she knew that this was a dinner party she couldn't afford to miss unless she wanted to lose her job in the police force. 'Waiting will make it all the better,' she assured Rick.

'I wasn't serious,' said Rick as they drove towards Chelsea. 'Guy would kill me if we didn't turn up.'

'You're the guest of honour, are you?' asked Cressida.

'Hardly, but he was very anxious that you were there.'

A warning bell sounded in Cressida's head. 'Why's that, do you think?' she asked.

'No idea,' said Rick, pulling into a tiny side street tucked away from the main road and parking outside a mid-Georgian house whose front wall was entirely covered by wisteria. 'The house will surprise you; it doesn't look much from the outside but Marcia's had it extended and it's pretty spacious inside.'

'How many floors?' asked Cressida, glancing up at a dormer window in the roof.

'Four, I think, including the basement.'

'You've been down in the basement?' asked Cressida, remembering his drawings.

Rick gripped her tightly by the elbow. 'Cressida, I'd rather not talk about Guy, Marcia or anything I might or might not have done here with them, OK?'

Cressida was surprised by his reaction. 'Of course. I didn't mean to pry, I was only interested.'

'You're special to me,' continued Rick. 'We've got something different; I feel closer to you than I've ever felt to anyone before and I don't want the past to spoil it.'

Startled by his intensity, Cressida could only nod, but his words had created a sense of guilt in her. She liked Rick and loved the sex they had, but she knew that she didn't feel the same about him as he did about her. Once again she wished that she didn't have to use him, especially if he was an innocent part of the conspiracy.

'You're the last to arrive, as usual,' said Marcia, opening the front door. Her blonde hair was loose on her shoulders and she was wearing a pink and grey beaded dress modelled on the style of the flappers. Privately, Cressida thought it was a mistake with a bust as large as Marcia's, but the effect was certainly eye-catching.

'Sorry,' said Rick with his most charming smile. 'You know what I'm like about time.'

'And you know what Guy's like,' said Marcia pointedly. 'He's been glancing at his watch for the past half hour. Come on, we'll go straight through to the dining room. If we don't eat quickly it will spoil.'

'Not the most relaxing of hostesses,' murmured Cressida.

'She's on edge because of Guy,' whispered Rick. 'He gets very uptight on evenings like these.'

Cressida knew that this was true the moment she saw Guy. His face had the tight, shuttered look that she'd come to recognise as signifying tension, and when he looked across the dining room at Rick his eyes were cold. 'Couldn't you tear yourself away from your latest work of art?' he enquired silkily, his eyes then moving slowly over Cressida so that it was unclear whether he meant Rick's drawing or Cressida herself.

'Sorry, Guy, the traffic was dreadful,' explained Rick, as an awkward silence fell on the room.

'Never mind, they're here now,' said Marcia brightly. 'Cressida, you're sitting in between Sir Peter Thornton and Marcus Lloyd. Rick, you're here, between Lady Bradley and Fliss.'

With a quick glance at Cressida, Rick took his place at the highly polished light oak table. He'd hoped to be sitting next to Cressida, but Fliss – the constant companion of Marcus Lloyd, hairdresser to the stars – was an acceptable alternative. Young, flirtatious and full of scandalous gossip, she had often enlivened a dull evening for him.

As the meal progressed, Cressida – with the help of Sir Peter – gradually got to know the names of the other guests. She was intrigued to note that the considerable age difference between Sir Peter and his exotic wife was reflected in another of the couples there. Lord George Bradley was in his mid-sixties but his wife Emily was in her early thirties.

She was disappointed that there was no sign of Lady Alice Summers, and somewhat surprised to realise that there was a spare man, Sir Nicholas Rodgers, who looked to be about 60 and was, according to Marcus Lloyd, newly divorced and highly eligible. 'Tonight must be rather a disappointment to him,' said Cressida. 'I can't see any eligible single women.'

'Apart from you,' said Marcus, whose hair was if anything even more carefully styled than Fliss's.

'I'm not eligible,' retorted Cressida. 'I'm here with Rick.'

'Are you two an item?' enquired Marcus.

'I suppose so, yes.'

He smiled a strange, secretive smile. 'Then no doubt

you know the delights that await us later on. I must say, he's taken up with a rather different sort of companion. The last time we were at one of these dinners together he brought along an extraordinarily tall and voluptuous redhead. She was the entertainment that evening though. You're not, are you?'

Cressida frowned. 'What do you mean?'

Marcus opened his mouth to speak but Sir Peter interrupted from her right side. 'Guy told us you've recently started work at the gallery, which presumably means you're the young lady who has to work with my daughter all day?'

Cressida had no option but to respond to him, and Marcus Lloyd turned to Rose Thornton who, dressed in a royal blue crepe evening dress with side splits and a low neckline, had the attention of every man in the room without making any effort at all.

After coffee and chocolate mints, all the guests moved into the living room which was on the first floor. There they drank liqueurs and chatted, and Cressida noticed a change in the atmosphere. Before it had all seemed very conventional and civilised but now there was an under-current of excitement, a tension in the air. And Guy's mood had changed during the meal, leaving him as relaxed as it was possible for him to be.

Cressida had watched him a lot during the meal. What intrigued her about him was the fact that although he seemed to take part in the general conversation, he actually spent a lot of time watching his guests, rather like an anthropologist watches specimens. They clearly fascinated him, but his fascination was tinged with more than a hint of contempt; a contempt which was quickly disguised whenever he was aware that he too was being watched.

As soon as her brandy glass was empty Cressida felt Rick's hand on her arm. 'We're all going down now,' he said quietly.

'Down where?' asked Cressida.

Guy moved to the other side of her and she felt him slip an arm round her waist. 'Marcia's very proud of her renovated basement. She likes her guests to go and admire it. Rather boring if you're not interested in such things but I find it's best to humour her. You might find it more interesting than you expect,' he added.

'The whole house has been renovated, hasn't it?' asked Cressida as the guests moved towards the door.

'Yes, at considerable cost, but Marcia does have impeccable taste.'

'It's a pity she can't paint, then you wouldn't need to pay so many artists,' laughed Cressida.

Guy shook his head. 'That wouldn't do at all. Marcia and I won't always be together, but I'll always need artists. I think it's far better not to mix business and pleasure.'

'You are partners in the gallery,' pointed out Cressida.

'True, but I own other galleries elsewhere that Marcia isn't involved with. I'm not a man to keep all my eggs in one basket.'

No, thought Cressida, I'm sure you're not, and she remembered the massive Interpol investigation that had so far failed to trap him. He looked at her steadily for a few seconds and then walked away, leaving Rick to escort her down the two flights of stairs to the basement.

'Unnerving, isn't he?' remarked Rick. 'I never know where I am with him.'

'I suspect that's what he enjoys,' said Cressida. 'He likes knowing that people are uneasy in his presence. It gives him some kind of ego boost.'

'It also attracts the women,' said Rick. 'Your predecessor nearly killed herself trying to get him to notice her, but she wasn't his type.'

Poor Sue, thought Cressida. The trouble was, it seemed she herself might be Guy's type, but she wasn't certain how well she'd handle things if he actually made a move on her. She was attracted, but at the same time afraid.

At the bottom of the stairs everyone waited for Marcia to open the basement door. She turned and gave her guests a dazzling smile. 'Here you are. I hope you enjoy the evening's entertainment. It's really been designed with Rick in mind, because he claims he's lacking in inspiration!'

'Or was, until he met you,' Guy whispered in Cressida's ear. She ignored him, linked hands with Rick, and moved into the basement.

She was expecting a dark room, but instead it was so bright that she almost took a step back as the light hit her. All the walls, originally old red bricks, had been plastered and then painted a shining white with a hint of blue. Large spotlights were dotted around the walls, which were stark except for at the far end of the room, where strange African fertility symbols had been hung, symbols that were menacing in their rich sexuality. It was a large room but had been fully carpeted, unlike the rest of the house where Marcia had chosen rich rugs to complement the beautiful wooden flooring.

Because Cressida and Rick were the last guests to enter the room, it took Cressida a few moments to work out why the other guests were all gathering on the opposite side of the room. However, when the group parted to make way for Guy, she had her first glimpse of what she swiftly understood to be the evening's entertainment that Marcus Lloyd had spoken to her about earlier.

The mid-section of the opposite wall had been draped with black and white silk material that shimmered beneath the beam from a spotlight. Standing against the backdrop, her fine-boned body twisted into a strange shape by the judicious use of metal fastenings fixed through the silk into the wall, was a tall blonde with grey eyes and very fair hair, slicked back off her face revealing high cheekbones and a generous mouth.

The woman, who didn't look to be much more than 22 or 23 to Cressida, was wearing a strange black silk dress. It fell to her ankles, but at the right-hand side of her body, which was totally exposed to the watching guests, the dress was slit to beneath her bust, revealing every inch of silky flesh from ankle to hip.

The material had fallen in such a way that the area between her legs was covered, although it was clear that the slightest movement would mean that she was to be totally exposed. The dress was backless with a deep plunging neckline that barely covered the lower half of her breasts, and had a cross-over back.

Because her left arm and leg were fastened to the wall with the left leg drawn up, her left thigh was also on display, and while the left arm was fastened below her waist her right wrist had been handcuffed above shoulder height. Round her neck there was a thin loose-fitting strip of leather that prevented her from moving her head more than a few inches.

Next to Cressida, Rick drew in a deep breath and when she looked at him she saw that he was staring at the young woman with a look of desperate hunger. 'Is she one of your models?' whispered Cressida.

Rick shook his head. 'No,' he whispered back. 'I've never used her, but I know who she is. She's – '

At that moment Guy walked up to the fastened woman and ran his hand with soft deliberation along the sensitive skin beneath her tightly upheld right arm. Cressida could feel the caress herself, felt her skin tense and tingle as his fingers moved so slowly and intimately over the other woman's flesh. Her belly felt swollen and hot.

'I'm sure most of you here tonight remember Lady Alice Summers,' he said politely. 'Poor Alice was telling me the other day that all of her friends have deserted her since Michael died. I knew this wasn't true and thought that it would be a nice idea to throw a little party for her so that you can all show her she isn't forgotten.'

Cressida couldn't believe that this was the woman whose cut-glass vowels had sworn so succinctly down the phone at her earlier in the day. She wondered what it must be like to stand there on display for people who'd known her as the wife of an important public figure and listen to Guy's words. The humiliation must be unbearable, but there was a terrible fascination about it that was arousing her with frightening speed.

'Nicholas,' continued Guy, looking at the recently divorced man with a thin smile on his face. 'I know you were always close to Lord Michael and his wife. Perhaps you'd care to come forward and move her dress a little to one side. I think that after ignoring her for so long most of you would like to see more of her now that you're here.'

Sir Nicholas Rodgers didn't need inviting twice. He hurried up to the fastened figure and caught hold of the edge of the flowing dress with both hands, drawing it up and away from her body then tucking it tightly beneath her trapped left knee so that she remained exposed to their view.

Cressida had expected Lady Alice to be naked beneath the dress, but she was wearing a black high-cut thong with three strips of leather riding over her hip bones on either side of her body. The thong was tight, the crotch pressing tightly against her vulva, and as Sir Nicholas moved away he couldn't resist lightly brushing his hand against the area between her thighs.

Cressida watched as Lady Alice's face tightened and she averted her face as far as she could from the watching crowd, but she couldn't disguise the tell-tale flush of pink that stained her pale, English-rose cheeks.

'Because poor Alice has been so neglected she's very anxious to make up for lost time,' continued Guy, his eyes scanning the watching guests whose sexual arousal was obvious from the way they were either touching their partners or pressing towards the imprisoned Lady Alice.

Cressida had never been in such an erotically charged atmosphere and she was both ashamed and excited by her own desire. She found that like everyone else in the room she couldn't tear her gaze away from Lady Alice, but when Guy stopped speaking she looked at him and for the first time saw his eyes burning with a feverish excitement that made her tremble.

'I think it would only be polite if we allowed one of the ladies to start the proceedings,' continued Guy. 'Cressida, as this is your first visit here perhaps you'd like to come and meet Lady Alice? I'm sure a new friend is almost more welcome than an old one since she feels that her old friends have let her down. What do you say, Alice? Would you like to meet Cressida Farleigh, Rick Marks's new girlfriend?'

Alice didn't reply, but it was clear Guy hadn't expected her to. Instead he looked steadily at Cressida, his eyes almost hypnotic in their power to draw her towards the front of the group. 'Cressida, please start the game for everyone.'

Rick released Cressida's hand and gave her a gentle push in the middle of her back. 'Better do as he asks,' he murmured.

In truth, Cressida didn't need Rick's encouragement – she was already moving towards Guy and the woman chained so provocatively to the wall behind him.

'What do I do?' she asked softly, hardly daring to look at either Guy or Alice but knowing that she must play her part if she was to keep Guy Cronje's confidence.

He smiled, and for once there was no sarcasm in the smile. 'Don't look so anxious, Cressida, you can do anything you like. There are no rules here, providing the pleasure is mutual. Just introduce yourself with a soft touch; the kind of touch you'd like to receive from someone who really cared about you.'

Cressida realised that she had no idea what to do. She'd never touched another woman in a sexual way

145

before, and tried to imagine what sort of touch she'd like to receive if this were happening to her. She looked to the fastened woman for guidance but Lady Alice's head was turned to the side and it was clear there would be no help from her.

Once she was standing close to Alice, Cressida found that it was the black leather thong covering Alice's vulva that most excited her. The material was tight over the lightly oiled body and almost of its own volition Cressida's hand moved towards the three strips that covered the right hip bone. She ran one fingernail down across the straps and then back up again, leaving a tiny mark on the white skin, and she saw the imprisoned woman's flat abdominal muscles ripple gently as her belly drew in.

Cressida was fascinated by the instant reaction and her hand moved down over the curve of the hip and the outer thigh until she could reach between the long colt-like legs and let her fingers stray over the tight leather crotch. Again the muscles of the abdomen moved and she heard Alice's breathing quicken.

Without realising it, Cressida had forgotten her surroundings; forgotten that there was a crowd of people watching her as she greeted the young blonde in this bizarre fashion. All she was aware of was a sense of power and a driving need for some kind of sexual satisfaction, either her own or for the woman she was touching.

Watching Cressida, Guy's pulse quickened with excitement. He had quite expected her to refuse to touch Alice, or at the very least make a half-hearted attempt at some mundane gesture. Instead, he could tell by the look of intense longing on her face that she was lost to everything but the eroticism of the moment, and he knew then that he had to have her.

He'd guessed that she must be more sensual than her appearance suggested, especially once Rick became besotted, but tonight she was displaying signs that she was more complex than even he had guessed, and at that moment he mentally dismissed Rick from the scene. Cressida must be his, and before too long.

'That's enough for now,' he said quietly. 'The others want to say hello as well.'

Brought back to reality, Cressida was overcome with embarrassment and she quickly stepped away from the leggy blonde, moving to Rick's side and trying to hide herself from the other guests. Rick smiled at her. 'You looked as though you enjoyed that.'

'Yes,' murmured Cressida, who didn't want to analyse her feelings.

'I can't wait until we can leave,' he muttered, but Cressida hardly heard him. She was watching Guy as he moved closer to Alice and slid a hand between her thighs, slowly massaging the taut muscles that were becoming uncomfortable as she remained fastened to the brackets in the wall.

'There, a new friend for you, Alice,' he whispered. Alice felt his hand press upwards against her vulva and beneath the thong her flesh started to swell and her outer sex lips opened slowly, allowing the thong to press directly against her hard, erect clitoris.

Marcus Lloyd was the next person to approach Alice, and after running his fingers through her hair sucked and licked the tops of Alice's rapidly engorging breasts. 'He used to be her hairdresser,' whispered Rick. 'I think he stopped taking her calls after her husband died. There's been some kind of scandal over the estate and as she wasn't ever one of the set her husband belonged to she's been deserted very fast. That's the way these people treat you,' he added.

Cressida noticed that Alice's heavy lidded eyes watched Marcus while he worked, and when he reached inside her dress and pinched each of her nipples in turn a small tremor ran right through the blonde's body as she had her first climax of the evening.

Cressida wished that she could come as well. It was unbearably arousing to watch the semi-clad haughty blonde being pleasured without any control over the situation, and if there hadn't been so many people in the basement with them she'd have leapt on Rick there and then, although the person she was watching the most closely was Guy Cronje, the man orchestrating Lady Alice's pleasure.

It was Marcia's turn next and she took a hairbrush from her handbag and moved it in circular motions all over Alice's exposed lower torso, although she avoided the area between her thighs. To Cressida's surprise this soon had Alice moaning aloud, her head twisting from side to side as much as the neck restraint would allow, and all the men pressed closer as they watched Alice gasping helplessly before she was shaken by a far stronger orgasm than her first.

Marcia stepped back and Cressida saw how Alice's skin was glowing red where the brush had touched her. When Sir Peter approached Alice, he rubbed what Cressida assumed to be a cooling gel over the same area, cooling and yet re-stimulating it at the same time. Rose moved to her husband's side and as Alice suddenly began to cry out for Sir Peter to stop, Rose crouched down and nipped sharply at the tender flesh on the inside of the blonde's right thigh.

With a scream of mingled despair and ecstasy Lady Alice Summers climaxed again, and this time her entire body was shaken and Cressida watched as all the muscles contracted beneath the surface of the pale skin. She tried to imagine what it must be like to be so tightly bound at such a time and found that the very idea was making her breathless with suppressed desire.

To her surprise no one suggested that Rick should approach Alice. Instead, the final part of the entertainment was left to Sir Nicholas Rodgers and Guy himself. Guy waited until Alice's body was still again and then he crouched down and very lightly circled her right ankle with his left hand, allowing his fingers to stray along the tense calf muscle and also down beneath the high arch of her narrow foot.

Cressida watched his face, which was in profile, and her own legs trembled simultaneously with Lady Alice's leg as she too felt the cruelly tender caress of the slim, knowing fingers. As his hands moved higher, massaging the aching muscles of Alice's right leg, Cressida shifted restlessly and felt herself growing damp between her thighs.

The atmosphere in the room was electric. Marcus Lloyd and his partner Fliss were no longer watching Lady Alice Summers – they were already wrapped in each other's arms and Marcus had his hands cupped tightly round Fliss's pert buttocks as he pulled her lower body against his erection.

Cressida moved even closer to Rick and waited for him to he put an arm round her, but he didn't. All his attention was on the woman on the opposite side of the room, and Cressida wondered if he was converting the scene into a drawing or simply mesmerised by the way her body had reacted to the variety of caresses it had received.

When Guy finally started to roll the black leather thong down Alice's legs, the guests all held their breath and for a moment there was total silence. Even Marcus noticed the change and lifted his head to see what was happening.

Because of the way the blonde woman was fastened to the wall, the garment couldn't be removed. Instead it was left just above her knees, at an angle that allowed everyone to view her light brown pubic curls and her vulva, swollen now by the stimulation she'd already received. 'Over to you, Nicholas,' said Guy with a tight smile. Sir Nicholas Rodgers quickly knelt and began to nuzzle between the blonde's separated thighs.

Cressida moved to the side of the room so that she could see what he was doing. His hands were holding Lady Alice's sex lips apart while his tongue was busily moving up and down her inner channel.

At first Alice ignored the sensations. Until this moment she'd managed to detach herself from everything that had gone on, and even her orgasms had been private because she'd closed her eyes and blotted out her so-called friends, assembled by Guy as a punishment for the second visit from her lawyers. It was a visit that Alice had been unable to stop.

Now though, as Sir Nicholas's tongue circled the entrance to her aching vagina and then flicked inside, she found that she was unable to forget her audience any longer.

She grew more and more excited as his tongue touched every side of her vaginal walls, and when it pressed against her G spot she moaned with pleasure and felt her breasts start to ache with rising desire.

He knew how to use his tongue to great effect, and within minutes she was writhing within the restrictions of the cuffs, her muscles sore and aching but her whole body on fire with what she knew was nothing more than pure lust. A lust that needed slaking, however great the humiliation.

She closed her eyes and tried to twist her hips so that he touched her exactly where she wanted, but immediately she felt Guy's cool, purposeful hands on her hips and a cushion being pushed between her lower body and the silk hanging of the wall so that she was even more exposed to view. And still Guy's hands kept her motionless, enabling Sir Nicholas to work at his own speed and control her reactions as he wished.

Time and time again Alice's body started to peak. The tightness would suffuse her pelvic area, her pulse would quicken and the blood drum in her ears, but just as she started to topple over the edge, Sir Nicholas would fail to supply that final, vital amount of pressure to enable her total release.

Cressida, watching with hot cheeks and dry mouth, realised what was happening from the way Alice was moaning and trying to move. Her own level of arousal was incredibly high now, and she understood only too well the blonde's need for satisfaction, but it seemed that Sir Nicholas, without intending to, was preventing the blissful satisfaction Lady Alice craved.

All at once, with an ear-shattering scream of frustration, Alice took matters into her own hands. Ignoring the pain in her arm and leg muscles and Guy's restraining hands, she pushed her body down as hard as she could so that the snake-like flickering of Sir Nicholas's tongue became fiercer and more rapier-like, but still it wasn't quite enough and to her horror Alice felt tears of frustration forming behind her closed eyelids.

Guy saw them and decided enough was enough. If Sir Nicholas Rodgers couldn't satisfy the frantic young widow then he'd have to make way for someone who could, and so Guy tapped him on the shoulder and indicated that he was to move away.

Alice felt the tongue slowly withdraw and cried out again, but within seconds Guy had taken his place. Opening her up with one hand, he slid his erection inside her while with other hand he slowly massaged the skin at the top opening of her sex lips so that her aching clitoris was at last stimulated. Immediately Alice's body spasmed furiously, arching away from the wall as a climax tore through her.

It lasted several seconds and Cressida watched in silence, wishing that she was the one enjoying the even, measured thrusts of Guy's penis and the sensation of his hand between her thighs. As Lady Alice finally slumped limply against her bonds, Guy withdrew and walked away from her, leaving Sir Nicholas to take her down.

The rest of the guests, knowing that the evening's

entertainment was over, were quick to disperse. They collected their coats and bags, said goodnight and vanished into the darkness, all of them hurrying home, consumed by sexual desires that had been activated by the scene they'd witnessed.

As Rick handed Cressida her bag, she realised they were the last to go and opened her mouth to thank Marcia for the evening. Before she could speak, Guy flung himself down into an easy chair.

'I'd rather you didn't go yet, Cressida. Marcia and I want to speak to you about the man we saw you with on Monday night.'

Chapter Eight

'Why don't you sit down again?' suggested Guy, watching the expression on Cressida's face with interest. 'This might take a few minutes.'

'What man?' demanded Rick, looking far more shocked than Cressida at Guy's words.

'He wasn't anyone special,' Cressida assured Rick. 'I had no idea you liked Indian food,' she added casually to Guy, as she took a seat opposite him.

'There's a lot you don't know about me,' he said flatly.

'We both like Indian food,' put in Marcia, crossing one leg over the other and absent-mindedly stroking her knee. 'I saw you too. The pair of you looked very intimate.'

As Cressida opened her mouth to give them the speech she'd already mentally rehearsed for just such a confrontation, the door opened and Sir Nicholas Rodgers put his head round the door. 'I'm running Lady Alice home now,' he said, smiling broadly. 'She realises that I never meant to ignore her after she was widowed. I was caught up in my own divorce and somehow never got around to calling. Too self-centred, that's my problem.'

'I'm sure Lady Alice is delighted,' replied Guy coolly.

'Seems rather pleased,' agreed Sir Nicholas.

Glancing over her shoulder, Cressida saw that Lady Alice Summers was now dressed in an impeccably tasteful lightweight summer suit complete with a double strand of pearls, and that her fair hair looked soft and curled round her face. There was no trace of the wanton abandonment they'd all witnessed earlier in the basement; only a gleam in her heavy lidded eyes gave her away.

'I thought they'd suit each other,' remarked Guy to Marcia as the two of them departed. 'That should keep her sweet for a time.'

'As long as he gets her off our backs,' said Marcia irritably, but when Guy shot her a warning look she tried to lighten her tone. 'I really meant off yours,' she added quickly. 'The way she's been pestering you has been highly embarrassing.'

Cressida knew that this wasn't the truth and that Marcia had made a mistake in mentioning any professional relationship with Lady Summers, but she stared into space as though she wasn't listening to a word they were saying, choosing instead to exchange an intimate look with Rick.

'Now that everyone else has finally gone,' said Guy smoothly, 'perhaps you'd like to answer our original question.'

'I don't honestly see what it's got to do with you,' retorted Cressida. 'I assume my private life *is* my private life. You don't pay me enough to consider I'm yours, body and soul, day and night!'

Guy smiled in appreciation. 'That's very true. In fact, we pay you very badly, but the world of art, like the world of publishing, isn't one where you get rich financially. The sense of satisfaction in promoting good works of art is meant to compensate for the lack of money.'

'If anyone's entitled to know about Monday it's Rick,

not you,' continued Cressida, certain that attack was her best line of defence.

'Again that's true, but we do have a special reason for asking. I'd be grateful if you'd bear with us and let us know,' said Guy quietly.

Cressida gave a very audible sigh. 'Marcia already knows,' she announced.

Guy turned his head towards his mistress, who looked more than a little surprised. 'I don't think I do,' she protested.

'But you asked me about him once before,' explained Cressida. 'He's the customer at the gallery who keeps coming in and asking me to go out with him. You saw him once and we talked about him then.'

Guy's fingers moved impatiently against the arm of his chair and Marcia frowned as she tried to remember. 'Oh yes, I do recall something like that happening,' she admitted at last. 'I didn't realise it was the same man on Monday night though.'

'Well it was,' said Cressida shortly. 'He's been such a nuisance that in the end I agreed to go out for a meal with him, but we didn't hit it off. I ended up walking out on him when he made a suggestion that I found offensive on a first date.'

Guy laughed. 'You sound like the original Miss Prim! Considering what you've spent this evening doing, and believe me I saw how much you enjoyed it all, what on earth could he have suggested that would offend you?'

'There's quite a difference between being here tonight with my lover and having a bizarre proposition made to you over an Indian meal on a first date,' insisted Cressida.

'What was the bizarre suggestion?' asked Guy lazily.

Unfortunately Cressida hadn't thought of one and she cast around in her mind for something that the others would believe. 'He wanted to dress up in women's clothes and let me make love to him like that,' she said wildly.

'He must have felt very confident that he could trust you to keep this secret,' said Guy thoughtfully. 'Do you know what he does for a living?'

Cressida didn't hesitate for a second. She was certain now that Guy and Marcia knew, and reasoned that it was unlikely that poor Tom, if he'd ever suggested a liking for transvestism, would have done so before she'd first learnt what his job was.

'Yes, of course,' she said with a slight laugh. 'At least, I think I do. He could have been lying, but I don't see why he should. He told me he was a detective sergeant in the police force.'

'Don't you think it odd that a policeman would open himself up to blackmail by telling you he wanted to dress up in women's clothing?' asked Guy. 'After all, it's scarcely likely to go down well with his colleagues!'

'I'd already told him about one of my fantasies,' said Cressida slowly.

Guy raised an eyebrow. 'It seems that Indian restaurants are the place to go if you want to become intimately acquainted with someone very quickly!'

'I didn't tell him there,' said Cressida. 'It was something that came up during one of our meetings at the gallery and I suppose it gave him the confidence to tell me his private desires. If his hadn't been so bizarre it wouldn't have mattered.'

'Lots of men enjoy dressing in women's clothing,' murmured Marcia. 'I've never found it impairs their performance in any way – quite the contrary in fact.' She gave a secretive smile.

'I'm afraid I wouldn't know,' retorted Cressida.

'What's your fantasy then, Cressida?' asked Guy. 'No doubt Rick's already acquainted with it, but out of sheer curiosity I'd love to know.'

'It's no big deal,' muttered Cressida awkwardly as she tried frantically to think what she could say.

'It was enough to make our police sergeant pretty bold,' Guy reminded her, and she knew by the look in his eyes that he hadn't yet accepted her story.

'I've always fantasised about making love out in the open, in a place where there's a danger of being caught,' she murmured.

'And has Rick brought this somewhat banal fantasy to life for you?' asked Marcia.

'That's my business,' said Rick, his voice tight with anger.

Guy sighed. 'How disappointing; I'm sure you could come up with something better given a little encouragement, Cressida. Never mind, fantasies are very personal things and perhaps it's only possible for you to fantasise within the limits of your sexual knowledge. Maybe tonight has changed your mind,' he added. 'Would you have liked to be Alice?'

'No!' said Cressida emphatically.

'What a pity,' said Guy as their eyes locked. 'I think I'd have enjoyed it if you were, but that of course is my fantasy, not yours! Well, time for the pair of you to get going. I expect you've got a lot to talk about.'

Cressida got to her feet. 'I hope you're happy now you've heard all the details of my private life,' she said angrily. 'You said you had your reasons for asking, but I don't believe you. I think you're just turned on by other people's secrets.'

Guy nodded. 'Perhaps you're right, but if that were true, then don't you think your secret must have been rather a let-down for us?'

'I hope so!' snapped Cressida, feeling far bolder now that the imminent danger of exposure seemed to have receded. 'I'm not here to slake your jaded appetites. Let's go, Rick.'

'I'll walk you to your car,' said Guy.

Once outside, Rick struggled to unlock the passenger door and Cressida felt her employer move up close behind her. Then, as Rick continued to fumble with the key, he pressed himself close to her and blew very softly on her neck.

He didn't speak, but Cressida shivered with a mixture of desire and nervous tension. She knew that this was the man she was expected to sleep with, the man wanted by Interpol and her true quarry, but suddenly she wasn't certain that she had the courage to go through with it.

Tonight she'd seen exactly what kind of a man he was. She'd witnessed at first hand his strange, darkly erotic brand of sexuality and been subjected to his sharp, all-seeing intelligence. For the first time she doubted her ability to cope with him if he chose her as a lover.

'Done it!' exclaimed Rick, opening the door with a flourish. Cressida climbed in and Guy helpfully bent down and tucked her skirt around her legs.

'I like the outfit,' he said quietly. 'So subtle and yet at the same time very erotic. It must have been designed with you in mind.'

'What did he say?' asked Rick as they drove off.

'He said he liked my outfit,' replied Cressida, still trembling without fully understanding why.

They drove fast and in silence for some time. Cressida couldn't think of anything to say that wouldn't make matters worse, so she waited for Rick to begin talking. Eventually he did.

'Are you sleeping with this policeman?' he asked angrily.

'No, of course not. Didn't you listen to a word I said back there? He fancies me, I made a mistake and agreed to meet him once in a public place, and that's the end of the story. He never meant anything to me. I just wanted to get him out of my hair.'

'Why didn't you tell me then? I'd have seen him off.'

'I didn't think it important,' said Cressida wearily.

'It wasn't much fun for me listening to you talking about your fantasies in front of Marcia and Guy.' Rick now sounded sulky.

'Then why didn't you step in and tell them to mind their own business?' asked Cressida. 'It was even less fun for me, but I didn't get a word of support from you. What kind of a lover does that make you?'

'It's difficult,' said Rick, quietening down. 'Guy's been very good to me; he makes me a lot of money and – '

'Fine, he pays you and he pays me which is why we were there tonight and why we had that strange, intrusive conversation at the end of the evening. If that makes sense to you then let's drop the subject, shall we?'

'Doesn't it make sense to you?' demanded Rick.

'Not really. Why should they care what I do in my own time?'

'They don't want me hurt,' said Rick lamely.

Cressida laughed. 'They don't care about your feelings, or anyone else's come to that. They're only interested in their own pleasures.'

'He was a *policeman*,' said Rick. 'Naturally they were interested.'

'Why? Don't they like policemen? Is there something illegal going on at the gallery that I don't know about?' asked Cressida, trying not to sound too interested.

'No, but the police are always making life difficult over stupid things. Marcia had a lot of trouble with them over the alarm at the gallery, and then two of the wealthiest collectors had their cars clamped right outside the place and the police were very unhelpful about sorting out a parking area for customers to use.'

'You'd think they'd have better things to do, like catching criminals,' said Cressida.

'Exactly! If your car gets stolen or your house broken into they aren't interested, but just park for five minutes on a yellow line or have the alarm that's rigged up to the

159

station go off a couple of times by mistake and they're treating you like a murderer,' said Rick angrily.

Cressida was interested to hear his view of her profession. She thought he had a fair point, although not where Guy and Marcia were concerned, because clearly their antagonism was based on more than Rick realised.

'His work did put me off a bit,' she confessed. 'I never think you can trust the police, particularly in the Met.'

'No, you can't,' agreed Rick. 'Half of them take bribes anyway.'

'Do they?' asked Cressida, genuinely interested. 'Why's that?'

'I've no idea, but Guy tells me it's common practice.'

'Clearly he didn't pay enough then if his favourite clients got clamped!' laughed Cressida.

Suddenly Rick pulled the car off the road and parked it outside a huge pair of wrought iron gates. He switched off the engine and turned to her. 'How would you like to realise your fantasy tonight?' he asked softly.

'Here?' asked Cressida in amazement.

'No, not right here at the edge of the road! I thought we'd go over the gates and make love in the grounds.'

'Whose house is it?' she asked anxiously.

Rick laughed. 'A high-ranking police officer's!'

Cressida couldn't believe she was hearing right. 'Are you sure?'

'Of course I'm sure. Guy pointed it out to me once. He was demonstrating how well the top brass live, although to be fair I think his wife's got the money.'

'Whose wife?' she asked, terrified that she already knew the answer.

'Detective Chief Inspector David Williams of the fraud squad!'

Cressida was grateful that the darkness hid her face from Rick. She wondered how she was ever going to make herself do what her lover wanted, knowing that if they were discovered she'd find herself face to face with her superior officer. For a few seconds she simply sat there, but then perversely she found that she was becoming aroused by the idea.

Williams was the man who'd put her in this position. He'd stressed time and again how important it was that she did whatever was asked of her in order to keep the trust of everyone involved with the gallery, and if he caught her and Rick together then he'd know she was carrying out his orders to the letter.

'Well?' asked Rick. 'Doesn't the idea turn you on? You said you wanted to do it out of doors where you might be discovered.'

'I was thinking of woods or a park, not a private garden,' protested Cressida, but her tone lacked conviction and she was already pulling on the door handle. 'He hasn't got dogs loose in the grounds, has he?' she queried.

'No, I'm not that stupid. There's some kind of security guy who sometimes patrols the grounds, but I think that's in the day and early evening. Like I said, his wife's got money and they're terrified of criminals with a grudge getting their hands on her.'

'I suppose he deals with some well-organised criminals,' said Cressida, starting to climb athletically up the left-hand gate.

'He certainly isn't involved with any petty crime,' muttered Rick. 'You're pretty fit,' he added as she landed inside the grounds ahead of him.

'I was always good on the wall bars at school!' she laughed, feeling her excitement level rising. 'Where do we go now?'

'Keep your voice down,' whispered Rick. 'Anyone would think you wanted to be discovered.'

A part of her did, but she obeyed and followed him as he moved in a crouched position along the high wall and down two small steps into an enclosed herb garden with an oval-shaped lawn in the middle.

'This will be perfect,' he murmured. Then his hands were fumbling with the pearl fastenings of her lacy top and as he undressed her, Cressida tugged at his dress shirt buttons and then, after unfastening the trousers of his evening suit, she slid her hand down inside them and encountered his rapidly swelling erection.

They were both breathing hard now, and when his mouth covered hers with a bruising intensity, she pushed her tongue between his lips and caressed the soft inside of his cheeks before sliding the tip of her tongue along his gums. Rick responded by stabbing his tongue into her mouth in mock sexual penetration and their breathing grew so loud that it was all Cressida could hear in the still night air.

Finally they were both naked and she felt Rick's hands pulling her down on to the grass, which was slightly damp with the dew. She lay on her back as he slid himself all over her, moving up and down and then circling his hips so that his penis made soft circles on her lower belly. His mouth was on her breasts now, nuzzling and licking as his hands moved between her thighs and started to massage the whole area until she was desperate to feel him inside her.

She'd never felt so free or so abandoned. Above her, stars shone in the clear night sky and beneath her back the soft grass seemed to mould itself about her in a gloriously primitive sensation that made her long to shout out with excitement. 'I want you inside me,' she told Rick. 'Quickly, I need to feel you fill me up.'

'Not yet,' said Rick, and to her surprise he flipped her over on to her front so that now it was her breasts and belly that were caressed by the damp grass, the coolness soothing the areas where Rick's stubble had grazed her nipples and the surrounding flesh.

Cressida ground her belly down into the earth, loving the sensation, and then she felt Rick's chest on her back and his pelvis hit her buttocks as his long erection slid

162

slowly up between her thighs until at last she felt it touching the entrance to her vagina.

'Hurry!' she cried, totally forgetting to keep her voice low, but Rick slid himself back down her body so that the brief tantalising touch of the tip of his glans was removed and she had to wait several seconds before he carefully eased himself back up her. Then she was again hit by the weight of his chest and pelvis and felt the teasing caress of his penis, this time swirling just inside her, arousing the achingly sensitive nerve endings at the opening there.

'Push right in!' she screamed, grinding her breasts down against the grass. 'Don't wait any longer. I want you inside me now.'

'Did you do it with the policeman?' demanded Rick, rotating his hips so that tiny sparks of pleasure ran through her vulva.

'No! Do it, Rick. Do it now.'

'Swear to me that I'm your only lover. Swear it,' hissed Rick, and she felt him starting to withdraw from her again.

'I swear it!' she yelled, driven frantic by her overwhelming excitement.

Unseen by either of them, a light went on at the top floor of the house and a security light that covered the driveway clicked on.

'Good,' said Rick with satisfaction, and he let one of his hands glide beneath her belly, turning the palm upward until it was resting against her pelvis. Then, as he began to thrust vigorously, he was able to feel his erection hitting his hand through her body. It was an incredible sensation, and every time he pushed forward and felt himself inside her he uttered a low growl of animal pleasure.

For Cressida the combination of these sounds and the sensation that she too had from the pressure of his hand beneath her provided an experience far beyond anything she'd had so far. Then, as the pressure mounted inside her and she felt the preliminary darts of achingly sweet pleasure spreading from between her thighs up through her lower belly, and as her breasts swelled and her tight nipples were tickled by the grass beneath them, she felt tiny drops of rain start to hit the parts of her back that weren't covered by Rick.

She was burning up inside with the impending orgasm, every sinew straining towards the moment of climactic release, and suddenly this heat, which she could feel escaping through her pores, was stimulated even more by the unexpectedly cool raindrops.

Rick continued to thrust fiercely, ignoring the rain as he concentrated on bringing them both to a climax, but the sensation of the rain sent Cressida into a frenzy of excitement as she writhed and twisted beneath her lover. Without realising it, her hands were clutching at the earth and she lifted her head towards the sky, relishing the incredible freedom of the moment as the hot, insistent throbbing that seemed to have been consuming her for so long exploded and her body felt as though the explosion had sent shards of red-hot larva through her whole body.

She had no idea how loud her scream of delight was, but Rick, who was about to come himself, quickly pushed her head down into the grass to try and muffle her scream. Her excitement only added to his and within a few seconds he too was bucking and groaning and his orgasm was also incredibly intense, spreading throughout his entire body and leaving him jerking and shuddering far longer than usual.

When he was finally finished, he collapsed on top of Cressida and then they rolled over on to their sides, arms locked around each other. Cressida laughed with pleasure. 'That was wonderful!' she enthused.

'As good as you'd imagined?' he murmured, pushing her damp hair back off her face.

'Yes, even better than my fantasy,' she assured him, almost forgetting that in truth she'd never had such a fantasy.

Rick pulled her closer and began to lick some of the raindrops off her shoulders and exposed breasts. Cressida squirmed with delight and to her surprise realised that she was becoming aroused again. She ran a hand over Rick's stomach and up across his chest, tweaking his nipples until they were as hard as her own.

'You're insatiable!' he said with a grin, but as his hand started to stray between her thighs they both heard the sound of a door slamming in the distance.

'We'd better go,' said Cressida, her desire vanishing now that the prospect of being discovered by Detective Chief Inspector Williams was becoming dangerously possible.

Rick hastily grabbed their clothes and whispered for Cressida to follow him. 'We'll dress in the car,' he hissed.

It was raining harder now and every drop on her sensitive flesh made Cressida flinch with an aching need that she didn't quite understand. It was as though the very slight discomfort was re-arousing her despite the danger of her situation.

When they reached the driveway they both realised that it was now brightly lit by a security light but they had no choice other than to go on towards the car. Somewhat ungallantly Rick was the first to start climbing the gate, but because he was hampered by carrying their clothes Cressida scaled the wrought iron quicker than he did. Just the same, as she twisted round at the top before letting go with her hands and dropping to the grass verge outside, she knew that she was fully illuminated if anyone was watching.

No one challenged them or even made themselves visible, and finally she and Rick were safely inside the car again, laughing and teasing each other as they put their clothes back on before Rick was able to drive away.

In some rhododendron bushes to the side of the drive, Detective Chief Inspector Williams smiled to himself. He'd always suspected that WPC Cressida Farleigh had hidden depths, and now he'd been proved right. She also had hidden assets, and he rather envied the young man she'd been with tonight. He was certain that before long Guy Cronje wouldn't be able to stop himself from trying to replace the young man, and then the police would literally be as close to him as it was possible to get. Returning to his house, the police officer woke his wife, who was startled but delighted by the urgent inventiveness of his lovemaking.

Because they were both soaked through, Rick drove straight to his flat, which was nearer than Cressida's, and once inside they hurried into his bedroom, peeled off their clothes again and then dried each other with thick towels.

Soon the warm, invigorating rub had rekindled desire in both of them and after a very short time Cressida reached hungrily for his swollen erection. They sank to the floor together and Cressida was delighted by Rick's frantic hunger as he placed her on all fours and then pushed himself deep inside her, grasping her hips firmly and pulling her tightly back against his groin.

Cressida's whole body was glowing from the towelling and every nerve ending was stimulated and ready for him as he pushed deeply inside her. Then, as her orgasm began to flicker teasingly in the depths of her belly, Rick pulled her upward so that they both remained on their knees but now her back was resting against his upper torso.

She was whimpering with need as his hand reached round between her thighs and he slipped two fingers between her sex lips until he encountered her clitoris, swollen with desire. The moment he massaged the base of its shaft the flickering climax started to build inside Cressida until her breasts were hard and aching.

With his one free hand, Rick began to massage her left breast, squeezing and releasing the sensitive burgeoning flesh so that Cressida moaned with delight and leant back, turning her head towards him. Rick's mouth immediately fastened on to hers and he matched the rhythm of his tongue with the rhythm of his thrusting buttocks.

Cressida felt as though she was going to explode as she remained balanced on the edge of orgasm, every fibre of her body ready for release. She could tell that Rick was ready to climax again and suddenly he squeezed her breast harder so that instead of simply pleasure her flesh experienced a tight aching sensation that drove her nearly wild with excitement.

Sensing that if he got it right they would both come together, Rick removed his mouth from hers and nipped softly at the tender flesh beneath her ear while at the same time he squeezed her clitoris lightly between two fingers so that the same strange dark ache now suffused Cressida's lower body too.

With all her senses titillated and aroused, her orgasm rushed over her without warning, a different orgasm from any she'd had before because her whole body was suffused with a bitter-sweet ache that only exploded into the usual liquid pleasure at the very last moment. But to her astonishment she was left feeling peculiarly dissatisfied. As Rick groaned and climaxed deep within her, Cressida wondered what it was that her body wanted, and why this wonderful moment of release hadn't been enough.

Later, as they lay together on the floor with Rick stroking her hair and whispering words of love to her, Cressida had to fight to keep her body calm and relaxed. Somehow Rick had released a hunger in her that she'd never known she possessed before, a hunger that Rick

167

himself didn't know about and probably wouldn't be able to comprehend.

'I want to show you something,' said Rick at last.

Cressida, who'd been lying in his arms thinking guiltily about Guy Cronje, smiled. 'What's that then?'

Rick grinned. 'Nothing sexual! It's my work, but not a side of my work that I usually let people see. Interested?'

Cressida was, but she wished that her undercover work wouldn't keep intruding on private moments of sexual bliss, even though she knew that she was only having the sexual bliss because of her work. 'Of course I'm interested,' she replied truthfully.

'Come up to the attic then,' he said, and she followed him up the tiny flight of wooden stairs. 'Remember that Holbein reproduction you saw the first time we made love?' he asked.

Cressida felt her pulse beginning to race. 'Yes, I think I do, although it isn't my most important memory of that night!'

'I should hope not,' retorted Rick. 'Well, at the time I told you I was just doing it for fun, as an experiment, remember?' Cressida nodded. 'That wasn't quite true,' continued Rick. 'Look, what do you think of these?'

He went over to the far wall and removed a large cloth. Beneath it were half a dozen paintings. To Cressida's eye they looked like a Canaletto, two Titians, a Holbein, and two Rembrandts. 'Well?' he asked anxiously.

'Where did you get them?' asked Cressida quietly.

Rick grinned like a delighted schoolboy. 'I painted them!'

Cressida stepped nearer and studied them closely. She was no expert, but she very much doubted if anyone would be able to tell the difference between these and original paintings by the artists, unless they used scientific tests.

'They're incredible,' she said honestly. 'Are they for Guy?'

Rick looked at her in apparent surprise. 'Hardly, they're not his kind of thing. No, I do these for people who want to pretend they own valuable paintings, just to impress other people with their wealth. You mentioned it once, but you thought Guy would be behind it, not me.'

'How do you get hold of the original paintings?' asked Cressida, gently stroking Rick's arm and shoulder as they talked in an attempt to keep him slightly distracted from the topic in hand.

'I don't. I copy them from the Tate or the National.'

'I thought you said you weren't very good at this,' persisted Cressida. 'That wasn't true – you're incredibly good – and you've obviously had a lot of practice.'

Rick frowned to himself, but Cressida was too busy studying his brushwork technique to notice. 'I didn't tell you the truth at first because it's so at odds with my own work,' he explained slowly. 'I suppose I pride myself on my creativity, but this isn't in the least creative. The trouble is, it makes me a nice lot of money, and commissions for my work aren't regular enough for me to give this up. I don't know whether to be proud of it or ashamed. I'm only telling you because I don't want there to be any secrets between us.'

'That's nice,' murmured Cressida, every professional instinct telling her that Rick was lying. Obviously he'd wanted to show her this work because he was proud of it and needed to share his achievement with her, but she was still convinced that it was Guy who used the paintings, swapping them for those that came into his hands for restoration and cleaning work.

'How do you make your contacts? Find the people who want to buy these paintings?' she asked.

'I network at the parties Guy and Marcia throw. They've also introduced me to quite a few of the newly rich. They're the ones most likely to want something in this line.'

'Then why doesn't Guy cash in on the market if it's so lucrative?' persisted Cressida.

Rick moved away from her and re-covered the paintings. 'Why do you keep on about Guy?' he demanded. 'Do you think I'm incapable of doing anything on my own? Or is it that you find him more interesting than me?'

'Of course not!' protested Cressida quickly. 'I suppose I've always thought of artists as being highly creative people who can't handle the practicalities of life. You're the exception to the rule it seems; clever, talented, sexy and with a sharp business brain.'

'I've never felt like this about a woman,' murmured Rick, bending down and kissing her lightly on the lips. 'You do love me, don't you?'

'You're the best lover I've ever had,' replied Cressida truthfully.

'That's not what I meant,' said Rick, his mouth turning down at the corners.

Cressida put a finger in his mouth and let him nibble on it as his hands clasped the back of her neck. 'I know, but it's the only answer I can give you right now. It's early days, Rick. Don't rush me.'

Rick began to kiss and caress her in earnest again, but Cressida suddenly wanted to get back to her house, sort out all that she'd learned that evening, and prepare her report for the following morning. Pulling away from Rick she moved towards the door.

'Not again!' she laughed. 'I need some beauty sleep. Shall I call a cab?'

She didn't expect him to agree, but apparently her inability to commit herself to him emotionally, together with her refusal to let him make love to her all night, had changed his mood.

'Yes, that's probably a good idea,' he muttered. 'I wish I hadn't shown you these paintings now.'

'Why?' asked Cressida as she followed him down into

the karate club's entrance hall where there was a phone. 'I'm really impressed.'

'It was a mistake,' muttered Rick, but he wouldn't elaborate and as soon as he'd seen Cressida safely into a cab he picked up the telephone again.

Chapter Nine

*A*fter Rick and Cressida left Marcia's house, Guy watched his mistress as she straightened cushions and tidied up some of the glasses. 'Leave that,' he said curtly. 'Your cleaning woman can do it in the morning. Tell me what you thought about Cressida's explanation of her dinner date with that policeman.'

'I didn't believe her,' said Marcia. 'Perhaps he was the man I saw at the gallery with her, but that doesn't mean he first met her there. As for all that nonsense about discussing their sexual fantasies, well, she simply isn't the type of girl who'd do that. I've watched her with Rick and although they're lovers she still seems to be keeping part of herself back from him. Why should she suddenly begin discussing sexual fantasies with a virtual stranger?'

'More to the point, why should he discuss his with her?' murmured Guy. 'No, I have to admit that I was unconvinced. It may well be that she lied because she felt we were prying into matters that didn't concern us, which would be reasonable, but in case there's a more significant reason for the elaborate story I think I'd better check her out.'

'How do you intend to go about it?' asked Marcia. 'I

suppose I could ring Sue. After all, she was the one who recommended Cressida for the job.'

Guy shook his head. 'No, I don't want Sue involved. Since she put Cressida forward the pair of them might be in on something together. I think I'll operate on a more personal level.'

Marcia's face tightened. 'Meaning what?'

'I think it might be necessary for me to get a little closer to our Cressida,' said Guy with a smile. 'Don't worry, I'll try not to enjoy myself too much! And I trust you know me well enough to feel certain that I'll take care of anything I feel needs my attention.'

'Yes,' agreed Marcia. 'But hopefully it won't take you too long to find out what you need to know.'

'Anyone would think you didn't trust me,' retorted Guy.

'You've never given me any reason to trust you,' said Marcia bitterly. 'Look at Lady Alice and Rose Thornton. I know perfectly well that you see them on their own as well as with their husbands.'

'I can hardly see Lord Summers now that he's dead,' pointed out Guy.

'I think it's time you left,' snapped Marcia. 'I'm tired after the evening's excitement.'

Guy rose from his chair and walked over to her, placing one hand on her shoulder in a gentle but restraining grip. 'You seem tense tonight, Marcia. I think you need to relax a little.'

The blonde woman shook her head. 'I just need a good night's sleep.'

'But you might lie awake for hours if you can't get rid of some of that tension. I tell you what, why don't you use the flotation tank?'

Marcia felt her stomach tighten at the prospect. This was something that always drove her into a frenzy of need, but there were times when Guy would manipulate her senses so skilfully that it could be hours before she

173

finally emerged from the tiny bathroom that had been converted into a flotation area, and sometimes even then she was more strung up than when she'd entered. It all depended on Guy's mood, and at this moment she couldn't judge that.

'The choice is yours,' said Guy.

Marcia struggled to decide what she most wanted, and in the end frustrated sexual desire, aroused by watching Alice earlier, won over common sense. She loved it when Guy took her to the boundaries of sexual excess, but it was the rare occasions when he pushed her beyond the limits she'd have chosen for herself that she resented it, although even then her pleasure was earth-shattering.

'Well?' asked Guy impatiently, glancing at his watch.

Marcia remembered that soon he'd be pursuing Cressida, and her last lingering doubts vanished. They'd have such an incredible time together that nothing Cressida could do would provide any threat.

'I think I'd like that,' she agreed.

Guy nodded and held the door open for her, standing back to allow her to go first up the two flights of stairs to the tiny room where sexual excess was the order of the day.

Before they entered the flotation room itself, Guy and Marcia went into a small room off it where Marcia removed her clothes as Guy prepared everything that would be needed later during her time in the tank.

Once she was naked he helped her into a very thin wetsuit that fitted her so tightly it seemed to be embracing her, but there were holes cut out between her shoulder blades, her thighs, her buttocks and in the middle of her belly, while her breasts protruded through circular holes that gripped the fullness of the outer edges, pushing them erect.

Marcia stared at herself in the mirror on the wall and knew that she looked incredibly sexy and desirable with her long blonde hair and firm, upthrust breasts, the nipples already hardening. Guy smiled and then fastened her hair on top of her head before picking up a water-proof blindfold. 'Let's go in,' he said huskily.

It was impossible for Marcia to see what he'd put inside the small black box he was carrying with him, and she trembled with rising desire. 'We will be on our own, won't we?' she asked at the door.

Guy shrugged. 'I haven't decided yet, but your chef is still around if I need him, isn't he?'

Marcia remembered Bradley and her last passionate encounter with him only a few nights earlier. 'Yes,' she whispered, her throat dry.

'Good; I'll put you in the tank and then I'll ask him to be on standby for the next hour. It's often more fun with three. You can have so much more variation when there's an extra pair of hands available.'

With that he opened the door into the already dark-ened room that was nearly filled by a wide bath that had fitted rings on both the sides. Marcia paused on the threshold, her eyes trying to adjust to the darkness of the room, but before they could, Guy had placed the water-proof blindfold round her and was tying it tightly at the back of her head. 'Remember, it's only by removing all visual stimuli that your other senses can be at their most intense,' he murmured, and Marcia did remember – she remembered very well.

Guy's eyes adjusted rapidly to the semi-darkness and within a few moments he was able to study the imposing figure standing before him, her full breasts protruding proudly through the clinging wetsuit. For a fleeting moment he tried to imagine what it would be like to have Cressida there instead of Marcia, but then he pushed the thought aside. Pleasures with Cressida were still to come. He was determined to enjoy tonight to the full and appreciate Marcia's more obvious but also more sophisti-cated charms.

Marcia stood waiting. Usually Guy helped her into the

heavily salted water immediately, but tonight she could hear him opening his black box and her body rippled as it waited to see what he had in store for it.

Guy pulled on a large latex glove that fitted over his hand but had holes in the end so that his fingers were free. The palm of the glove was covered with probes of varying sizes and after a slight pause, just long enough to get Marcia tense with anticipation, he pressed the palm of the glove against the area of her belly that was exposed by one of the cut-out areas. Then he began to massage, gently at first but soon more deeply, and as he did his fingers dug into the wetsuit around her flesh until he heard her breathe in quickly as the blissful tingles began to fill her lower body.

For Marcia it was like being licked by hundreds of knowing tongues, and whenever Guy pressed the glove more deeply against her flesh a heavy ache filled her belly and her thighs started to shake despite the fact that she knew her first orgasm would be delayed for a long time yet. Once he knew that she was near the edge of a climax, Guy switched his attentions to her breasts, and as she felt the insistent massaging on the undersides of her rounded globes Marcia moaned with desire.

Guy worked systematically over every exposed area of her body, except for the space between her thighs which he avoided for the moment. While he was massaging and kneading her buttocks Marcia felt a rush of heat suffuse her entire body and her head started to go back in a reflex action which alerted Guy to the danger of an early climax.

'I think we should stop there,' he said calmly. 'You haven't really relaxed at all, have you? Time for the flotation part of the session. I'll help you into the water and then fetch Bradley. He may be useful later.'

Despite the fact that they had been lovers for over a year now, Marcia still didn't totally trust Guy. His behaviour was too unpredictable, his changes of mood too swift, for her ever to relax totally with him, and her body was taut with tension as he led her towards the bath of water.

'Why are you so tense tonight?' he murmured, running his fingers over the nape of her neck. 'You know how much you enjoy this.'

She did, but not the fact that she was blind and helpless. 'I'm too vulnerable,' she said sharply.

There was a short silence. 'Then I'd better let you go,' said Guy slowly. 'You can use the flotation tank on your own and see if that's sufficient to relax you, but I hope you won't mind if I don't stay around to watch. I might get a little bored, I think.'

Marcia cursed her stupidity. She knew that it was the very fact that she was totally under his control that excited her so much. If he were to go and leave her alone in the room then there would be no special sexual charge; no undercurrent of danger that added so much to their sex life. He'd be gone, and she would be alone and bored, because Bradley was no substitute for Guy.

'No, don't go,' she said quickly. 'I didn't mean that. It's the waiting that's put me on edge. You've made me wait too long.'

Guy laughed. 'You've got some time to wait yet, but at least we can get you in the water. Here, let me lift your leg in. Lean on my shoulder.'

The water was pleasantly warm, very buoyant and about six inches deep. Marcia's head rested on a floating headroll and a rubber ring was placed beneath her hips so that the area below her hip bones was more easily accessible for Guy.

'Arms here,' she heard him murmur, and then each of her wrists were strapped into the rings on the sides of the bath and she was floating in the darkness with the water lapping soothingly against the areas where her wetsuit left her flesh exposed.

177

'I'll put on a little music for you while I fetch Bradley,' said Guy. 'That should relax you even more.'

She heard him switch on a Mozart tape and then heard the click of the bathroom door as he went to fetch her young chef. Alone in the dark, her breasts, belly and buttocks still tingling from their earlier massage, Marcia was left to contemplate what sexual delights awaited her when her lover and his companion arrived.

Despite the music, she heard the two men approach and moved her head blindly on its support. 'Keep still,' said Guy calmly. 'You know you can't see anything. Just relax, let yourself go, and make your mind a blank. I'll switch on the jets so that the water stays warm.'

Now Marcia felt tiny currents of slightly warmer water rising up beneath her, and when they tickled against her buttocks and the sensitive flesh at the backs of her knees that were also revealed by the suit, she sighed with delight.

'That's better,' said Guy in a gentle voice, and at last Marcia began to relax.

Above her sightless eyes, Bradley was standing waiting with an ice bucket in his hands. At a nod from Guy he bent over the supine form of his employer and, using a pair of stainless steel tongs, carefully placed a large cube of ice on each of her breasts.

The contrast with the warmth of the water and her previously relaxed muscles was almost cruel, and Marcia gave a cry of shock as the ice cubes, trapped by the edges of the wetsuit, stayed perched on her breasts and began to melt.

As the ice-cold drips trickled across the swollen surfaces of her breasts, Marcia arched her belly upward off the supporting ring, and Guy firmly pushed her back down. 'Let the water take your weight, float on it and keep weightless,' he reminded her. This was the part that was always difficult, because as her arousal grew Marcia's body became tight with desire and it needed incredible self-control to remain limp on the surface of the salt water. Guy waited. He always enjoyed this moment, the point in time when Marcia had to subdue her natural inclinations and force her body into submission in order to gain her pleasure.

When she was finally level on the water once more, revelling in the heat of the tiny jets beneath her and the rapidly melting ice, Guy fitted a piece of plastic over the cold tap of the nearby basin and then, without any warning, he played a jet of cold water over Marcia's belly and watched the muscles twist and ripple beneath the surface of the skin.

Marcia tried to move herself away from the jet, but this was impossible because the bath was narrow and her arms were fastened. She felt the pin-pricks caused by the water spreading through her whole abdomen and then down towards her thighs and vulva. A climax began to build but almost immediately the water was turned off and the ice cubes removed, and she was left floating with her body aroused but unsatisfied.

Whenever that happened Marcia's pelvic area would start to ache, and her hips moved without her knowledge to try and ease the restless need that was consuming her. Then she felt Guy's hand slide beneath her in the water and he carefully slipped an anal plug into the space between her buttocks.

The plug was wide and spread the walls of her rectum, touching every sensitive surface so that the ache of frustration in her pelvis increased and she gave a whimper of protest. Guy only laughed. 'What do you think, Bradley? Should we let her have a climax now or make her wait a little longer?'

'She needs to come,' said Bradley quietly, and Marcia could have sobbed with gratitude.

'In that case, you may give her her first orgasm,' said Guy casually. 'Use this waterproof vibrator; it works very well at times like this.'

179

Marcia's buttocks tightened around the anal plug as she sought to give herself additional pleasure, and the stimulation this caused meant that sparks of hot excitement rushed through to her vagina where Bradley was slowly passing the tip of the vibrator over her swelling labia and around the area of the clitoris.

The vibrations from this, together with the sensations from her rectum, at last gave Marcia the release that she so desperately sought, and as she tightened all the muscles in the lower half of her body a shudder ran through her as the overstretched nerves at last found momentary relief and the pleasure engulfed her.

As soon as she'd climaxed the vibrator and the anal plug were removed and she heard Guy ordering her to let herself go totally limp once more so that she was again floating calmly on the surface of the water.

'I can't,' protested Marcia. 'I'm still aroused. I need more.'

'You won't get more until you relax again,' said Guy, and she heard him start chatting to Bradley as though she wasn't even in the room. Marcia forced herself to take slow, deep breaths and to listen to the music that was still playing softly in the background. Finally, after what seemed an eternity, she knew that she'd achieved what Guy had demanded.

'I've relaxed,' she said loudly, hoping that he wasn't going to simply unfasten her wrists, remove the blindfold and call it a day as he had done two or three times before. Guy wasn't; tonight he too was in the mood for more.

'I'm going to give you a special massage, Marcia,' he whispered, and then she knew why he'd used the anal plug and she felt her body shaking with delight. This was one of the things she enjoyed him doing most to her, and she found that she could hardly breathe she was so excited. She also knew that very few women liked him doing it, and felt sure that Cressida wouldn't take pleasure from it despite the fact that Guy was such an expert.

She heard the snap of the latex glove as he put it on his hand, and then his other hand was beneath her, spreading a waterproof jelly around her anal area. When the protected hand started to tickle lightly around her anal rim, Marcia exhaled with gratitude at the prospect of the pleasure that lay ahead.

Very slowly Guy eased his index finger into her back passage and at the same time Marcia contracted her anal muscles and inhaled, before relaxing them and exhaling. The sensation that this aroused in her brought her close to ecstasy. A heavy warmth seemed to fill her rectum but the heat also spread up through her entire body and a delicious tremor kept running through her nervous system as he gently vibrated the finger.

Once he felt her start to shake, Guy slowly turned his finger in a rotating movement, pushing against her delicate tissue until finally he was able to move deeply enough inside the rectum to massage her coccyx before lazily pressing against her sacrum bone through the flesh in a zig-zagging move that drove her wild with ecstasy.

Marcia was totally out of control now as the muscles of her abdomen coiled and slithered in response to his touch. She thrashed around on the surface of the water, screaming for Guy to keep going, to probe harder and more deeply as the heavy, hot sensation expanded until she thought that it would totally consume her.

Her body was swollen with excitement, her belly pressing up through the gap in the wetsuit and her breasts so full that the watching Bradley couldn't resist bending down and drawing each of the rigid nipples in turn into his mouth where he nibbled and sucked on them, increasing her frenzied movements in the water.

As her orgasm continued to build, Marcia was almost afraid of how it would feel when it finally broke. For Guy, the sight of the normally controlled blonde helpless and screaming in a delirium of need was too much, and without thinking he withdrew his finger from her rectum and, ignoring her cry of disappointment, tore off his clothes before climbing into the bath and crouching over her floating body.

Marcia hardly had time to whimper her despair before Guy was thrusting his erection between her swollen labia, allowing the head to play briefly over her clitoris before sliding himself inside her vagina.

Now that her vaginal walls were being stimulated, the pleasure centre started to move there, but then Bradley decided to re-insert the anal plug and suddenly Marcia found that both entrances were full. As Guy managed to press down above her pubic bone with one hand, massaging her clitoris through its protective hood of flesh, her body at last erupted into a shattering climax that had her sobbing in total abandonment as the agony of her previous frustration was finally broken.

Guy felt her internal muscles shuddering and gripping him tighter than he could ever remember. Even he was shaken by the power of her orgasm, so that when it was over and she lay limply on the surface of the water he wondered briefly whether or not he was doing the right thing in pursuing Cressida when this blonde-haired woman was capable of such intense sexuality.

As usual, Guy returned to his own home soon afterwards, and as he was putting his key in the lock he heard his phone ringing.

'Hello?' he said quietly.

'Guy, it's Rick here. I thought you ought to know that Cressida seemed unduly interested in my reproduction painting work tonight,' said Rick nervously.

Guy's fingers tightened round the cordless phone. 'How does she know about it?' he asked softly.

'It was my fault,' confessed Rick. 'We'd had a fantastic evening, you know what it's like, and I wanted her to share everything with me. Well, not everything, but my work – my talent if you like.'

'I don't *like* any of this,' retorted Guy. 'Go on.'

'Well, I thought she'd just say how brilliant I was, how multi-talented, that kind of thing!' laughed Rick nervously. 'The trouble was, she kept trying to get me to say that I did the work for you.'

'What did you tell her?' enquired Guy calmly.

'That it was a sideline of my own. That I sold the works to the *nouveau riche* who were out to impress their friends.'

'Why did you have to say you sold them to anyone?' demanded Guy angrily. 'Wasn't showing off your talent enough? Some people do that kind of thing for a hobby, you know.'

'I know, only I thought that if she knew I did other things then she might realise I wasn't quite as broke as I appear to be. She's not as keen on me as I am on her, I know that, and I'm sure it's because she thinks I'm always going to be hard up. This was my way of showing her that I do earn other money, apart from the work I sell at the gallery.'

'You cretin!' snarled Guy. 'If, as you surmise, Cressida isn't as much in love with you as you'd like, it isn't likely to have anything to do with money. She's not that kind of a girl. You could be a millionaire and still not have that vital sexual chemistry for her. It's a sad fact of life and I wish you'd asked me before showing her the paintings. Now you've put a lot of people at risk and probably all for nothing.'

'You don't know anything about the sexual chemistry between us,' protested Rick. 'Anyway, I've let you know now; I could have kept it to myself.'

'Yes, and put your own income in jeopardy,' Guy pointed out, less than impressed by this apparent display of unselfishness. 'If she's a spy and finds out what's going

183

on then you'll be a loser just as much as the rest of us, won't you?'

'I don't know what to do now,' confessed Rick. 'I knew I'd made a mistake as soon as she started questioning me, and I think she sensed it.'

Guy sank down into an armchair and thought for a moment. 'Leave it all to me,' he said at last. 'Marcia and I have already agreed I need to find out more about her. Set up an evening out for next Tuesday – say you're going to take her to dinner, then you'll be struck down by a nasty virus and I'll take your place.'

'You're not to hurt her,' said Rick sharply.

Guy laughed. 'Hurting her was the last thing on my mind! I'm sorry, Rick, but you've blown your chance with her. From now on she's mine and in case you start getting overcome by an attack of jealousy at any stage, I'd like to remind you that unless I continue to recommend your work you won't do very well. I'm the one with the contacts, and should you displease me there are plenty of other artists, like your friend Kevin, for instance, who are equally talented in that particular direction.'

'Kevin's useless!' shouted Rick.

'His own work's terrible, but his reproductions are excellent. Now get off the line. I need some sleep, and I'm sure you do too. I hope your last night with Cressida was one to remember,' he added with a chuckle.

As soon as he replaced the phone his laughter died away. It looked as though Cressida wasn't all that she appeared to be and that was worrying. On the other hand, the prospect of becoming more intimately acquainted with her was distinctly appealing. With that pleasant thought he went to bed.

On the Tuesday morning Cressida was extremely busy. The previous day Leonora had been exceptionally sulky even by her standards and today she hadn't bothered to put in an appearance at all. When she failed to ring in Cressida asked Marcia if she should telephone to find out what the problem was.

'I don't think so,' said Marcia lightly. 'Guy isn't anxious for us to keep her on. He says she's become a liability that even his friendship with her father can't overcome. In other words, she's got a schoolgirl crush on him and he wants her out!'

Cressida wasn't bothered about losing Leonora – she'd never been good company – but at least she'd been an extra pair of hands, and as the summer progressed the gallery was getting busier and busier. She was pleased that at least she'd be seeing Rick that evening. Detective Chief Inspector Williams had made it plain he was anxious for her to keep a close eye on Rick's reproduction paintings. Even without that order, she was in the mood for some more good sex with him.

At lunchtime she finished wrapping a painting for a customer and then started to collect her things together before leaving for her break. When the phone rang she was tempted to leave it, but seeing that Marcia was busy at the far end of the gallery she sighed and picked up the receiver.

'Yes?' she said abruptly.

'Cressida, is that you?' asked a familiar voice.

'Rick! Sorry, I was about to go for lunch and must have sounded a bit brusque. What time are you picking me up tonight?'

Rick coughed down the line and then she had to wait while he blew his nose. 'I'm really sorry, but I'm not going to be able to make it after all. I've got this summer flu virus that's going about and I feel lousy.'

'Oh no!' protested Cressida. 'I mean, I'm sorry, of course, but I was really looking forward to seeing you.'

'I was looking forward to seeing you,' said Rick, and there was no doubting the sincerity in his voice. 'I know it's late to let you down and I wondered if – '

'Shall I come round and soothe your brow?' suggested Cressida. 'I'm quite a good nurse and I'm sure you're not too ill to see me. I know what men are like. You've probably only got a cold.'

There was another rather long bout of coughing. 'Honestly, Cress, I'm pretty rough. You don't want to catch it, but I was talking to Guy on the phone a moment ago and when I told him about our date he said that perhaps you'd like to take Marcia's place at a dinner he's got to go to tonight. She's apparently got to see her mother who's not well and he needs a partner.'

Cressida looked down the gallery to where Marcia was laughing and chatting with a customer. 'She hasn't said anything to me about her mother being ill,' she said doubtfully.

'I hardly think Guy would have made it up,' retorted Rick before he was overcome by another fit of coughing. 'Look, I'll have to hang up. Guy said he'd be in touch with you during the afternoon to see if you could make it.'

'I'll ring you tomorrow,' promised Cressida, but Rick had already put the phone down.

For some reason Cressida's appetite for lunch had vanished now. She knew that this was an important moment. Although going out with Rick had been good for her police work, going out with Guy – the man wanted by Interpol – would be considered far more advantageous, but she was scared.

For one thing, her policewoman's instinct told her that there was something wrong about all this. Rick had coughed too much and despite blowing his nose loudly he hadn't sounded full of cold. Then there was the fact that Marcia's mother had so conveniently been taken ill on exactly the same night as Rick.

Common sense told her that this meant Guy had planned it all, but whether he'd planned it because he was suspicious of her or simply because he fancied her she didn't know. The former seemed more likely, although he had made it clear that he was attracted to her on Saturday night.

'Something wrong?' asked Marcia as her customer left.

Cressida shook her head. 'Not really. It was Rick on the phone and he's got some flu bug so we won't be going out tonight.'

'That makes two of us,' said Marcia sympathetically. 'I was meant to be going to Lord and Lady Truscott's dinner party with Guy tonight but I got a call from the nursing home to say that my mother's not very well and I've had to cry off.'

Cressida studied the other woman carefully. She sounded genuine enough, and there was no suggestion from her that Cressida should take her place. 'I'm sorry about your mother,' she said politely.

Marcia gave a rueful smile. 'Don't be; she's always having "turns" but she'll probably outlive me! Aren't you meant to be at lunch?'

'Yes,' murmured Cressida, finally picking up her handbag and getting to her feet. 'I'll only take half an hour today – that way you can get a break as well. Are you going to replace Leonora?'

'That depends on a lot of things,' said Marcia slowly. 'The final decision will rest with Guy. He prefers to keep the number of people we employ as low as possible. A small, efficient unit is what he aims for, and sometimes it's difficult to get people you can trust. We've been so lucky with you!'

Blushing with embarrassment, Cressida hurried out of the door, and Marcia smiled to herself. She'd be interested to hear what Guy found out about Cressida during the next week or two.

When Guy called in at the gallery that afternoon and invited Cressida out, she accepted with as enthusiastic a smile as she could manage. There was no choice. She'd rung her chief in her lunch break and he'd been over the moon with excitement, so all her personal fears had been put firmly to one side. Even if Guy was suspicious of her, and Detective Chief Inspector Williams had agreed he might well be, she still had to play along with him and learn what was going on behind the scenes at the gallery.

'I'll pick you up at seven-thirty,' he told her before he left. 'It's pretty formal but they're a very nice couple. Hugo, that's Lord Truscott, is sixty-five, but his wife Venetia's only in her early thirties so it's never stuffy there!'

'You know a lot of men with much younger wives, don't you?' remarked Cressida casually.

Guy's eyes narrowed. 'Do I?'

'Well, yes. There were quite a few at Marcia's on Saturday night.'

'I suppose that's what being rich does for men. They can keep casting off their ageing wives and taking on new young things. Probably they truly believe the women are in love with them too!'

'No doubt the women believe it as well,' remarked Cressida. 'Money's a great aphrodisiac, or so they tell me.'

'I take it from that, you don't know this from personal experience?' asked Guy.

Cressida shook her head. 'The few really wealthy men I've met have never held any sex appeal for me, but maybe I just happened to meet them on the wrong day!'

'Maybe you're looking for something else,' suggested Guy, leaning over the desk. 'I have a feeling you're more attracted by danger than money.'

'Danger?'

'Yes, I think that beneath that placid surface you enjoy living a dangerous secret life,' said Guy.

Cressida forced herself to look directly into his dark brown eyes. If he was suspicious about her true reasons for working at the gallery then now was the moment to try and allay his suspicion. 'You're quite wrong,' she said firmly. 'I'm rather a timid person I'm afraid.'

'Well, I shall have to try and teach you some courage,' he whispered.

Cressida felt goosebumps rising on her forearms, as though she was sitting in a draught, and for a moment she was almost hypnotised by the look in his eyes as he searched her face for clues.

'I hope I don't need courage for the dinner party tonight,' she said lightly, but both she and Guy heard the slight catch in her voice as she fought to control the strange feeling that his proximity created.

'None at all; wear one of your most alluring dresses and leave the rest to me. It will be a good night out, I promise you.'

She remembered his words when she was dressing. For once she decided to go for a conventional little black dress, which she felt would be safe, but it also looked very sexy. It was short and made of flowing crepe with tiny diamanté shoestring shoulder straps. She dressed it up with large silver earrings and a diamanté necklace and wore her highest heels to accentuate her long legs and shapely calves. Then she sprayed herself lavishly with Dior's Dune, checked her make-up and hair, and decided that she definitely did look good enough to partner Guy.

For a brief moment she wondered what Tom would make of her now, but quickly dismissed the thought. He'd be horrified at the change in her, and since it was a change that she rather enjoyed she wondered where that left her and Tom when her undercover work was over and Guy was behind bars. She was surprised at how disturbing she found that idea, and when he rang the doorbell she was still frowning. 'Not late am I?' he asked, glancing at his watch.

Cressida shook her head. 'No, I was thinking about something.'

'Nothing very nice by the expression on your face!' his eyes assessed her and he gave a brief smile. 'Nice; not your usual style but definitely nice. Rick's done you good.'

'He didn't make the dress,' retorted Cressida, wishing she hadn't thought about what was going to happen to Guy when she finally managed to trap him.

'Maybe not, but he certainly taught you something about discreetly displaying your feminine charms. You've changed a lot since you joined the gallery, you know.'

Cressida climbed into his XJS and thought how much better he looked in a dinner jacket than Rick. 'I hope I've changed for the better,' she said teasingly, deciding that a small display of flirtatiousness was called for since she had to encourage his interest.

'It's always a good thing when women start to learn the truth about themselves,' said Guy quietly. 'Mind you, I think you've still got a long way to go before you discover the real you.'

'Why do you imagine you know the "real" me better than I do?' asked Cressida with a laugh.

'Because I've watched you very closely over the past few weeks, and women are my hobby.'

'Then I'd better take your word for it,' said Cressida with mock resignation.

Guy turned and smiled at her. 'There's no need to take my word for anything. I hope I'll have the opportunity to show you precisely what I mean.'

Suddenly Cressida's breathing felt constricted as she realised that she was now totally committed to following this through. She had to go wherever Guy Cronje chose to lead her, because only then would her superiors be able to finally close the net about him, but that journey could well be far more frightening than she'd appreciated. Frightening, but also highly pleasurable too, because as he'd said, he was a man who'd made women his hobby and probably knew more about their bodies and responses than anyone she'd met.

'Not cold are you?' he asked, pulling off the road and into the drive of a house near Hampstead Heath.

'No, someone must have stepped on my grave,' she replied.

Guy parked the car behind several others at the front of the double garage, then got out and walked round to open the passenger door for her. 'Don't worry, Cressida,' he murmured. 'Before the night's over you'll feel much warmer, I promise you.'

Chapter Ten

Cressida stepped into the vast four-storey house with Guy's hand resting on her elbow, and as she glanced about her at the beautifully decorated hall with a wide redwood staircase leading off it, she thought how lucky she was to have been given the chance to live like this even for a short time.

Her host, Lord Hugo Truscott, was a very tall, well-built man. He had curling light brown hair and a friendly but clearly sensuous face with widely spaced brown eyes and a full mouth. His wife, Venetia, was another leggy blonde whose ankle-length, figure-hugging lime green dress with a plunging neckline and side splits left little to the imagination. She kept her arm possessively in her husband's, and gazed adoringly at him every few seconds. Cressida wondered why nearly all men chose blondes at this stage in their lives.

'Marcia sent her apologies,' explained Guy briefly. 'This is Cressida, a friend of mine, who very kindly agreed to take her place. It's Marcia's mother again,' he added.

Hugo nodded. 'Marcia's loss is our gain, my dear,' he said to Cressida. 'Do come through. I think everyone's here now. It's the usual crowd, Guy. Venetia, darling, get Cressida a drink and take her through into the reception room, would you? I'd like a quick word with Guy before we join you.'

Venetia flashed a dazzling smile at her husband, which faded the moment she and Cressida were alone. 'What would you like?' she asked politely.

'A dry martini please,' said Cressida. 'I hope we aren't late,' she added.

Venetia shrugged. 'No later than Guy usually is; we all know that he can't tell the time, but of course he's forgiven because he's so gorgeous. I'm rather surprised Marcia put her mother first tonight. She's quite possessive of Guy normally.'

'She knows me too, so I suppose she knows I'm safe,' responded Cressida.

Venetia glanced pointedly at Cressida's legs. 'If she knows you well I can't believe she imagines you're safe at all. Quite the opposite really. Are you and Guy staying the night?' she added eagerly.

Cressida shook her head. 'Good heavens, no! We don't have that kind of a relationship.'

Venetia sighed. 'What a bore! I was so looking forward to the night. I hope Marcia's mother gets better soon.'

Totally baffled by this line of conversation, Cressida followed her hostess into the reception room which, despite its size, was packed with people. Within a few minutes several of the men had introduced themselves so that when Guy finally returned she was having rather a nice time.

'Glad to see you're not a wallflower,' murmured Guy, putting an arm around her waist as he smiled thinly at the two men she'd been talking to. They quickly drifted back to their partners.

'Everyone's very friendly,' said Cressida demurely.

'That's one way of putting it I suppose!'

'Our hostess seemed to think we'd be staying the night;

in fact, she was very put out when I said you and I didn't have that kind of a relationship. Why should it matter to her?' asked Cressida.

Guy frowned. 'Venetia's very pretty to look at but she does talk too much. Don't worry about it, it's nothing to do with you. Good, we're going in to dinner, I'm starving.'

Dinner was excellent, the quality of the food more than equalled by the quality of Lord Truscott's wine cellar, and when the meal ended and the guests drifted into various rooms, Cressida felt quite light-headed.

'Did you give your telephone number to that chap who was sitting on your left?' asked Guy.

'I may have done, I can't really remember,' admitted Cressida. 'I think I could do with some more coffee!'

'It's lucky for you I'm not the jealous type,' he remarked. 'Look, I've got to go upstairs and take a look at some of Hugo's paintings. Are you interested? Or would you rather stay down here and chat to your new-found admirer?'

Cressida's head cleared immediately as her professional instinct took over but she pretended that she was still feeling slightly befuddled. 'I think I'd like to look at some pictures,' she said, resting her head against his shoulder. 'Are they like Rick's pictures?'

'Silly girl!' commented Guy lightly, but although he seemed taken in by her behaviour Cressida knew that it was possible he was acting too and that he was actually watching her reaction closely. She wished that she wasn't so affected by his physical closeness and the smell of the aftershave he used.

They followed Hugo up a flight of stairs and then their host unlocked a heavy wooden door and led them through into a long room with paintings hung on all the walls. 'My family have been avid art collectors for years,' he explained to Cressida, as she stared about her in astonishment. 'There's everything here from fourteenth-century Italian painters to Guy's very own Rick Marks, although he's kept in the bedroom at the moment as he proves quite a turn-on for us both!'

'What was it you wanted me to see?' asked Guy.

'It's this Correggio – "Madonna and Child". You can see it's filthy dirty and I do feel some responsibility about that because when I married for the second time – you know, the one before Venetia – it got put in the attic by mistake. Do you think you could do something with it for me, or is it too risky?'

Guy stepped up to the painting and studied it carefully, while Cressida watched from a few feet away. She hardly dared to breathe as he worked his way over it inch by inch because she knew that if he agreed, if he actually said in her hearing that he'd get the picture restored and when it was returned the police got Lord Truscott to have it examined by experts and it was found to be a forgery, then he was trapped.

'Yes,' he said at last. 'I'm sure we can do that for you.'

As he spoke he turned and looked straight at Cressida. She was watching him closely but the moment he caught her eye she glanced away, hoping she didn't look as though what she'd witnessed mattered as much as it did.

'I take it you're interested in art, my dear,' said Hugo Truscott as he took the Correggio down off the wall and began to protect it with bubble wrap and board. 'Who's your favourite painter?'

For a terrible moment Cressida's mind went blank, and she was aware that Guy was waiting with interest for her answer. 'Francis Bacon,' she said abruptly.

Guy smiled. 'Why's that? Are you fascinated by the screaming popes? I watched a programme once where a psychologist came up with the theory that the popes weren't really screaming, they were trying to draw breath. Francis Bacon's brother had drowned when he was young and it was this image that haunted him.'

Cressida knew then that Guy was definitely suspicious

of her and that the trap had been cleverly laid, but luckily, thanks to her crash course in art, she was able to cope. 'His brother didn't drown,' she corrected Guy. 'He died of an asthma attack, and Francis Bacon himself suffered from asthma, so it is possible that the pope series depicts men gasping for air, but personally I don't believe that. Anyway, it isn't those pictures I like.'

'Really? Which is it then?' asked Guy with interest.

'"Three Studies for Figures at the Base of a Crucifixion." It's the sense of desperate anguish and blind impotence that's so overpowering.'

Lord Truscott gave a small cough. 'Right over my head I'm afraid. Give me an old master any time. Quite a knowledgeable young lady you've got here, Guy.'

Guy smiled thinly. 'Isn't she just!'

'How long will it take for you to get the Correggio in shape?' continued Hugo, handing the parcel to Guy.

'Quite a time I imagine; it's in pretty bad condition. I'll ring you and let you know more precisely when I've had a word with our restorer, OK?'

It was gone one in the morning before Guy and Cressida finally left Lord and Lady Truscott's, and even then Venetia made it plain she was reluctant to let Guy go. 'Bring her back another time,' she whispered, too quietly for her husband to hear but still within earshot of Cressida. 'It would have been divine if the pair of you had stayed tonight.'

'Far too soon for that I'm afraid,' retorted Guy, but he was smiling as he and Cressida made their way to the car.

'Why does she like people to stay overnight?' asked Cressida. 'Does she parade around in some skimpy little outfit over breakfast the following morning? Is that how she gets her kicks?'

'Not exactly,' murmured Guy. 'Don't worry about it, it isn't important. Look, before I run you home I ought to put this picture in my safe. We pass my place on the way back. Do you mind if I stop there for a moment?'

Cressida's mouth went dry. 'Whatever suits you best,' she murmured, feeling her heart start to race. If Guy decided to make a play for her now then she had to go along with it. Her body was more than willing but there was something about him that made her uneasy and she realised that she was missing Rick's easy-going companionship. Not Tom though; she never missed Detective Sergeant Tom Penfold these days.

Guy's house was one of a row of terraced Victorian houses with a low white fence around the front garden. When he stopped the car outside he turned to Cressida. 'Do you want to wait here or come inside for a moment?'

'I might as well come inside,' said Cressida, well aware that this was what Detective Chief Inspector Williams would want her to say, even if her natural instinct was to remain safely where she was.

'I hoped you'd say that,' said Guy quietly.

He took her through the tiny hall and into a surprisingly comfortable drawing room with a highly polished wood floor and what looked to her like the original Victorian fireplace. There was a long sofa in a rich shade of autumnal red with matching chairs, while the draped curtains and rugs were bottle green.

'Take a seat; I'll only be a few minutes,' said Guy with a brief smile. 'Would you like a drink while you wait?'

Cressida shook her head. 'I think I had more than enough at the dinner.'

While he was gone she looked around her more carefully, surprised that the decor wasn't modern. This seemed like a comfortable family home rather than somewhere that a man like Guy Cronje would live. She got up and was examining a polished sideboard when he finally returned.

'I picked that up at an auction,' he commented, putting an arm round her shoulders. 'It was quite a bargain.'

197

'This room isn't at all like I expected,' said Cressida, incredibly aware of the touch of his hand on her bare flesh.

'Really?' Guy's fingers eased under the slim shoulder straps of her dress and stroked the flesh beneath. 'What did you expect then?'

Cressida swallowed hard, trying to ignore the almost hypnotic stroking movement of his hand. 'Something more modern.'

'I'm afraid I'm not like you; I'm not a Francis Bacon type of man at all! Let's sit down for a few minutes. I've made some coffee since you seemed to think you'd drunk too much alcohol.'

Cressida was scarcely aware of what he was doing until she found herself sitting on the large sofa and sinking back into the soft cushions. Guy watched her through hooded lids and studied her face as she slowly allowed her guard to drop and her lips parted as she gave a sigh of pleasure.

'What about the coffee?' she murmured.

'In a moment,' said Guy. 'Let me make you really comfortable first.' Bending down, he removed her sandals and then lifted her legs up on to the sofa so that she was lying along the length of it with her head cushioned on the padded arm at the end. 'That's better,' he whispered, and she felt his hands massaging her aching insteps.

It felt delicious and gradually her whole body relaxed so that when he eased the skirt of her dress higher up her thighs she didn't even pretend to protest because she wanted the pleasure to continue.

'Close your eyes,' whispered Guy. 'Concentrate on the feelings.' She obeyed, but was aware that now he too was sitting on the sofa and then he lifted her legs and positioned her thighs over his. 'Do you trust me, Cressida?' he asked quietly, his hands moving up her inner thighs.

She knew that she shouldn't, that he was the last person on earth who should be trusted, but the feelings were so erotic and her body so aroused that she never even hesitated. 'Yes, of course I do,' she murmured. Because her eyes were closed she didn't see the smile of satisfaction that crossed his face.

'That's good,' he assured her. 'Very good indeed.'

All thoughts of doing this for her chief had long since gone from Cressida's mind. This was for her, and she was relishing every moment of it. When Guy carefully removed her panties she felt nothing but gratitude that at last he could touch her where she most wanted to be touched.

Guy spread some of the massage oil that he'd brought back from his bedroom with him over his fingers and then carefully, using only the lightest of touches, he lubricated the whole of Cressida's genital area, including the highly sensitive perineum. As his fingers moved over the thin layer of skin, Cressida wriggled with excitement and lifted her hips a little to allow him easier access.

Once she was thoroughly lubricated, Guy softly circled his fingers in the area round her vagina, stroking her outer sex lips and tugging with almost unbelievable lightness on her pubic hairs so that the sex lips were lifted and he could see her inner lips swelling as her excitement increased.

For Cressida the hot liquid sensation that he was arousing was unbearable because it made her want so much more. She longed for the piercing sharpness of an approaching climax, but Guy continued his slow, relentless teasing as she squirmed more and more desperately against the soft cushions.

At last he moved his fingers between her sex lips, circling closer to her aching clitoris. When he finally drew the tip of his middle finger around the swollen bud she gasped with delight, and noticing her response he continued with the circling movement until she felt the start of the throbbing sensations behind the mass of nerve endings, a throbbing that promised her the blissful release of an orgasm.

Guy watched her closely and pushed her dress up higher so that he could see her pelvic muscles tense, and then he felt her lower torso arch towards his fingers in a straining need for stronger stimulation. At that precise moment he stopped circling her clitoris and instead went back to stroking her inner thighs and pulling on her pubic hair so that Cressida's eyes opened in surprise and for the first time since he'd begun she looked directly at him.

'Why did you stop?' she asked.

'Because I want to make it last,' he said with a smile, brushing her hair off her forehead with his right hand. 'Rick might have liked to do things in a hurry but I prefer to savour every moment. You'll find it's much better for you as well.'

Cressida thrust her body upward. 'No!' she protested. 'I was about to come then. I didn't want you to stop.'

'I asked you if you trusted me and you said you did,' he reminded her. 'Just for tonight, let's do it my way. Now close your eyes again and leave it all to me.'

By now the incredible tension that always preceded a climax had dissipated and Cressida's body, although aroused, was no longer on the brink of release. With infinite patience and pleasure, Guy began to raise the level of arousal once more. Cressida felt his fingers gliding along the thin skin between her front and back passage, delicately teasing the sensitive nerve endings there until it felt as though all her internal organs were coiling and knotting as slithering snakes of pleasure writhed inside her.

This time Guy waited until she was moaning with need and then took her clitoris between the finger and thumb of his left hand, gliding across the oiled tip with the softest touch imaginable and once more the hot, desperate need mounted as he kept up a steady dependable rhythm that helped her body climb higher and higher towards its goal.

Now the sexual tension and tightness threatened to consume her and Cressida started to lose control as her body began to thrash about on the sofa. Her mouth was swollen and pink, her breasts so tight that they had risen up, revealing far more cleavage than earlier in the evening, while the nipples stuck out through the thin black material, whose touch only increased the stimulation of Cressida's body.

Guy felt his own breathing quicken at the sight of her so wantonly thrashing around beneath him but still he kept her waiting and as she uttered a tiny mewing sound and began to arch off the sofa he stopped all stimulation and bent over her. 'Wait just a little longer,' he whispered. 'Next time you'll come, I promise.'

Cressida's lower belly and pelvis ached with frustration and she moaned in dismay at his words, but without the wonderfully clever movements of his fingers she felt her approaching orgasm slowly vanish yet again and turned her head to one side so that Guy couldn't see the disappointment that she knew must be visible on her face.

He didn't need to; her taut muscles, the tell-tale sexual flush on her breasts and neck and the involuntary twitching of all her muscles told him better than any expression how frustrated and desperate she was, but this was the way Guy wanted to play her, and his pleasure in watching her was almost as great as hers would be when she was finally able to come.

He waited until her body had started to descend from its high level of arousal and then with cruelly exquisite care he began the entire process again, massaging the crevices at the tops of Cressida's thighs, rotating the muscles of her lower belly with his fingers and pressing lightly against her pubic bone until she was once more moving restlessly beneath his touch and uttering tiny cries that drove him wild with desire to possess her, a desire that he didn't intend to fulfil that evening.

For Cressida this third arousal was painful in its intensity. All of her senses were now so finely honed that everything had a keener edge to it and the strange coiling sensation deep within her seemed tinged with a dark edge that was only just pleasure but affected her more deeply than anything that had gone before.

Guy knew that Cressida had to come soon or the moment would be gone. Carefully he stroked the side of the stem of her clitoris and her whole body jerked with pleasure. Sustaining that movement he also slid a finger of his other hand inside her vagina until he was able to locate her G spot, now as engorged and firm as her clitoris after all his foreplay. Then, with great care, he stimulated both the side of her clitoris and her G spot in the same rhythm, and Cressida felt as though she was about to explode.

She pushed herself against his hands, bore down with her clitoris and moved her hips in an effort to finally release herself from the all-consuming tension, but then Guy murmured 'Now!' and as he spoke he changed the rhythm of his finger against her clitoris so that he was flicking at the stem with a soft padded fingertip. At last Cressida's climax erupted and she heard herself screaming out in an ecstasy of gratitude and pleasure as her internal muscles finally contracted and released in an incredible bitter-sweet orgasm.

When it was over she opened her eyes and stared at Guy, who was looking down at her with an unfathomable expression on his face. Reaching out, he touched her briefly on the side of her mouth in a gesture that was almost affectionate, but then he stood up and glanced at the clock.

'I must take you back,' he said calmly. 'We both have to go to work in the morning.'

Cressida knew that she should have been grateful for

his detachment. After all, she wasn't in love with him and however expert a lover he proved to be she had to remember that she wasn't really an assistant at his art gallery. She was a working policewoman on an under-cover assignment of international importance. Unfortunately she didn't feel grateful; she felt confused and let down after his display of tenderness and the incredible pleasure he'd given her.

Luckily her years of police work enabled her to hide her feelings well. 'You're right,' she said lazily, pulling down her dress and swinging her legs off the sofa. 'I never did get that cup of coffee either!' she pointed out as they left the house.

'Next time,' promised Guy, and relief flooded over her – professional relief because after this Detective Chief Inspector Williams would certainly expect her to keep intimate with Guy until the operation was successfully concluded.

'Does Rick help with renovations like the one you got tonight?' she asked Guy before he dropped her off.

'Rick? Good heavens no! He's creative; restoring and cleaning old paintings is a very specialised job and not usually one that creative people are interested in. What made you think he'd be involved?'

Cressida realised that because she felt so relaxed and languorous she'd made a mistake. She was certain that Rick would be asked to copy the Correggio and had totally forgotten that as far as Guy was concerned she knew nothing about copies or large-scale fraud. 'I only wondered if that was another way for struggling artists to make some extra money,' she said lightly.

'Rick isn't a struggling artist, he's a highly successful one and in a few years time he won't need me or my gallery,' said Guy shortly. 'Here we are. I expect I'll see you tomorrow. I'll have to call in at the gallery to arrange for Hugo's picture to be examined by our expert. Goodnight, and I'm very glad you were able to take Marcia's place!'

'I'm glad too,' replied Cressida, and she was.

As soon as she got indoors and played back the messages on her answerphone, she found one from Detective Chief Inspector Williams asking her to call him the moment she got back. Reluctantly, because she was afraid of giving away precisely how intimate an evening it had been, she called her chief's number.

'Cressida, thanks for ringing back. How did the evening go?' he asked. She told him everything, except for what had happened on the sofa in Guy's house. 'What about your stay at his place?' he asked when she finished.

Cressida hesitated. 'What stay?'

'We had you followed – for your own protection, you understand – and our man said that you spent over an hour at the house Guy Cronje is renting. What happened during that time?'

'He rents it, does he? That explains why it wasn't quite what I expected!' she exclaimed.

'No doubt he wants to be free to leave the country at a moment's notice. The place belongs to a friend from years back. So, what happened, WPC Farleigh?'

It was plain her superior expected an answer and Cressida knew that she was going to have to admit that they'd become rather more than casual friends, although not yet lovers in the full sense of the word.

'We chatted and got to know each other on a more personal level,' she said curtly.

'Did you sleep with him?' asked her chief eagerly.

'No,' retorted Cressida.

'For heaven's sake, I hope you're not going to go all coy on us now!' he shouted. 'You've got him hooked, so make the most of it.'

'He didn't ask me to sleep with him, and I'm not in the habit of making the first move with men,' said Cressida shortly. 'Don't worry, sir, I'm sure it won't be long before both you and he get what you want.'

'What I want is to see that man behind bars,' snapped Detective Chief Inspector Williams. 'Peter Thornton's one of my closest friends and if I find that he's been swindled by this con artist and we let him escape I'll never forgive myself, or you either come to that. Do I make myself clear?'

'Perfectly clear, sir,' said Cressida, suddenly desperately tired as the adrenalin of the night's excitement died on her. 'Don't worry, tomorrow I'll make sure Lord Truscott's picture has been logged in the renovation book and then, when it's returned, we can get Hugo to call in an expert and you'll have caught Guy red-handed.'

'Only if we establish a firm link between him and the people who clean the paintings,' pointed out her chief.

'I think the link between him and the artist who does the replica is probably just as good,' said Cressida, wishing she could banish Rick's face from her mind.

'True, very true. Well, you get some beauty sleep now and from tomorrow you'd better concentrate on making yourself totally irresistible to the man. It's amazing how careless men are when it comes to pillow talk.'

'I've got a feeling he doesn't go in for any talking afterwards,' said Cressida, but her chief had already replaced his phone.

The next day she was surprised to find that Guy was at the gallery before her, and Marcia looked equally startled. He smiled at Cressida and as he walked past her ran a hand through her hair. 'You look tired!' he laughed. Cressida blushed, and Marcia gave her a hard look before turning and following Guy into their office.

Later that morning a customer bought a painting by one of their newest artists and wanted it framed there and then so that she could take it with her to a birthday lunch as a present.

'You'd better go into the framing room and see if there are any of the plain black frames left,' said Marcia to Cressida. 'I do wish Polly came in some mornings as well, or at least told us more about her work.'

'It's all right, I know what I'm looking for,' Cressida assured her.

The framing room was at the far end of the gallery, up three steps, and as usual it was crowded out with discarded old and new frames all stacked haphazardly in piles. Polly didn't have a tidy mind.

Cressida put on the light as the room was dark and then jumped with surprise as she realised that Guy was already in the room. He glanced at her thoughtfully. 'You look guilty, Cressida. What's the matter? Are you doing something you shouldn't be doing?'

'No, of course not!' she laughed, hoping he only meant at this moment but suspecting that he meant far more. 'You startled me, that's all.'

'You startled me last night,' he responded. 'I guessed that you were a very sensual young woman, but your responses were even better than I'd hoped. How would you like to go to dinner tomorrow night?'

'That would be lovely,' she murmured.

'Good, I'll pick you up at seven as it's quite a drive. I prefer to eat out of London, especially when the weather's as hot as it is now. You can dress casually – I want it to be a really relaxing evening for us both.'

'That sounds wonderful,' she said truthfully, but then Marcia came in and Guy quickly slipped away leaving the two women alone together. Cressida quite expected some kind of trouble from her employer, but Marcia didn't say a word. She simply took the black frame from Cressida's hands and went back to the customer.

She maintained her icy politeness all day and by the time Cressida left work she was certain that Marcia must have given her agreement, however reluctantly, to Guy making a move on Cressida, which had to mean that they were both suspicious of her. The trouble was, Cressida was more excited about the prospect of an evening out with him and what might happen after their meal than she was about the opportunity of finding out about Hugo's painting. Her unusual lack of professionalism shocked her.

Because she felt guilty, Cressida decided that the least she could do was call in on Rick on her way home. If she caught him up and about and looking perfectly well then she'd know that her suspicions about the previous evening being a set-up job were right, and that would help to keep her on her guard the following evening.

At first Rick didn't answer his door, which made her think she might have been wrong after all, but then after her second ring she heard his footsteps on the stairs and when he opened his front door he had a paintbrush stuck behind his right ear. His face went pale when he saw her. 'Cressida!' he exclaimed in surprise.

She nodded. 'That's right, it's me. You're lucky I didn't bring a Thermos of soup and a bunch of grapes or you'd have looked even sillier than you do now.'

'I don't know what you mean,' blustered Rick, oblivious to the brush behind his ear.

'Well, you seem to have made a miraculous recovery from the incipient bubonic plague that was troubling you when you rang me yesterday,' she pointed out.

'I felt really bad for twenty-four hours,' he protested. 'In fact. I've only got dressed this evening because I thought it might do me good. I didn't really feel well enough to get up.'

'But you're painting,' Cressida pointed out.

'Of course I'm not!' snapped Rick in a robust denial that contradicted his statement about feeling frail.

'Really? Is the brush behind your ear some new kind of decoration, like a nose stud or something?' enquired Cressida with interest. Rick reached up and grabbed hold of the brush, but it was obvious that he couldn't think of anything to say. 'What are you painting?' continued Cressida, pressing hard now that she had him at a disadvantage. 'Your new "puppet woman" with the torn jacket?'

'Of course not. If you must know I find some painting therapeutic, which is why I've decided to try my hand at a bit this evening. Why are you in such a temper about it? You should be pleased I'm not at death's door.'

'Should I?' asked Cressida quietly. 'I think you're wrong there because I get the feeling I've been dumped. You've handed me over to your boss, the worthy Guy, haven't you? You were never ill, you didn't even have the suspicion of a sniffle, you were simply obeying orders and handing me to him on a plate. Well, I don't like that. I thought we meant something to each other. It seems I was wrong.'

Rick's eyes were anguished. 'Come in,' he said suddenly. 'We'll talk about this properly. You are special to me, I promise, but I can't afford to get involved. My work has to come first and Guy felt you were distracting me from it.'

'Really? I remember him saying that I was your muse, your inspiration!'

'Cressida, please come inside. I really do need to talk to you,' he begged, but Cressida knew that she couldn't do as he asked. In the first place she wasn't really in love with him and it wouldn't be fair to pretend that she was, and in the second place she didn't dare risk losing her contact with Guy at this vital stage.

'I don't think so, Rick,' she said calmly. 'You see, whatever the truth was behind last night's invitation, it doesn't matter now. Guy and I had a marvellous time and I'm going to see him again tomorrow. I only called in to tell you that we were finished.'

Rick's face fell. 'I see,' he said quietly.

'No protests? No arguments?' enquired Cressida.

Rick shook his head. 'I don't expect you to understand,

it's all too complicated, but I can't argue and I can't try and compete. I only hope he doesn't hurt you too badly. I know you didn't love me, but please, Cressida, don't fall in love with him. He doesn't understand the meaning of the word, and I don't want to see you become another of his victims.'

'Take care of yourself,' said Cressida quietly, acutely aware of the fact that when she brought down Guy and Marcia, Rick would be charged as well, even if it was only as an accessory, and his punishment was likely to be harsh.

'I will,' promised Rick, but she knew he didn't understand and felt a pang of conscience at what she was doing to him.

Later, after she'd got home and talked to Detective Chief Inspector Williams, she felt less guilty. Defrauding innocent people and abusing their trust was despicable, as her chief had pointed out. All the same, when she went to bed that night she was still looking forward to the following evening with far more anticipation than she should have been. Her sexuality, which had once played a secondary role to her career, was now beginning to take precedence over everything else, and she couldn't wait for the touch of Guy's hands on her body again.

The next day she managed to get into the main office while Marcia was out to lunch, and there in the 'Renovations' file, which inexplicably was still under the letter 'E', she found the new entry that was so vital to her case. Lord Truscott's Correggio had been booked in and she was able to take a photograph of the entry with the tiny camera she'd been given at the start of her assignment. When she returned to her desk she was surprised that she didn't feel a greater sense of triumph.

Cressida wore a calf-length white summer dress with a bold pattern of blue and yellow shells and fishes on it for her second evening with Guy. The dress buttoned down the front, which she thought might well prove useful if things went as she hoped, and in the V of the neckline she wore a tiny pearl on a slender gold chain that had been a present from her godmother on her twenty-first birthday. She knew that her choice had been right when she saw Guy get out of his car wearing a single-breasted blazer over a blue and white shirt with a button-down collar, dark grey slacks and a maroon, white and navy striped tie. He looked casual but smart, and she saw a fleeting smile of approval on his face as she greeted him, but it was quickly gone and within a few minutes they were on their way out of London.

'Where are we going?' she asked with interest.

'It's a surprise,' he told her. 'I'm like that – full of surprises.'

'I can imagine,' said Cressida with a laugh.

Guy glanced sideways at her. 'Yes, I expect you can. After all, you're a girl who enjoys surprising people, aren't you? I mean, we take on this smart, demure creature and the next thing we know she's having a wild affair with Rick Marks, the most revered erotic artist of the day. I'm beginning to think you deceived us at your interview.'

A slight coldness touched the nape of Cressida's neck. 'Deceived you?'

'You pretended to be someone you weren't,' he said smoothly.

'No, you *assumed* I was someone I wasn't. There's quite a difference,' said Cressida quickly.

'Is there? Not that much of a difference, not in the "I say what I mean is the same as I mean what I say" class, is it? In order for us to make an incorrect assessment you have surely had to mislead us?'

'Not at all. Perhaps you're just not very good at assessing people. Try using a psychologist when you employ people; some of them are trained to help firms do just that. I think that's pretty amazing.'

'So do I!' Guy laughed. 'I prefer to use my own amateur brand of psychology and if I do make mistakes, let's hope they're all as rewarding as you've turned out to be.'

'*If* I was a mistake I was Marcia's, not yours,' pointed out Cressida, finding the verbal sparring a considerable turn-on.

'And Sue's,' said Guy.

'Sue's?'

He laughed. 'Yes, Sue! Your predecessor and long-time best friend. Don't tell me you've forgotten her already. How is she? What's she doing now?'

Cressida's mind went blank. She was totally unprepared for the question and since telling the truth – 'As a matter of fact she's back on the beat as a WPC' – was out of the question she floundered around trying to think of something acceptable.

Unseen by her Guy smiled to himself. 'I take it you're no longer such good friends as you were a few weeks ago?'

'The trouble is,' said Cressida, his remark giving her inspiration, 'Sue's a bit jealous of me these days. She liked working at the gallery and seems to resent the fact that I've taken her place.'

'Why did she leave us then?' asked Guy idly.

Cressida went cold. She couldn't remember what reason Sue had given for handing in her notice, and she was beginning to feel like a mouse being tormented by a particularly sadistic cat. 'Because she fancied you and wasn't getting anywhere,' she blurted out, deciding that a half-truth was the safest thing.

'Yes, I rather thought she did,' murmured Guy. 'Does she know anything about you and Rick?'

'Yes, and that's when we lost contact. She must have fancied him too and she couldn't understand why I'd succeeded when she hadn't. She's used to getting any man she wants,' she added truthfully. 'I think most girls who look like her do.'

211

'She was just another blonde airhead,' said Guy dismissively. 'What you saw was undoubtedly what you got. I prefer more interesting packages. The wrapping may not be quite as eye-catching, but the contents generally prove to be more exciting.'

'I don't think I like being told my wrapping isn't as attractive as Sue's!' laughed Cressida.

'I don't think it bothers you one iota,' retorted Guy. 'Do you know where we are?' he added. Cressida shook her head. 'We're about to go through Maidenhead – the lock's on your left. A little further on there's my favourite eating place. I hope you enjoy it as much as I always have.'

Cressida stared out of the car window at the people strolling along the side of the river dressed in their flimsy summer clothes and she tried to relax, but Guy's questions had unsettled her and when he turned left and they drove along a wood-lined road with virtually no one else on it she felt her unease increase. Without any address to give her chief she knew that there was no chance of anyone tailing her, and it was beginning to look as though tonight was the first time she might need help.

Guy swung the car off the road and along a wide track that led them deep into the woods. 'Nearly there,' he said cheerfully.

'You mean there's a restaurant in the middle of the woods?' asked Cressida.

'Not exactly; I told a small fib,' murmured Guy, and Cressida felt a touch of fear. The woods seemed totally deserted and when the car drew to a halt they were surrounded by nothing more than tall trees and thick shrubs with the occasional sound of birdsong for company.

'Get out,' said Guy softly.

Cressida didn't argue. She opened the passenger door and stood by the car, her eyes scanning the scenery for any possible escape route.

'You look worried,' continued Guy, walking to the back of the car and opening the boot. 'You've also gone silent, which isn't like you. What's the matter?'

'I'm a little confused. I thought we were coming out to dinner,' she replied, relieved that her voice didn't sound as nervous as she was feeling.

'So we are. Here, help me get the picnic basket out, will you? I thought that given your fantasy for making passionate love in the fresh air, this was a good place to spend the evening. Or have you lost interest in that particular dream?'

'No,' said Cressida, her legs going weak with relief. 'It's still something that excites me.'

'Good. I'm sure Rick did his best to make all your dreams come true, but hopefully I can make it even more memorable for you,' said Guy, spreading a rug on the ground and taking a bottle of wine out of the hamper. 'Here, let's have a drink first, shall we? What should the toast be do you think?'

'To the success of the gallery?' suggested Cressida.

'Perhaps, but I think I'd like to make it more personal. Let's say, may all your wishes come true, Cressida, whatever they may be.'

Cressida looked at him, registered the way his eyes were searching her face, and knew that while he might not be certain exactly what she was up to he definitely knew that she was playing some kind of game and that she wasn't really what she was pretending to be. 'I've got a better idea,' she said quickly. 'Let's have a toast to our true selves.'

'True selves?' he asked with a frown.

'Yes, let's toast the people we really are rather than the people we pretend to be. I'm sure you know as well as I do that no one is quite what they appear.'

Guy's mouth lifted slightly at the corners. 'How astute! Very well then, to our true selves.'

They both sipped from the cut-glass wine goblets he'd

brought with him, carefully wrapped in damask napkins, and then as Cressida reached into the hamper for something to eat his hand closed round her wrist. 'I think we'll eat later,' he said softly. 'I can't wait any longer. I've been thinking about this all day and I'm afraid my self-control is beginning to fail me.'

Cressida stared at him and felt his fingers gently stroking the inside of her wrist in a caress that triggered a rush of desire in her. 'I think you're right,' she murmured.

'I know I'm right,' said Guy, and pushing the hamper to one side he started to unbutton her dress.

Chapter Eleven

Guy gave a sigh of contentment as he peeled off the dress and saw that beneath it Cressida was wearing only a white G-string. He pressed her down on the rug and for a moment she closed her eyes as he started to caress her upper arms and softly kiss the corners of her mouth. As soon as he saw her eyes close Guy pushed her arms up above her head and then, before she realised what was happening, he'd drawn a piece of cord out of the hamper and tied it round her wrists. Cressida's eyes flew open and she stared at him anxiously, suddenly wondering if it was all a trick and now that he had her hands fastened he intended to question her about her undercover work.

'Don't look so anxious,' murmured Guy. 'This is all part of the pleasure. Stand up now and move over here.' He guided her a few metres away from the rug, moving deeper into the woods, and then threw the end of the cord over an overhanging branch of a tree so that she was standing with her arms tightly extended upward. When he pulled on the cord to tie it she had to go on tiptoe which meant that her calf muscles were stretched. With only her G-string to cover her she felt horribly vulnerable to any passer-by, as well as to Guy himself, but despite this the blood was racing through her veins and her whole body surface tingled with a strange excitement.

'You look incredible,' murmured Guy, standing back to study her. 'Rick would adore you like this! Just one more touch and then we can really begin to live out your fantasy.'

'I didn't ask to be restrained,' said Cressida breathlessly.

Guy laughed. 'I know, but you love it, don't you? It makes you feel like the woman in the picture you admired so much; both mistress and slave at the same time.'

'Yes,' she muttered, and then jumped with alarm as he walked behind her and slipped a dark band of material over her eyes. 'Tell me to let you go if you don't like the game,' he whispered, his breath warm against her neck, but Cressida didn't want him to release her. Her body was clamouring for his touch and she knew that her sex lips were already swelling as she started to become aroused by the entire dangerously erotic set-up.

She heard Guy move away from her again and then she felt his fingers at her mouth. 'Eat this,' he told her quietly, and very slowly slipped an olive into her mouth so that she could savour the salty tang as she sucked and then crunched on it. When he brought her a second olive he teased her with it, pressing it against her lips before ordering her to put out her tongue so that he could place it on the tip as the liquid in which it had been bottled left a trail down her chin. As she ate it he licked at the briny juice, his tongue teasing her chin and the top of her bare breasts where a few drops had spilled.

Cressida's breathing was rapid and after she'd finished the second olive Guy allowed her to drink a little wine from one of the goblets, but when she tried to drain the goblet he moved to the back of her and tipped the rest of the chilled wine down her spine.

With a gasp of surprise Cressida began to squirm against her restraint and her hips twisted in an effort to find some kind of stimulation lower down her body. 'Not yet,' Guy told her, his voice kind but firm, and then he licked the back of her body with tiny flicking movements of his tongue as he drank the wine. By the time he'd finished Cressida couldn't stop herself from squirming with rising excitement and she kept making tiny noises of pleasure.

For a few minutes after that she was left alone, and to her horror she heard the sound of voices in the distance. 'Guy, someone's near us!' she called but he didn't answer her and when she heard a car door slam she grew frantic. She could imagine only too well how she must look, and the thought of a stranger witnessing her body, stretched tightly with arms extended upward and swollen breasts jutting out shamelessly, was too dreadful to contemplate. Then she wondered if the car door that had slammed had been Guy's, and if he'd left her there in the woods as a punishment because he knew what she really was and intended to humiliate her in retaliation.

To her surprise all these fears only served to increase her arousal. Her belly felt hot and swollen as she remained suspended from the tree branch with her senses screaming for stimulation. She would never have believed it possible to feel so aroused when she was utterly helpless in the hands of a man considered to be highly dangerous but it was true and it made her realise that before this she'd never known anything about her own sexuality.

'What's the matter?' asked Guy softly, and she gave a whimper of relief.

'I thought other people were here and that you'd left me,' she admitted, her voice catching in her throat.

Guy ran a finger idly over her left nipple which was swollen and erect. 'It doesn't seem to have affected you in any adverse way,' he remarked, then he tweaked the nipple hard and to Cressida's shocked embarrassment a shudder ran through her as her body rushed into a small orgasm. 'In fact, it's been positively beneficial,' he continued. Cressida kept silent.

'Is this what you fantasised about?' asked Guy, his right hand resting on her lower back in a gesture that seemed to Cressida to be one of almost tender support as her orgasm slowly died away. 'Is this how you imagined your open-air sex?'

'No,' whispered Cressida. 'It wasn't at all like this.'

'And when Rick tried to make your dream come true, was that like this?' persisted Guy. Cressida shook her head, longing for him to start touching her again because even the sensation of his hand against her naked back was arousing her.

Because of the way she'd been tied up every muscle and sinew in her body was taut, making the nerve endings more responsive to stimulation. When she felt a strange soft pricking sensation over her abdomen she gasped and jerked against the tension of the cord around her wrists, but almost immediately the sensation moved to the insides of her tensed arms, swirling around the crook of her elbow and then down her inner arm to the inside of her wrist. The movement was repeated again and again, and slowly the delicate tingles began to spread throughout other areas of her body and her whole pelvic region began to ache with frustration.

'Guess what I'm touching you with,' murmured Guy.

'A brush,' said Cressida immediately. 'A man's hairbrush.'

'Wrong,' he retorted, and then he was caressing her inner thighs with the same instrument, and now the feelings began to spread upward towards her vulva and she felt her lower body trembling with desire and the thrill of dangerous pleasure.

'Guess again,' he instructed her, but despite concentrating desperately on the feeling Cressida couldn't put a name to it. 'You're showing a regrettable lack of imagination!' he laughed, and then she felt him part her sex lips and run the bristles lightly over the exposed area so that the tip of her clitoris was briefly touched and her body tried to jackknife in on itself with the shock of the sharp, searing streak of pleasure. 'One more guess,' murmured Guy as Cressida whimpered with frustration.

'I don't know!' she shouted.

'Here it comes again. Try harder,' he suggested, and she tensed in anticipation of the indescribable thrill that once more shot through her as her clitoris received a painfully tender caress that caused all the mass of nerve endings there to send out spirals of hot liquid heat which made her entire pubic area tense and throb.

'It's an old-fashioned shaving brush,' explained Guy when her ragged breathing eased a little. 'I thought you'd enjoy that. Now I think I'll try something rather different.'

Tight, aching and swollen with need, Cressida was forced to remain a prisoner, tied to the tree while he once more went away. She wished that she could have him in her power like this for just a brief moment in order to make him suffer in the same delicious manner, but she knew that Guy wasn't the kind of man who'd be willing to do that. Rick was, but she no longer wanted Rick; it was this man she wanted. This man, and everything he could teach her about her body.

She heard him behind her and when he kissed the nape of her neck she sighed in relaxed pleasure. 'That's nice,' he murmured. 'You really sound as though you're enjoying yourself.'

'I am,' she admitted. 'But I'd like to have another orgasm now.'

'Soon,' he promised her. Now he pulled her G-string down her legs and cupped her tightly rounded buttocks, and then he was parting the cheeks of her bottom and she felt him spreading a cold jelly-like substance around the

219

rim of her anus. She pushed her belly forward in an attempt to get away from him, but he simply put an arm round her bare waist and pulled her back into position.

'You'll love this,' he assured her. 'Trust me.' Then he carefully parted the fair-skinned globes and inserted a short but thick anal plug, well covered in lubricating jelly. Cressida stiffened against this unexpected invasion. 'Relax,' he whispered, his tongue sliding down the side of her neck until she shivered in response. 'I'm going to move it very slowly in and out and as I move it in I want you to tighten your muscles around it, then relax them as I withdraw it. You should enjoy the sensation, but you must relax.'

Cressida knew that she had to trust him and obeyed his instructions to the letter. As the device was carefully eased in and out of her back passage she used her muscles as he'd described and within a few seconds realised that he was right. Bitter-sweet piercing sensations lanced through her from front to back, not only giving pleasure but also increasing her need for stimulation of her clitoris. Soon she was panting heavily, crying out for him to touch her between her thighs, and still she was blindfolded and naked in the middle of a public place.

'You're utterly shameless,' said Guy, leaving the anal plug in and walking round to the front of her, his hands running down the sides of her body as it jerked and twitched with sexual tension. 'What are you?'

'Shameless,' she admitted proudly, no longer caring in the least but revelling in the delicious feelings that were almost consuming her.

'Tell me what you want now then,' he commanded.

'I want to come.' Cressida begged him, thrusting her hips forward and trying to part her legs as much as her awkward stance would permit.

'I want to possess you,' said Guy, his voice deep and quiet. 'I want to take you now, standing like that, tethered to the tree, helpless and desperate. Does that make me the master, or the slave?' As he spoke he continued to caress her, running his hands all over her naked body, which was hot and covered with a fine sheen of perspiration.

'I don't know,' admitted Cressida. 'Please Guy, let's talk about that afterwards. I want you inside me, now.'

'You seem hot,' he said thoughtfully, and suddenly a fine spray of water covered her swollen body as he directed an atomiser spray of scented water over her. He watched her taut belly draw inward and her nipples become even more engorged and finally he couldn't stand it any longer himself and to Cressida's delight he was suddenly standing in front of her. He pushed her naked back against the trunk of the tree as his penis slid slowly inside her. Then he moved with great care, gliding in and out of her aching vagina in steady movements, making sure that each time he drove fully into her, her clitoris was stimulated by contact with his pubic bone. At the same time his hands massaged her breasts, and then he pushed them both upward so that he could fasten his mouth around each of the nipples in turn, sucking hard on the aching little buds until she could have cried with ecstasy.

Cressida wanted the feelings to go on and on. Every part of her was on fire, but the pleasure was all centred in one place, behind the hard, aching nub of her clitoris. She'd never had a man move so slowly and steadily, and the pressure built deep within her pelvis until she tightened all her internal muscles as she tried to precipitate the elusive final orgasm.

When she did this she felt the anal plug touching the walls of her rectum and this drove her into a frenzy of desire as even more stimulation was added to her body. Her muscles tightened around Guy so that now he too lost control of himself, and his movements became as

221

frenzied as hers as he drove on towards the moment when he could at last allow himself sexual release.

Just before he came he removed a hand from one of Cressida's breasts and, sliding it down her between their bodies, he pressed his fingers into the soft flesh just above her pubic bone. She felt the heavy ache spread downward through her vulva and when it met the jagged sparks of pleasure darting from her clitoris her orgasm was finally triggered and all her muscles seemed to go into a mad spasm as even her fingers, held forcibly high above her head, twitched in an involuntary response to the waves of sexual satisfaction washing over her.

Hearing Cressida's groans of satisfaction Guy allowed himself to come as well, and for the first time he found that when his climax was over and his almost painful sexual tension was at last dissipated he didn't feel the need to withdraw immediately. Instead he stayed where he was, his penis still inside Cressida as his hands moved gently over her face so that he could remove her blindfold.

For a few seconds they stared into each other's eyes, but surprisingly Cressida was the first to break the contact between them, and then Guy understood how his other women must have felt when he withdrew both mentally and physically as soon as the moment of pleasure was over.

'Quite a good fantasy, I think,' he said shortly as he unfastened her wrists and let her down. 'After that the picnic may seem rather tame!'

Cressida found that she had very little appetite for the delicious food that was presented to her a few minutes later. Instead she lay on her side, propped up on one elbow, sipping wine and watching Guy as he ate. Every now and again he would reach out to stroke her ankle, or run a hand up her lightly tanned leg, his fingers dancing a teasing path beneath her long dress.

'You have lovely bones,' he remarked idly, nibbling on

a tiny salmon mousse quiche. 'They're so delicate and feminine.'

'There's something I have to ask you,' said Cressida, wishing that his fingers didn't have such a powerful effect on her because once again her nipples were hardening and she started to remember the wonderful moment when she felt a climax start to build within her.

'What's that?'

'When I was tied to the tree just now, did someone come by?' she enquired anxiously.

'Does it matter?' asked Guy.

'Yes, it does. The last thing I can afford is to have people seeing me naked and aroused in a public place,' she retorted hotly.

Guy eyed her thoughtfully. 'The last thing you can afford. What do you mean by that? Do you have famous parents or something? Would your nakedness make the front page of the tabloids?'

Cressida realised that once again she'd made a mistake. That was the trouble with good sex, it made her over-relaxed and careless. 'Of course not, but my mother's not well and I wouldn't want to upset her,' she said lamely.

Guy didn't look as though he found this very convincing but he didn't query it. 'As a matter of fact a courting couple did pull up near my car. They both got out, but then I think they must have realised they were interrupting something rather special and they drove off again.'

'I knew I heard a car door slam,' said Cressida.

'It didn't seem to put you off,' remarked Guy with a brief smile. 'Can't I tempt you with anything from the hamper? I'd hate you to fade away; your curves are exactly to my liking at the moment.'

'I don't think gaining your approval is my prime objective in life,' commented Cressida with a laugh. 'However, as I like my shape too I'd better try and eat something. Some of the pâté would be nice.'

Guy spread pâté on a cracker and handed it to her.

'Here you are then. You know, I'm quite surprised to hear that gaining my approval isn't your prime objective. I rather thought it was.'

Cressida forced herself to keep calm and nibbled at the biscuit. 'Why do you say that?'

'Because Marcia told me, and she's very rarely wrong when it comes to that kind of thing. Her feminine intuition is very strong.'

'Maybe she guards you so jealously that she sees danger where there isn't any,' suggested Cressida.

'In this case it seems she was right. If she'd been wrong we wouldn't be here tonight.'

'That doesn't mean I went out of my way to gain your approval. In fact, I'd have thought that would have had the opposite effect on a man like you.'

'Then perhaps you were simply being extra clever and making yourself aloof to catch my interest.'

'You know, you're incredibly conceited,' said Cressida with a smile. 'Why should you be so special?'

'I've no idea,' said Guy, his hand moving in soft circles around the inside of her left knee. 'I hoped you might be able to tell me.'

'I didn't think you were special at first. I never even wanted to go out with you when Rick was ill. I admit I think you're special now, but that's quite different from gearing my entire lifestyle to attract you. To be honest, Guy, I've never done that in my life and I don't think I ever will. Until our two dates, sex has never been that important to me.'

'Better not let Rick hear you say that,' said Guy.

Cressida felt uncomfortable. 'Rick was fun,' she admitted. 'He showed me there was more to life than – '

'Tom?' suggested Guy helpfully.

Luckily Cressida was now on her guard. 'Tom?' she queried with a frown.

'Yes, Detective Sergeant Tom Penfold, remember him?'

She paused for a moment. 'Oh yes! The customer from

the gallery who took me out to dinner. Well, if you put it like that I suppose Rick did show me that there was far more to life than men like Tom.'

Guy's eyes, which had been fixed on her face, returned to her figure. 'Undo your buttons,' he murmured. 'I want to stroke your breasts while we talk.'

Although Cressida's body would like nothing better she knew that in order to keep her mind sharp she didn't dare let him. 'Not yet,' she protested. 'I need more time to recover.'

'Nonsense,' said Guy. 'I'm not suggesting another sex session, just some physical intimacy. What's the matter? Are you afraid you'll lose control again?'

He was too near the truth for comfort but she let him move closer to her and helped him unfasten her buttons so that he could softly massage her breasts, which immediately began to swell in his hands, the light blue veins becoming more obvious as she started to become aroused.

'Tell me about yourself, Cressida,' he whispered. 'I want to know about your childhood, your school days, and when you first began to get interested in art.'

'All right,' agreed Cressida, who had a well-prepared background story. 'But only if you tell me your life history when I've finished.'

'I might,' he said evasively, and as his fingers teased the soft undersides of her breasts she lay with her head in his lap and slowly told him her story, a story that had been worked out in every detail by her superior officers.

When she'd finished she could hardly speak because her chest felt constricted by her rising need for Guy to make love to her again. As her voice trailed away he bent his head and nipped hard at one of her engorged nipples. She gave a tiny squeal of mingled shock and excitement. 'What a good memory you have,' he said idly. 'I couldn't recall every detail of my life so accurately, but plainly you have a very good memory for detail.'

225

'And for pleasure,' she said softly, reaching up for him.

He looked down on her but he didn't smile. 'Yes, and for pleasure,' he repeated thoughtfully. By now Cressida was lying sprawled on her back with most of her top buttons unfastened. Guy quickly unfastened the rest of them but left the dress on her, like a long loose jacket. 'This is going to be very special,' he promised her, and she felt a fluttering in her solar plexus as her body anticipated what he might mean.

Her eyes were closed and she was taken by surprise when his hands began to turn her on to her stomach, where she realised that her hips, belly and pubic area were now resting on a large, soft pillow. 'You didn't just bring food with you!' she joked.

'No,' said Guy seriously. 'I was prepared for everything. Make sure you press your body down against the pillow; it will give you the stimulation you need at the beginning, while I'm doing other things.'

Cressida didn't have any time to wonder what the other things were because as she obeyed and pressed her aching flesh down into the soft pillow, Guy flipped her dress up over her back and then gently removed the anal plug which he'd left in after untying her from the tree. She remembered to let her muscles go slack and was rewarded with a kiss at the base of her spine that made her press herself down even harder against the pillow, grinding her hips in order to stimulate as much of her vulva as possible.

'The plug should have helped to stretch you,' murmured Guy to himself, and suddenly Cressida began to tense. 'Keep relaxed,' he reminded her. Then she felt one of his fingers, lubricated with a cold jelly, moving inside her rectum, circling around and touching every surface in his quest for maximum arousal.

Tiny streams of hot liquid seemed to run through her and when she maintained the pressure of the pillow against her belly it ached with need. She felt full and engorged, as though her body wasn't large enough to encompass all the sensations Guy was engendering.

Her breasts ached too, and without thinking she put her hands on them, squeezing the erect nipples before circling the surrounding tissue with her fingers. She heard Guy give a quiet laugh, and then suddenly he lifted her lower body off the pillow and while one hand parted her buttocks the other remained firmly beneath her, his hand sliding downward until his fingers located her clitoris.

He played with it for several minutes, massaging it through its protective hood until she felt hot and swollen with desire, then easing the hood back and alternatively stroking and flicking the side of its stem.

Cressida was uttering animal-like gutteral sounds as the intensity of the stimulation increased, so that when Guy finally started to ease his erection inside her rectum she didn't hesitate for a moment but instead tightened her internal muscles as he'd taught her earlier.

The force of her muscular contraction almost made Guy ejaculate immediately and he quickly moved his hand from her clitoris and massaged her lower belly instead so that for a second or two she lost her rhythm and allowed him time to regain control. He'd never known a woman revel in the combination of sensations so quickly and her clear delight and ecstatic reactions were an aphrodisiac to him.

Very slowly and carefully he began to move himself in and out of her, but he was careful never to overstretch her or make any sudden movements that might cause discomfort. As a result, the amazing hot, dark excitement spread through Cressida and when Guy lifted her buttocks a little higher she lowered her forearms so that now her aching breasts were on the pillow.

When Guy's fingers returned to her clitoris, streaks of white light flashed behind her closed eyelids as the forbidden pleasure continued to consume her and she felt the first tiny trembling sensations that heralded the contractions of her orgasm. 'I'm coming!' she shouted, and before the words were out of her mouth Guy felt her body rippling and tensing around him so that they came together in a frenzied moment of bliss that flooded through Cressida's veins with such force she felt a moment's fear before the pleasure finally peaked and then slowly began to ebb.

Guy carefully withdrew and when he turned her on to her back and saw the glazed look of satisfaction on her face he couldn't resist parting her legs. Then, with her thighs resting on either side of his waist, he lowered his head and tongued at the incredibly sensitive tissue surrounding her bud of pleasure.

For Cressida, just coming down from the most intense climax of her life, this light moist caress was almost too much to bear, but her body responded instantly and once more her muscles spasmed in a short, painful orgasm that lifted her just as the previous one was dying away and she heard herself groan in a mixture of delight and despair. 'No more,' she pleaded as her body muscles began to soften and relax. Reluctantly Guy released her.

'You're incredible,' he murmured, kissing her stomach and the soft sensitive skin of her hip bones. 'I just want to make love to you for ever.' At that moment, Cressida couldn't think of anything she'd like better either.

Later, when they were packing away the picnic things, she fell quiet. It had been an unforgettable evening and Guy's inventive lovemaking had been tempered with such sensitivity and tenderness that she felt consumed by guilt over what she was doing to him. She found it difficult to meet his eyes knowing that as soon as possible she would be handing him over to the fraud squad, and he'd learn that she too had been nothing but a fraud, except that she wasn't faking any longer. She was falling in love with him, and it was like a nightmare come true.

'I don't want you to come into work tomorrow,' he said

when they finally arrived back at her house in the early hours of the morning.

'Why not?' asked Cressida.

'Because I want you to rest. We're going out again tomorrow night, to a very special party, and I think you need some rest after this evening!'

'What kind of a party?' enquired Cressida, trying to work out what this all meant.

'We're going to visit Sir Peter Thornton and his wife Rose. I'm sure you remember them – they were at Marcia's dinner party.'

'Leonora's parents,' said Cressida.

'Well, he's her father but Rose is just another step-mother. You will come, won't you? It's important to me that we're there together.'

'Why not Marcia?' demanded Cressida.

Guy put an arm round the back of her seat. 'Do you want me to take Marcia?' he asked.

In a way she did, because she knew that one of Sir Peter's pictures had been taken away by Guy for cleaning and that at this meeting he might well return it, which meant that the swop would have been accomplished and she would be forced to reveal the truth to Detective Chief Inspector Williams, but it was her job and no matter what her personal feelings were she had to go through with it now. 'Of course not,' she said quietly.

'That's a relief! I'll collect you at eight. Don't worry about what to wear. I'll bring something with me and you can change before we go. You see, it's a rather special evening.'

'Fine,' said Cressida, and then to her surprise Guy leant over and kissed her on the mouth, his lips suddenly fierce against hers as though he was trying desperately to make her his, although she knew that he was not a man who would ever want to possess any woman totally.

Her call to her chief that night was brief, and while she made it clear that she and Guy were now lovers she kept all the details to herself. When he heard about the following night's visit to his friend, Detective Chief Inspector Williams could hardly restrain his delight. 'I think we've nearly got him now!' he crowed down the phone. 'You're doing brilliantly, WPC Farleigh. I just hope it isn't too much of a trial for you.' She heard him laugh as he hung up.

It took her several hours to get to sleep as her sense of duty battled with her new feelings for Guy, feelings that she felt sure were reciprocated. Even though he might not be capable of the kind of commitment she would have liked, she sensed that he was attracted to her in several ways, enjoying her company as well as her body.

At six the following morning, after only an hour's sleep, her phone went and she stumbled out of bed convinced for some strange reason that it was Marcia calling to make a scene. It wasn't; it was Detective Chief Inspector Williams.

'I had to call you,' he said shortly, his voice curt to the point of rudeness. 'It seems that the Matisse we gave to the gallery for cleaning has been returned and examined by our experts. It's the original.'

'The original!' Cressida's heart gave a thump and she failed to keep the relief out of her voice.

'It's hardly something to rejoice about,' her chief pointed out. 'If it had been a fake we would have known for certain that we were right and any information you got would simply have been the necessary corroboration. Now your findings are vital. You have to tie in everyone who works on this; Marcia, Guy Cronje and that artist fellow you went out with before Guy.'

'Rick Marks,' said Cressida slowly.

Her boss laughed. 'That's right, the excellent climber of gates, Rick Marks. I saw you both that night. You were showing commendable devotion to duty. I was proud of you! Remember, you probably haven't much time. I imagine that by now Cronje is having enquiries made about you and it won't be difficult for a man like him to get to the truth within a few days. You must nail him as soon as possible. If what you told me about Sir Peter's true then it might well be that you can do it tonight.'

'Yes, I think it might,' said Cressida slowly, remembering Sir Peter's Holbein that had been entered in the renovations book.

'Excellent! Good luck then. We'll be near you tonight, but not too close. He's clever and we don't want to scare him off.'

Once she'd been woken Cressida found it impossible to get back to sleep. Instead she drank endless cups of coffee as her mind went over and over the previous evening. The truth was that she didn't want to come to the end of the assignment and walk away knowing that she'd helped put Guy, Rick or even Marcia in prison. They'd all played such an important part in changing her, in making her aware that there was more to life than police work and basic sex. She felt more liberated and confident in her sexuality since working at the gallery. It seemed a poor way to reward them, and for the first time she was ashamed of what she was doing.

'It isn't as though the owners lose out,' she said to herself as she popped some bread in the toaster. 'The insurance companies pay in the end.' But she knew really that this wasn't the point. Fraud was a serious crime, and so was abuse of trust, which Guy was doing to his friends. If she trapped him by the same method then perhaps there was a strange kind of justice in it, but it still didn't make her feel good.

After she'd rung in and told Marcia she had a migraine and wouldn't be going to the gallery that day, she went back to bed and managed a few hours' sleep. She knew that it was important she didn't look tired tonight, when Guy had made such a point of her staying at home to rest.

During the afternoon, as she bathed and did her hair and nails, she had time to wonder if he'd wanted her absent for other reasons. In order to collect the false painting to give Sir Peter perhaps, or to give himself and Marcia time to look into Cressida's background uninterrupted. Anything was possible, and she knew that whatever the truth of it Guy wouldn't give anything away when he collected her. He was far too professional for that, and she would have to rely on her instinct and training to see her through the night.

He arrived on time, carrying a soft holdall in his hand, and after he'd kissed her passionately he put the holdall down and unzipped it. 'I expect you'd like to see what you're going to wear,' he said with a smile. Cressida nodded. 'Go ahead, take it out then,' he instructed her.

Cressida reached inside, glowing with excitement. She'd already decided that it would probably be something long worn with a mask, as a masked ball theme seemed the type of party Sir Peter Thornton and his wife Rose would enjoy.

However, inside the holdall were three items of clothing, and none of them were anything like Cressida had imagined. Firstly she drew out a black satin half-cup bra, underwired, with shoestring straps and a black and white embroidered lace centrepiece and side panels. This was followed by a pair of matching embroidered transparent briefs with a black satin panel that would at least preserve her modesty a little, and finally there was a short, long-sleeved black kimono.

Cressida spread the three garments out on the sofa and shook her head in disbelief. 'I can't go out to dinner wearing these!' she exclaimed.

Guy looked surprised. 'Why not?'

'Because I'll look ridiculous! What will the other guests be wearing? I mean, even a pyjama party doesn't produce this kind of outfit. Well, not the ones I've been to.'

'We're the only guests,' said Guy quietly.

Cressida stared at him. 'What do you mean?'

'I mean precisely what I say. You and I are invited to

dine with Sir Peter Thornton and his wife, and this is the way Sir Peter wants you to dress. Marcia's done it before now, although that was for Lord Summers and his wife when he was alive. I'm hoping you'll prove to be a better companion than she was then. She failed to get into the spirit of the dinner and disappointed poor Michael, which meant that Alice didn't have such a good time as she'd hoped either.'

'I've no idea what you're talking about,' said Cressida, but she was beginning to feel very nervous indeed, especially when she realised that she had to go tonight, no matter how outrageous the demands Guy was placing on her might be.

'We're not just guests,' explained Guy, 'we're also the after-dinner entertainment. You see, men like Sir Peter, older men with much younger wives, frequently have problems satisfying them physically and quite often the sight of another couple making love proves to be the turn-on they need to get started. That's how it was with Lord Summers, and that's the way it is with Sir Peter as well. Rose often feels very neglected, and I'd like her to enjoy herself tonight.'

'You mean, we're going to make love in front of them?' asked Cressida, stunned by his words.

Guy smiled at her. 'Yes, and if you look as fantastic as you looked last night then Sir Peter's a very lucky man.'

'I can't,' said Cressida flatly.

Guy stroked the side of her neck and nuzzled her ear. 'Of course you can. You're a born exhibitionist. You loved it when you thought there were other people in the woods yesterday; it increased your excitement. You said so yourself and I could tell by your responses. Well, this will be even better.'

'I don't want him to touch me,' said Cressida, horrified at the prospect of ending up like Alice in Marcia's basement.

'Of course not. The whole point of this is that he finds

he can't keep his hands off Rose. It would be rather a waste if he used up his energy on you. Come along, Cressida, don't go all conventional on me at this late hour. I thought I knew you, but it seems I may have made a mistake.'

He started to put the clothes back in the bag and Cressida immediately snatched them away from him. 'No, you didn't make a mistake,' she assured him. 'I was taken by surprise, that's all.' It was true, she had been taken by surprise, but now she was beginning to warm to the idea. It was lucky that she was, because Detective Chief Inspector Williams would certainly be very displeased if she failed to attend the meeting between Guy Cronje and his personal friend Sir Peter Thornton, especially if at that meeting a fake picture was handed over to the unsuspecting older man.

Guy gave a sigh of relief. 'That's wonderful,' he whispered. 'Now put it all on, I'll wrap a cloak that I've got in the car round you and we can be on our way. You won't regret this, Cressida. It will be the most exciting evening of your life.'

'I hope you don't regret it,' said Cressida softly.

Guy raised his eyebrows. 'Why should I?'

She swallowed hard, knowing that she simply couldn't warn him. 'I might disappoint you when it comes to the action,' she explained.

He shook his head. 'I don't think so, Cressida. In fact, I find it hard to believe you'd ever do anything that would disappoint me.'

She wished he'd never said those words because they echoed through her head for the entire drive and when she climbed out of his car and he took her hand, giving it an encouraging squeeze before they entered their hosts' house, she wanted to cry for all that they were both going to lose in the very near future.

Chapter Twelve

Neither Sir Peter Thornton nor his wife showed any surprise at the clothes that Cressida was wearing beneath her cloak, which were in stark contrast to Guy's charcoal striped, three-piece suit and burnt orange open-necked shirt, and after a pre-dinner sherry and some polite smalltalk the four of them moved into a dining room which Cressida thought had probably originally been intended as a study.

It was beautifully decorated, with pale blue walls and matching blinds, hangings and tablecloth in a blue and white replica of the Frey print, 'Gonesse'. The ladderback chairs had heavily padded seats, a fact which pleased Cressida as she had nothing to cushion her legs since all her clothing ended just below her hips.

'I think I'd rather like to work at the gallery,' remarked Rose as they ate their first course of tiny strips of smoked salmon and salad. 'Everything's so well hung there!' She laughed and reached over to stroke Guy's thigh.

Cressida realised then that Rose and Guy must at some stage have had an affair, but Guy carefully removed her hand and started talking to Sir Peter about stocks and shares. Rose, looking rather put out by his rejection, fell silent.

It seemed an awkward meal to Cressida, and not in the least erotic, but when the dessert arrived that all changed. It was a delicious mixture of crumbled sticky meringue, creamy vanilla ice cream and real apricots. As soon as they'd been served Guy picked up his spoon, dipped it into Cressida's bowl and started to spoonfeed her. When a few crumbs of meringue escaped from her mouth he leant towards her and slowly licked them away before softly kissing the corners of her mouth.

Cressida saw that Sir Peter was watching them closely, his own dessert untouched as he stared with rapt attention at his guest. Rose however ignored them and ate in a distinctly unerotic sullen silence.

When all of Cressida's dessert had gone, Guy ate his own, but as he ate he kept reaching across and gently caressing the exposed tops of her breasts through the open front of her kimono. Once or twice he allowed a finger to slip lower and tease one of her nipples, which soon started to swell so that they were clearly visible through the satin bra.

'I think we'll take coffee in another room,' said Sir Peter in slightly strangled tones. 'Rose, my dear, bring it upstairs if you please.'

He led his guests into the same bedroom where, unknown to him, Guy and Rose had made love to Leonora and her boyfriend a few weeks earlier. There he settled himself back on the bed, sitting propped upright against a mound of pillows. 'As soon as Rose gets here you can continue,' he said to Guy, giving Cressida a rather shy smile of appreciation.

Cressida was surprised to find that she didn't feel shy. She felt surprisingly comfortable with what was happening, and she thought this was partly due to the fact that Rose was obviously not enjoying it as much as her husband. She was jealous, and she couldn't hide it. The moment Rose joined them she too went and sat at the head of the huge bed she shared with her husband, and her short shift dress rose up to enable him to easily caress her thighs if he wished.

'Cressida, come and lie down across the foot of the bed,' said Guy, taking her by the hand and leading her towards the other couple. Then he slipped off her kimono and spread her across the width of the bed with a pillow beneath her head and another one beneath the middle of her back so that her belly was lifted higher.

'Where shall I begin?' he asked her quietly. Cressida's breasts were already aching from the caresses they'd received during dinner and she touched them with her right hand. 'Say it,' he urged her. 'Sir Peter likes to hear women begging for what they want.'

'I want you to start by massaging my breasts,' said Cressida, and higher up the bed Sir Peter's breath caught in his throat and he reached over to his wife who parted her legs slightly so that he could stroke the soft skin of her inner thighs as the pair of them watched their guests. Rose was beginning to enjoy herself because Cressida was good, and when Sir Peter was sufficiently aroused he was an expert lover.

Guy poured massage oil into his hands and then carefully removed Cressida's bra before starting to massage the swelling globes until her nipples turned dark red and stood proudly erect. Then he tongued at each of them in turn, alternating between rolling his tongue around the circumference of each nipple and drawing them into his mouth with gradually increasing pressure until finally he nipped sharply at each of them in turn and Cressida's belly arched off the pillow in a jerk of excitement.

Now Guy moved down to the exposed abdomen, and he massaged in the oil so slowly and carefully that a heavy sweet ache suffused every inch of her stomach and she felt slithers of tight excitement moving deep within her. Her breathing became more audible and Sir Peter's hand crept higher up his wife's leg until he was stroking her vulva through the silk fabric of her panties. Rose squirmed with eager pleasure, but she kept her eyes on Guy and the slender young woman beneath him. She'd never imagined him capable of such tenderness.

For Cressida the rising desire was like a forest fire, starting with a tiny spark but quickly spreading so that within a few minutes it was threatening to consume her. However, Guy slowed the pace, anxious that the display shouldn't be over too soon. This wasn't just for Sir Peter's benefit, he was enjoying himself as well – enjoying Cressida's responses and her frantic need for the pinnacle of ecstasy that only he could help her attain.

Some of the massage oil trickled into the creases at the tops of her thighs which made Cressida give a muffled cry of pleasure, but to her disappointment Guy didn't continue there. Instead he moved and began to massage her feet, creeping with cruel deliberation up her legs until she felt that she'd scream at him if he didn't soon reach her vulva and clitoris which were aching with a painfully tight throbbing sensation.

Finally Guy spread her legs a little wider and began to massage her pubic area, then when he knew she was desperately aroused he slid two fingers inside her and began to play with her cervix, slowly moving it around. With a soft cry Cressida shuddered and found a moment's relief in her first orgasm.

'She came!' exclaimed Rose. 'That's much quicker than Marcia's ever managed her first orgasm.'

Cressida opened her eyes and looked at Guy. 'I didn't know you and Marcia had done this here,' she murmured.

'It wasn't the same,' said Guy quietly. 'She never really lost herself in the sensuality of the moment. You're my perfect partner. I'm going to start all over again now, but I'll finish differently.'

His words heightened her anticipation, as he'd known they would, and by the time he'd worked his way down her breasts, over her belly and then up her legs again she was in such a state of high sexual tension that she was trembling all over. Rose, unable to resist the temptation, slid down the bed and softly ran a hand across Cressida's upthrust stomach, watching the gentle ripple of the muscles as the other woman's body reacted instantaneously.

'She's ready to come again,' she whispered to Guy, who nodded and then slowly inserted a pulsating vibrator inside her, easing it in a little at a time so that Cressida's whole body twisted and turned with despairing need.

Guy carefully watched for the tell-tale clenching of Cressida's fingers and then he eased back the hood of her clitoris and drew circles round the pulsating flesh at the same time as the vibrator flooded her with glorious sensations. Almost immediately Cressida felt the tension tighten to an almost unendurable level and then her taut muscles spasmed and she was flooded by the liquid warmth of her second climax.

Sir Peter was now so aroused that Rose had freed his erection and was caressing the rim of the glans, trying not to obscure his view of the other couple while at the same time heightening his pleasure. His fingers were inside the leg of her panties and just after Cressida's second climax Rose had her first orgasm. She knew from the way her husband was responding to the show that it would be the first of many.

By now Cressida was so lost in the sexual sensations that all she wanted was another orgasm, but this time with Guy inside her. He knew instinctively what she needed, but made her tell him. 'Say it,' he urged her. 'Tell us what you want.'

'I want another orgasm, but I need to feel you in me; to tighten myself around you so that we come together,' she pleaded, arousing Sir Peter so much that he nearly came there and then.

'That sounds a very good idea,' murmured Guy, and stripping off his clothes he lay across the foot of the bed and then pulled her on top of him, her legs on either side of his body, her hands on his lower chest and her back resting against the tops of his thighs as she lowered herself on to his straining penis. 'Work for it, Cressida,' he urged her. 'Let them see you milking me. Prove that it's the man who's the puppet, not the woman.'

His words reminded her of Rick's drawing in the gallery, the one that had first awoken her dormant sexuality, and suddenly she took control, easing herself up and down on him, caressing his nipples with her sharp nails and clenching and unclenching her internal muscles so that time and again Guy was on the point of coming but every time she felt his body start to spasm she kept totally still and refused him all stimulation.

Soon he was as frantic as he'd been used to making her, and when he cried out, begging for release, she felt a surge of triumph. As Sir Peter threw himself on the panting Rose, Cressida increased the tempo of her rhythm, and when Guy's body tensed she continued the stimulation until he was finally allowed to come. He shouted out incoherently in gratified triumph and relief.

All four of them were collapsed on the bed, their breathing still uneven from their exertions, when the front door bell rang. Rose lifted her flushed face from the pillows and stared at her husband. 'Who on earth can that be at this hour of the night?'

'I've no idea,' he retorted. 'Unfortunately we gave Marie the night off so one of us had better go and see.'

'I'll go,' said Rose. 'Don't move, any of you,' she added with a smile. 'I'll be back very soon!' Pulling a robe round her she hurried down the stairs.

Cressida was only vaguely aware of what was going on because Guy was holding her close, telling her how wonderful she'd been and how there was even better to come. For a brief time her real purpose in being with him was forgotten and she revelled in the sheer sensuality of it all. The respite didn't last very long.

'I think you'd better come downstairs,' said Rose suddenly from the bedroom doorway. 'Marcia and Rick are here and they say they have something urgent that they need to talk to us about.'

'I'll stay here,' murmured Cressida. 'It's bound to be business and you don't need me.'

'I'm afraid we do,' said Rose, her voice cold. 'Marcia says that there's something we should all know about you.'

All the warmth and pleasure of the evening vanished and Cressida felt as though someone had thrown a bucket of cold water over her. Shivering slightly she got off the bed and began to pull on her skimpy items of clothing, wishing that she had some other clothes with her that left her less vulnerable at such a moment.

Guy watched her quizzically. 'This sounds interesting, don't you think, Cressida?'

'I'm not in the best condition to think,' she replied, her brain racing as she tried to work out what she was going to do if her back-up failed to materialise and her cover had been blown.

'Well, I think we should at least go and talk to them after they've taken all this trouble to come and find us. It isn't like Marcia to interrupt my social evenings unless it's something very urgent.'

'We'll join you in a few minutes,' said Sir Peter, who plainly wanted to spend a little more time with his wife.

'That's fine,' said Guy agreeably. 'It will give me a chance to hear what this is about. Come along, Cressida. You must be as curious as I am.'

The moment they entered the drawing room Cressida realised from the expression on Marcia's face that the other woman knew the truth about her. She hardly dared look at Rick, but when she did she knew that he too had learned her true identity, and that this knowledge had both hurt and angered him. She didn't care too much about that, but what she did care about was how Guy would react and whether she was going to get out of Sir Peter's house alive.

'Love the outfit!' drawled Marcia, her eyes skimming over Cressida's skimpily clad body. Cressida tried to clutch the tiny kimono more tightly round her but then gave up. It was a little late for modesty.

'What's happened?' asked Guy with interest. 'I hope the gallery hasn't caught fire?'

'The gallery's safe, for the moment,' replied Marcia, 'but you and I have had our fingers badly burnt by Miss Cressida Farleigh here, or perhaps I should call her WPC Farleigh to be absolutely correct.'

Guy's fingers, which had been linked lightly round Cressida's wrist, tightened. She tried to twist free but failed in the attempt. 'What do you mean?' he asked curtly.

'I mean that Cressida is an undercover police spy. She was put into our gallery by the fraud squad, who wanted to catch you before Interpol did.'

'How do you know this?' he asked.

'I followed Detective Sergeant Tom Penfold to a pub late last night and told him that Cressida was having an affair with you,' said Rick. 'I pretended that it was such an intense affair the pair of you were thinking of getting married and he went berserk. Within minutes he was telling me the whole miserable story. He felt sorry for me, you see, because I'd been taken in by her too.'

Guy spun Cressida around and pinned her against the wall. 'Is this true?' he demanded, his mouth a tight line against the sudden pallor of his face.

'Guy, please, don't hurt me. I was given a job to do. I didn't have a choice,' protested Cressida, wishing that she believed he had a better nature to appeal to but since she didn't, playing for just a little more time.

'Is it true?' he repeated, his hands hard on her shoulders.

'Of course it's true!' said Marcia. 'She's only here tonight because of the Holbein. As for that man who brought us in a Matisse, he was another policeman, a cover-up for the fact that we caught her snooping in our files.'

Guy frowned. 'The Holbein?'

'That's what Tom Penfold told me,' said Rick. 'Haven't you given it to Sir Peter yet?'

'Shut up, both of you!' snarled Guy, turning back to Cressida. 'For the last time, Cressida, is this all true?'

Cressida was terrified by the expression on his face, and also by the realisation that this was the end for her and Guy. Never again would she feel his hands on her body, or enjoy the glorious searing pleasure that only he had ever been able to give her. He was everything she could have wished for in a man, and she was going to lose him, either to prison or by ending up in the bottom of some quarry deep in the countryside where she'd probably not be discovered for years. She began to tremble but made herself look him in the eye.

'Yes,' she admitted. 'It's all true.'

To her amazement he released his grip on her shoulders, stepped away from her and laughed. 'How you've wasted your talents, Cressida. You should have gone on the stage! I could have sworn that you were really enjoying yourself with me, and I'm not an easy man to fool.'

'I was,' she whispered. 'That wasn't an act, but I still had a job to do.'

'So when you begged me to enter you, when you implored me to give you an orgasm, to finally let you come, that was genuine, was it?' he asked mockingly,

243

and she blushed furiously at the look on the faces of Marcia and Rick.

'Please, don't talk about it,' she begged him.

'Why not? You've done plenty of talking to people while we've been together, although presumably not about our sexual excesses! I must congratulate you. You totally misled me. In fact, I'd begun to grow alarmingly fond of you. How lucky for me that you weren't what you appeared to be. I was quite nervous about falling in love for the first time.'

His words were like hammer blows to Cressida and she flinched inwardly, but she knew that no matter how calm he seemed he must even now be plotting how to get rid of her and make his escape. She tried to block out her personal feelings.

'Now you know I'm a spy I've no doubt I'll "vanish" like Lord Summers' paintings,' she said crisply. 'Before I do, perhaps you'd like to tell me exactly how you did it.'

'I thought you'd worked it all out,' he said with a half smile. 'You seem very certain that you know what we're up to, so you tell me.'

'I know that you cheat your so-called friends by offering to renovate paintings for them and then having them copied. Presumably once you feel sure that they've been taken in by the copy you sell off the originals to private buyers around the world. What I don't know is who your contacts are, or who does all the work for you. I can't believe Rick's the only artist you use.'

'Perhaps you should have been a writer,' murmured Guy. 'Your imagination is certainly fertile enough.'

Cressida laughed. 'You're not going to try and tell me we're wrong are you? That Interpol and the Fraud squad are following the wrong man, and that you didn't switch Lord Summers' paintings? Or that the Holbein you're about to return to poor Sir Peter is the same one he gave you?'

Guy shook his head. 'No, I'm not going to try and tell

244

you that.' He reached out towards her and Cressida pressed herself tightly against the wall, but all he did was softly stroke her breasts through the flimsy material of the bra. 'You've such a lovely, responsive body,' he said to himself. 'I shall really miss it.'

'Stop playing with me!' shouted Cressida, realising that time was running out and determined to hear the truth from him whatever happened to her. 'Tell me what you've been doing.'

'He hasn't done anything wrong,' said a voice from the doorway. 'He's only done what his friends have asked him to do.'

Turning her head, Cressida saw Sir Peter Thornton standing in the doorway. 'What do you mean?' she asked in bewilderment.

The older man sighed. 'It's all rather pathetic I'm afraid, but although you're right about Guy having copies made of my Holbein and poor Michael's two paintings it was because we asked him to. Lord Summers, like me, had a much younger wife and, also like me, he had trouble keeping her sexually satisfied. That's bad enough, but if you want to keep them despite your sexual failings you have to shower them with gifts. When most of your money's tied up in family trusts or entailed it isn't as easy as you'd imagine, so several of us resorted to asking Guy to sell off some of our art treasures.

'It was all done perfectly legally. We gave him the proof of ownership certificates and he sold them discreetly for us, replacing them with almost undetectable forgeries. Lord Summers broke the law, because the pictures were part of his estate, and I've done the same with my Holbein, but Guy hasn't done anything wrong. We never even told him we weren't free to sell them, although no doubt he guessed. He's a very discreet middleman and invaluable to stupid old men like me who spend their final years trying to keep beautiful young women at our sides.'

Cressida could hardly believe her ears. 'You mean, both you and Lord Summers *knew* what was happening?' she demanded, as she heard the sound of screeching tyres on the gravel drive.

'We instigated the whole business, as have many other elderly titled men around Europe in recent years,' he said sadly.

'And Guy didn't do anything wrong?'

'He was helping out his friends, nothing more.'

Guy laughed. 'I think someone had better open the front door. There are several PC Plods hammering on the wood right now.'

Stunned by what she'd heard and wanting to weep at what she'd lost because her bosses had got it all so wrong, Cressida could only stare helplessly at Guy as the police rushed in to rescue her.

'Good God, Cressida, cover yourself up!' shouted Tom, dashing across the room and wrapping his jacket round her.

As Guy, Marcia and Rick were handcuffed and bundled away, Guy glanced back at her and grinned. 'Yes, cover yourself up, you abandoned hussy!' he said mockingly. 'Time to return to sex on Saturday nights with the lights out I think.'

'It wasn't him!' protested Cressida as she watched Guy being taken away. 'He didn't do anything. Ask Sir Peter here, he'll tell you.'

'Come along, Cressida,' said Tom gently. 'You're in shock, but you've done a wonderful job. I just hope you recover from all this. I can't bear to think about what you've gone through in order to nail that bastard.'

'Oh, shut up!' yelled Cressida, pulling herself free and throwing his jacket to the floor. She turned to Detective Chief Inspector Williams. 'If you want to hear the truth about this scam you'd better talk to your "good friend" Sir Peter here, and then decide whether or not you want to press charges.'

As her chief stared at her in stunned amazement she walked proudly out of the house in her skimpy underwear and short black kimono, climbed into one of the waiting cars and was driven away, leaving Tom open mouthed behind her. All she wanted now was to get home and be allowed some time to weep in private for everything that she'd lost.

Three weeks later Cressida was wandering around her house, wishing that her four-week compulsory recovery leave was over so that she could return to police work. Being alone with nothing to do all day, wondering where Guy was and whether Marcia was now enjoying the incredible sexual pleasure he'd once given her, was driving her mad.

She knew from what Tom had told her on his one brief visit, a visit that had ended abruptly when she'd told him that she no longer wanted their affair to continue, that Guy, Marcia and Rick had been released without charge and that so far no charges had been brought against Detective Chief Inspector Williams's friend Sir Peter Thornton either. Cressida had a shrewd suspicion that it never would be. Men of that type tended to stick together. The old boys' network still flourished and she had no doubt that the entire investigation would be quietly dropped.

None of which helped her. Her whole life had been changed by the assignment, and now she was expected to return to her old life and pick up the threads of what she realised had been a very mundane existence. Even her work no longer held the appeal it had once done, because she was totally consumed by her need for Guy.

When the front doorbell rang she thought it was the postman with a parcel she was expecting and held out her hand without looking at the waiting man properly. 'What do you want – money?' asked Guy. 'I'm the one who should be asking for compensation, don't you think?'

Cressida stepped back in shock as he pushed his way into the house. She couldn't tell if he was angry or not, but she felt a rush of gratitude that at least she'd managed to see him one more time. 'Are you leaving England?' she asked nervously, noticing that he was carrying a small suitcase.

'Yes,' he said shortly. 'Why are you wearing that dreadful pleated skirt?' he added. 'It makes you look terrible.' With that he reached forward, unhooked the clip at the side and watched it fall to the floor. 'That's better. I don't care for the blouse either. Will you take it off, or shall I?'

Cressida felt a mixture of fear and arousal. 'You're angry with me, aren't you?' she said quietly.

'Yes, if you must know I am. Here, let me assist you.' Before she quite knew what was happening her blouse was off and she was standing in front of him in her cotton briefs, sensible bra and bare legs.

'At least you aren't wearing tights,' he commented, looking around the room until he saw what he was looking for. 'Move that footstool over to the wall,' he demanded, and when she hesitated he pinched one of her breasts hard in his right hand so that familiar darts of dark pleasure seared through her.

Quickly she obeyed, and immediately he lifted her up so that she was standing on the footstool with her back against the wall. 'Keep still,' he instructed her, and then he undressed himself until he was totally naked.

'Draw the curtains,' murmured Cressida. 'Please, someone might see.'

'I thought you enjoyed that possibility,' he reminded her. 'We don't need darkness, you and I. We know each other too well for that. As for the neighbours, who cares?'

'I do,' she protested, but then her voice was stilled by the feeling of his mouth on her throbbing breasts and his hands on the sides of her waist as he began to arouse and titillate her flesh until she was moaning and whimpering in frantic need.

'Ask for it,' he urged her. 'I want to hear you ask me again, like you used to.'

'Please, make love to me properly,' she beseeched him, her body rippling and trembling with desire. 'I want you more than I've ever wanted anyone.'

Immediately he pushed her panties to one side and then he was thrusting inside her, sliding into the welcoming moistness of her vagina and easing himself in and out as his right hand pressed down on her lower belly, causing a sweet ache of rising desire that made her squirm against the wall. When his fingers finally located her clitoris and flicked lightly at the throbbing bud she felt him push deep inside her at exactly the same moment and immediately she came in an uncontrollable rush that swept upward through her body. Every millimetre of her flesh was scorched by the red-hot waves of orgasmic release. Seconds later Guy came too, and he gasped with the intensity of his own orgasm as he drove into her, slamming her back against the wall in a ferocious moment of possession.

When it was over he lifted her off the footstool and placed her in front of him. 'There, a reminder of the old days,' he said curtly.

Flushed, tousled and sated, Cressida grabbed hold of his arm. 'I don't want you to go,' she said fiercely. 'I can't bear to think I'll never see you again.'

His eyes, which until then had been dark and shuttered, widened and a light seemed to flicker in their depths. 'Are you sure?' he asked. 'You won't have a regular job any more. I never stay long in one place. I like to travel. It stops me getting bored.'

'I know now that I was always bored,' said Cressida. 'I didn't start living until I met you. I can't go back to my old life, and if I lose you I don't know what I'll do.'

Guy picked up the small suitcase he'd brought with him and handed it to her. 'You've got twenty minutes to pack. I've bought us two one-way tickets to Venice. I think that there you'll be able to continue your learning curve about life, love and art.'

'Twenty minutes?' asked a stunned Cressida. 'But . . .'

Guy shrugged. 'It's up to you.'

She knew then that there was no choice. No matter what happened in the future, no matter how short a time she had with Guy, this was what she wanted. And if she played her cards right she was certain that she could keep him by her side for as long as she wanted him, because they were two of a kind, and if he hadn't felt the same he'd never have called on her or bought the tickets in the first place. 'I'll be ready in fifteen,' she promised him.

Guy watched her run up the stairs and for the first time in his life he felt contented. 'That's good,' he said with a smile. 'In a short time we can become members of the mile high club!'

Cressida threw a few things into the case, scribbled a letter of resignation to her chief and then dashed back down the stairs again. 'Ready!' she said breathlessly.

'What about Tom?' asked Guy, taking the letter from her hand.

'Tom who?' she asked with a mischievous grin and Guy laughed. 'Quite right, Tom who! You know, Cressida, I've waited a long time to meet a woman like you, a woman who was as clever as she was sexy, and now that I've found you I don't think I'm going to let you go without a fight.'

'That's nice to know,' said Cressida as they left the house. And it was. It was even nicer to know that soon they'd be making love in a plane, miles above the surface of the earth, and already her wanton body was tingling with anticipation. 'I hope the flight isn't delayed,' she murmured as they walked into the airport.

'If it is we'll write a postcard to Sir Peter Thornton,' said Guy with a laugh. 'I'm sure he'll be pleased to know that some good came out of the mess you managed to land him in!'

'I should feel guilty; especially about Rick and Marcia,' admitted Cressida later as they adjusted their seatbelts in preparation for take-off. 'I don't though. What does that make me?'

'A very sexy and desirable woman,' said Guy. 'Anyway, you needn't worry. Marcia and Rick are now a very happy if unlikely duo. She's gone quite Bohemian.'

As his hand caressed her knee Cressida relaxed back into her seat. 'You know, the gallery was the best thing that ever happened to me,' she admitted.

'I brought you along a little memento,' said Guy, reaching into his flight bag and handing her a parcel wrapped in brown paper.

She untied it and stared down at Rick's drawing of 'The Puppet'. Her stomach lurched in exactly the same way as it had when she'd first seen it. 'That's when I knew,' she said quietly. 'That's when I began to understand about myself.'

'Then we'll hang it over our bed in Venice as a permanent reminder,' said Guy with satisfaction.

'Who do you think *is* the puppet?' she asked him quietly.

Guy shook his head. 'I've no intention of telling you, either now or in the future,' he said firmly, but Cressida knew already. It was the man who was the puppet, and it was this knowledge that had given her the courage to leave her past behind and fly into an unknown but exciting future with this darkly fascinating, sexy and enigmatic man at her side.

LOOK OUT FOR THE ALL-NEW BLACK LACE BOOKS – AVAILABLE NOW!

All books priced £7.99 in the UK. Please note publication dates apply to the UK only. For other territories please contact your retailer.

Also to be published in October 2009

THE THINGS THAT MAKE ME GIVE IN
Charlotte Stein
ISBN 978 0352 34542 4
Girls who go after what they want no matter what the cost, boys who like to flash their dark sides, voyeurism for beginners and cheating lovers ... Charlotte Stein takes you on a journey through all the facets of female desire in this contemporary collection of explicit and ever intriguing short stories. Be seduced by obsessions that go one step too far and dark desires that remove all inhibitions. Each story takes you on a journey into all the things that make a girl give in.

ALL THE TRIMMINGS
Tesni Morgan
ISBN 978 0352 34532 5
Cheryl and Laura decide to pool their substantial divorce settlements and buy a hotel. When the women find out that each secretly harbours a desire to run an upmarket bordello, they seize the opportunity to turn St Jude's into a bawdy funhouse for both sexes, where fantasies – from the mild to the increasingly perverse – are indulged. But when attractive , sinister John Dempsey comes on the scene, Cheryl is smitten, but Laura less so, convinced he's out to con them, or report them to the authorities or both. Which of the women is right? And will their friendship – and their business – survive?

To be published in November 2009

THE AFFAIR
Various
ISBN 978 0352 34517 2
Indulgent and sensual, outrageous and taboo, but always highly erotic, this new collection of Black Lace stories takes the illicit and daring rendezvous with a lover (or lovers) as its theme. Popular Black Lace authors and new voices contribute a broad and thrilling range of women's sexual fantasy.

FIRE AND ICE
Laura Hamilton
ISBN 978 0352 34534 9
At work Nina is known as the Ice Queen, as her frosty demeanour makes her colleagues think she's equally cold in bed. But what they don't know is that she spends her free time acting out sleazy scenarios with her boyfriend, Andrew, in which she's a prostitute and he's a punter. But when Andrew starts inviting his less-than-respectable friends to join in their games, things begin to get strange and Nina finds herself being drawn deeper into London's seedy underworld, where everything is for sale and nothing is what it seems.

SHADOWPLAY
Portia Da Costa
ISBN 978 0352 34535 6
When wayward, sophisticated Christabel is forced to take an extended country holiday she foresees only long days of bucolic boredom and sexual ennui. But she has reckoned without the hidden agenda of Nicholas, her deviously sensual husband, and the presence of unexpected stimuli within the grounds of a brooding old mansion house. Soon, she is drawn into a web of transgressive eroticism, where power and pleasure shift and change like the shadows playing across Collingwood's secretive walls. Drenched in this unusual and kinky atmosphere, Christabel learns lessons the jaded city could never teach her.

To be published in December 2009

ON DEMAND
Justine Elyot
ISBN 978 0352 34543 1
Brief encounters in the bar, seductions in the pool or a menage in the elevator –
this haven for the hedonistic promises as much heat, steam, lust and excitement
as those who pass through it can handle. Conferences end with a bang; a gym
instructor offers extremely personal training; illicit liaisons abound and flourish in
the luxuriously appointed rooms. The daring sexual exploits of the staff and guests
are often seen through the eyes of the Receptionist, who is on her own quest to
snare the attentions of the charismatic Manager. Does the woman who offers a
discreet venue for the indulgence of every secret desire and fetish – from satin
sheets to rubber masks – have anything to offer him?

FIONA'S FATE
Fredrica Alleyn
ISBN 978 0352 34537 0
Held hostage by the infamous Trimarchi brothers, Fiona Sheldon and her friend
Bethany must submit to the Italians' sophisticated desires while her husband
Duncan attempts to find the money he owes them. But Duncan is more concerned
to free his mistress Bethany than his quiet wife.

FULL EXPOSURE
Robyn Russell
ISBN 978 0352 34536 3
Attractive but stern Boston academic, Donatella di'Bianchi, is in Italy to investigate
the affairs of the Collegio Toscana, a school of visual arts. Two new friends, Kiki Lee
and Francesca, open Donatella's eyes to a world of sexual adventure with artists,
students, and even the local carabinieri. A stylishly sensual erotic thriller set in the
languid heat of an Italian summer.

ALSO LOOK OUT FOR

THE BLACK LACE BOOK OF WOMEN'S SEXUAL FANTASIES
Kerri Sharp
ISBN 978 0 352 33793 1
The Black Lace Book of Women's Sexual Fantasies reveals the most private thoughts of hundreds of women. Here are sexual fantasies which on first sight appear shocking or bizarre – such as the bank clerk who wants to be a vampire and the nanny with a passion for Darth Vader. Kerri Sharp investigates the recurrent themes in female fantasies and the cultural influences that have determined them: from fairy stories to cult TV; from fetish fashion to historical novels. Sharp argues that sexual archetypes – such as the 'dark man of the psyche' - play an important role in arousal, allowing us to find gratification safely through personal narratives of adventure and sexual abandon.

THE NEW BLACK LACE BOOK OF WOMEN'S SEXUAL FANTASIES
Edited and compiled by Mitzi Szereto
ISBN 978 0 352 34172 3
The second anthology of detailed sexual fantasies contributed by women from all over the world. The book is a result of a year's research by an expert on erotic writing and gives a fascinating insight into the rich diversity of the female sexual imagination.

Black Lace Booklist

Information is correct at time of printing. To avoid disappointment, check availability before ordering. Go to www.blacklace.co.uk
All books are priced £7.99 unless another price is given.

❏ SOUTHERN SPIRITS Edie Bingham ISBN 978 0 352 34180 8
❏ THE TEN VISIONS Olivia Knight ISBN 978 0 352 34119 8
❏ WILD KINGDOM Deanna Ashford ISBN 978 0 352 34152 5
❏ WILDWOOD Janine Ashbless ISBN 978 0 352 34194 5

BLACK LACE ANTHOLOGIES

❏ BLACK LACE QUICKIES 1 Various ISBN 978 0 352 34126 6 £2.99
❏ BLACK LACE QUICKIES 2 Various ISBN 978 0 352 34127 3 £2.99
❏ BLACK LACE QUICKIES 3 Various ISBN 978 0 352 34128 0 £2.99
❏ BLACK LACE QUICKIES 4 Various ISBN 978 0 352 34129 7 £2.99
❏ BLACK LACE QUICKIES 5 Various ISBN 978 0 352 34130 3 £2.99
❏ BLACK LACE QUICKIES 6 Various ISBN 978 0 352 34133 4 £2.99
❏ BLACK LACE QUICKIES 7 Various ISBN 978 0 352 34146 4 £2.99
❏ BLACK LACE QUICKIES 8 Various ISBN 978 0 352 34147 1 £2.99
❏ BLACK LACE QUICKIES 9 Various ISBN 978 0 352 34155 6 £2.99
❏ BLACK LACE QUICKIES 10 Various ISBN 978 0 352 34156 3 £2.99
❏ MORE WICKED WORDS Various ISBN 978 0 352 33487 9 £6.99
❏ WICKED WORDS 3 Various ISBN 978 0 352 33522 7 £6.99
❏ WICKED WORDS 4 Various ISBN 978 0 352 33603 3 £6.99
❏ WICKED WORDS 5 Various ISBN 978 0 352 33642 2 £6.99
❏ WICKED WORDS 6 Various ISBN 978 0 352 33690 3 £6.99
❏ WICKED WORDS 7 Various ISBN 978 0 352 33743 6 £6.99
❏ WICKED WORDS 8 Various ISBN 978 0 352 33787 0 £6.99
❏ WICKED WORDS 9 Various ISBN 978 0 352 33860 0
❏ WICKED WORDS 10 Various ISBN 978 0 352 33893 8
❏ THE BEST OF BLACK LACE 2 Various ISBN 978 0 352 33718 4
❏ WICKED WORDS: SEX IN THE OFFICE Various ISBN 978 0 352 33944 7
❏ WICKED WORDS: SEX AT THE SPORTS CLUB Various ISBN 978 0 352 33991 1
❏ WICKED WORDS: SEX ON HOLIDAY Various ISBN 978 0 352 33961 4
❏ WICKED WORDS: SEX IN UNIFORM Various ISBN 978 0 352 34002 3
❏ WICKED WORDS: SEX IN THE KITCHEN Various ISBN 978 0 352 34018 4
❏ WICKED WORDS: SEX ON THE MOVE Various ISBN 978 0 352 34034 4
❏ WICKED WORDS: SEX AND MUSIC Various ISBN 978 0 352 34061 0
❏ WICKED WORDS: SEX AND SHOPPING Various ISBN 978 0 352 34076 4
❏ SEX IN PUBLIC Various ISBN 978 0 352 34089 4
❏ SEX WITH STRANGERS Various ISBN 978 0 352 34105 1
❏ LOVE ON THE DARK SIDE Various ISBN 978 0 352 34132 7

BLACK LACE NON-FICTION

To find out the latest information about Black Lace titles, check out the website: www.blacklace.co.uk or send for a booklist with complete synopses by writing to:

Black Lace Booklist, Virgin Books Ltd
Random House
20 Vauxhall Bridge Road
London SW1V 2SA

Please include an SAE of decent size. Please note only British stamps are valid.

Our privacy policy
We will not disclose information you supply us to any other parties. We will not disclose any information which identifies you personally to any person without your express consent.

From time to time we may send out information about Black Lace books and special offers. Please tick here if you do <u>not</u> wish to receive Black Lace information. ❏

Please send me the books I have ticked above.

Name ....

Address ....

....

....

....

Post Code ....

Send to: Virgin Books Cash Sales, Black Lace,
Random House, 20 Vauxhall Bridge Road, London SW1V 2SA.

US customers: for prices and details of how to order
books for delivery by mail, call 888-330-8477.

Please enclose a cheque or postal order, made payable
to Virgin Books Ltd, to the value of the books you have
ordered plus postage and packing costs as follows:

UK and BFPO – £1.00 for the first book, 50p for each
subsequent book.

Overseas (including Republic of Ireland) – £2.00 for
the first book, £1.00 for each subsequent book.

If you would prefer to pay by VISA, ACCESS/MASTERCARD,
DINERS CLUB, AMEX or MAESTRO, please write your card
number and expiry date here: ....

....

Signature ....

Please allow up to 28 days for delivery.